DATE DUE

At ....on swelled within Will. In the ....tant, ne was pulling Arianna into his arms, positioning her on his lap, pressing his lips upon hers.

From the very first second of their contact he felt himself begin to glow with their combined energies. She was strong and beautiful in his arms, and with her touch came a sort of quickening. He was filling up. He was becoming alive. Arianna hungrily drank from him, taking all the passion he could give her and at the same time demanding even more.

For those few moments the grief of losing his daughter passed between them but his loss, now shared, became less of a deep well and more of a physical longing for the comfort only Arianna could give him.

"I want you," he muttered against her neck.

In answer she nodded. Her hands slid along his stomach, back and shoulders. "You're real! Dear God, you're real!"

Spirited Away

Pamela Labud

ZEBRA BOOKS
KENSINGTON PUBLISHING CORP.
www.kensingtonbooks.com

*To my husband Bill,
my real life companion and hero,
and my daughters, Jamie and Caitlin,
who share their mom with the computer every day.*

Chapter One

A steady rain fell, soaking the early morning. In its midst loomed Newgate prison, like a dark demon rising in the gray dawn. Thick, angry clouds gathered on the horizon, matching the stormy expression of the man who stood gazing out a narrow opening on the lowest level of the prison. Ignoring the moans and cries from his fellow prisoners, Will Markham waited for the first shards of daylight to cut into the darkness.

A storm was brewing, but not the kind that swept across the city with the approaching winter. The tempest raged, its power growing with each moment that passed. The former captain of the merchant ship *Persuasion* knew its like, for he had weathered such storms too many times in his life. A dark beast that raged just beyond his senses, threatening destruction and leaving no quarter as it tore a path through his battered soul.

In the distance, the keening sound of the wind rose to a high pitch, but Will heard none of it. Neither did he feel the sharp sting of the ropes that bound his wrists.

Hands fisted, he ignored the numbness in his fingers and the ache in the muscles of his arms and shoulders. He only waited for the storm to come, the one that he would face one final time. The one that would take his life.

"He's in the last cell on the right," the jailer's coarse voice growled in the distance.

Will tensed. They were coming for him. It wouldn't be long now.

He continued gazing out the window, wincing at the sound of heavy footfalls as men approached. He remembered the jailer well. The merchant captain grimaced. His body still bore the heavy, fist-sized bruises of their first meeting. Held down and pummelled for his resistance, Will learned fast that he no longer could command his own fate. It hadn't stopped him, though. He'd fought them every day, each time receiving harsh punishment for his insolence.

A small smile briefly lifted the corners of his mouth.

They had not broken him, no matter how hard or how many times they'd struck him. The jailer and prison guards would never know that the scars of his other hurts ran much deeper than any they could ever inflict.

The small door opened and the light of a candle glimmered inside. Two men entered. The jailer, a heavy barrel-chested man, looked down his bulbous nose at the man he'd been summoned to accompany to the condemned man's cell. An expression of distaste spread across his wide, ruddy face when he glanced at Will.

The other was a short, bent man, nearly bald, his white hair neatly combed to one side. His eyes were round as coins and the light blue color of an early summer sky. Wrapped in a coarse, brown overcoat, the stranger nodded.

"Captain Markham," he said. "I am Thomas Donnelly, the vicar of St. Patrick's Parish. I've come to sit with you in your final hour."

For a moment, Will said nothing. " Go away. I don't want any visitors."

"No man should face the end alone," the vicar said in a tone meant for comfort.

"I have been alone for most of my life. I don't mind."

"I'll not leave you." Donnelly crossed his arms.

Will shrugged. "Do as you will, I don't care either way."

"Get it done, there's not much time," the jailer ground out. Turning, he left the clergyman alone with Will.

For a moment, the two men stood silent, the only sound in the room that of the heavy cell door being pulled shut behind them. The vicar jumped slightly when the key clicked in the lock.

Taking a deep breath, the clergyman held up his hand. "My son, shall we sit?" He motioned toward the small cot in the corner of the room.

Will said nothing and remained standing, his gaze returning to the window.

Without further word, the visitor sighed, walked to the cot, and sat down. He cleared his throat. "I've come to offer you comfort and to hear any confessions you might wish to make."

White-hot anger burned in Will's chest. "I've no need of comfort and I've nothing more to say."

"I don't think you mean that. It may be your final chance for salvation. A chance to beg for God's mercy."

Will bit back a hollow laugh. "He has showed me no mercy my entire life. I don't expect He'll make the effort now."

"There is no harm in asking, is there?"

Will considered his statement. The picture of himself on his knees, fists raised and prayers coming from his lips, slipped into his mind. He knew to the depth of his soul that it would be a vain attempt.

Instead, the twisted features of another sliced into his thoughts.

It was Richard Barrons, the man who had robbed him of his business, his dignity, and his very life's blood. Will choked down his anger, feeling it rise in him like bile.

"It doesn't matter. I've received no justice, I've no need of any other platitudes."

"My son, each of us has committed sin. Perhaps if you asked forgiveness . . ."

"My sins are of no import. Nothing could remove the stain of them from my soul. I seek only one thing and I shall not speak of it until the last."

"Such anger will not ease your passing."

Will sent him a cold glance. "I don't want it to be easy."

The clergyman clicked his tongue thoughtfully. "Still, it is my vocation to offer succor to those in your circumstances. Will you at least let me pray over you?"

Will lifted his bound hands before him. "Do as you will, I have no means to stop you. Just know it will make no difference."

Will turned away from him, clamping his urge to vent his anger upon an innocent man. He would speak no more.

Behind him, the vicar began praying, his quiet voice lyrical and smooth in his well-practiced litany. Will heard none of it. He only listened to the sound of the wind bellowing in his mind; the tempest was rising and sending out its siren's call. The storm would come to claim him soon.

The ornate carriage pulled into Newgate's courtyard and a single, well-dressed figure stepped out. Several men rushed up to welcome him, but Richard Barrons scowled at them, his long stride scattering them as he approached the entrance.

Of them, one short, round figure stepped into Barrons' path. "Mr. Barrons, I presume? I am Jacob Calvin, assistant to Lord Blevins of the Magistrate's office. I've been sent to meet with you and discuss your request to visit the prisoner."

"Where is he? I want to see Markham one last time."

"Mr. Barrons, this is most irregular," the man stuttered. "We usually don't allow civilians on the premises so close to the time of the execution. You are welcome to wait in the yard with the rest of the crowd."

Barrons whirled on the man. "I'll see him now. I have the Prince Regent's permission." He reached inside his overcoat and thrust the folded decree at the magistrate's lackey.

The man blew out a flustered breath. "If you wish, sir, but he's already receiving his last prayers. If you'd like to follow me, we'll go out to the yard and wait. It won't be long."

"It had better not be. I've business to attend to. It's the Prince's hope that I might be able to gain information from the blackguard. He attacked a naval vessel and stole a valuable shipment of weapons headed for the war in Spain."

"Yes, well, these things take as long as they take, you see." Calvin wilted as Barrons cast him a hard stare.

A sharp wind rushed between them, sending a squall of chilling rain across the yard. Barrons cursed under his breath. He'd nearly been too late. Reaching up, he pulled his overcoat tighter around his neck cloth. "Very well, but I'll not be put off for long."

The lackey nodded gratefully and motioned to the others to clear the way.

Barrons followed, his head bent against the weather. He'd labored long to reach this moment—it would be the pinnacle of his success and he would not be denied. Damn the weather, the rutted roads, and the broken carriage wheel that had delayed his arrival. He'd very nearly missed the chance of witnessing his enemy's final defeat.

Rounding the corner of the building, they entered the walkway where the prisoner would be led to the gallows. Barrons stared at the door, his gaze unrelenting, willing it to open.

"It shouldn't be long now," Calvin said.

"I'll wait." Barrons's eyes never left the door.

Too well he remembered the face of Will Markham, the surprised expression when Barrons had held his pistol against the merchant captain's chest, and then the haunted look of an enemy defeated when he'd been led to the prison to face his fate. Only seeing the fear of death would satisfy Barrons's appetite for the final destruction of the man who had been his biggest competitor on the open sea.

If that had been all that William Markham had been to Barrons, it might have been enough. But the fool didn't know of their other connection, the one that threatened Barrons's very existence. Instead, his plan to defeat the captain and elevate himself in the midst of society had been a stroke of sheer brilliance.

The temperature seemed to dive dramatically as Barrons gloated over his victory. No matter, he thought, as he folded his arms around his chest. The fire of his achievements burned hot in his belly and it was enough to warm him against the early morning chill.

"It's time," the jailer said. He opened the side door which led from the prison proper to the gallows yard.

Will was roughly pushed out into the morning light for the onlookers to gawk at, his clothing torn and covered with grime, his step uneven. Led down the walkway, he neither looked at the crowd nor gave his jailers any notice. Just as the small entourage reached the gate another figure stepped into their path.

"I see you've not yet learned how to approach your betters."

Will held his head high and glared at the rugged features of his accuser.

"Barrons," he grunted.

"Captain Markham. How fare you these days? I hear Newgate's provided special accommodations. Rooms fit for a king, eh?"

Will made no response to the other man's taunting.

"Still silent? You yet have a chance to save your neck, you know. Tell me the location of the arms shipment and you'll yet walk away from the gallows."

"To do what? Spend the rest of my life in prison squalor? To be transported to God knows where? Even if I knew where the guns were, do you think I'd trade such valuable information for that kind of life?"

"I wouldn't think that death would be all that attractive to you. Especially after you did nothing while your crew died. I imagine, if there is a hereafter, their ghosts will be anxiously awaiting your arrival."

"I had no choice. You held me belowdecks, you bastard."

"But your crew didn't know that, now did they? They believed that you'd thrown in with me and saved your own neck like a sniveling coward."

Will lurched forward, but was held steady by the two prison guards that flanked him. "I ought to kill you!"

"An empty threat coming from a man a few yards from his destiny, don't you think?" Richard's expression hardened. "Where is the shipment?"

"I don't know where it is. I didn't take it," Will said, his fists clenched, his arms pulling against the ropes that bound him.

"Then all the worse for you."

Will lunged again, nearly toppling the guards as he did.

"I may die today, Barrons, but mark my words. One day you will taste your own blood! Death may stop my sword now, but it shall not conquer my vengeance!"

"Brave words coming from a man almost dead." He turned to the jailer. "Let's be done with this."

Will was half dragged, half carried, up the steps. He knew the time for fighting had passed, but he fought them still. Just as he reached the foot of the gallows, the vicar stepped in front of him.

"My son, this is your last chance. Will you ask the Lord's forgiveness that He may save your eternal soul?"

"The only thing I ask is for the death of Richard Barrons. Beyond that, I want nothing."

Before he could say more, the executioner stepped forward. "Let justice be done." Taking Will by the shoulder, he pushed him to stand beneath the noose.

Will resisted them no more. Only revenge colored his thoughts, a picture of his blade piercing the black heart of his enemy. Nothing but darkness lived in him now, his final hope for justice disappearing with each passing second.

He stared across the crowd of people who had gathered that morning to see the man they thought of as a pirate executed. The rumbling crowd had quieted to excited anticipation, their whispers forming small clouds of vapor in the chill air.

It didn't matter what he said now. No one knew that Will Markham had been as good as dead for months. His heart had practically ceased its beating when the only person he'd ever truly loved had been wrapped in a canvas bag and thrown over the side of Will's own merchant ship. There was nothing left inside him except rage against his accusers and anger at God for the innocent life that had preceded his journey to the grave.

The executioner placed the hood around his head so that everything was obscured from his sight. Will paid it no mind. So loud was the anger roaring in his ears, Will didn't hear the final pronouncement of his sentence, nor did he feel the rough hemp as it was secured around his neck. When the trapdoor fell from beneath his feet and his own weight pulled him downward, Will heard only his thoughts, damning the man who watched him die.

Richard Bartholomew Barrons stood at the foot of the gallows and watched his one-time competitor dangle at the end of the rope. The hangman's dance, as gruesome as it had been, was the pinnacle of his success. With William Markham's demise, his plans had been set in motion.

"Well, Mr. Barrons? What did he say?"

Jacob Calvin stepped forward, the long, black robes of his office swirling about him like a summer storm at midnight.

"He did as I expected. Begged for his life. In the end the blackguard has paid for his crimes." Barrons tempered his words with a small, sneering grin.

"But what of the arms? Did he tell where he'd hidden them?"

Barrons took a long, slow breath, savoring his moment of triumph. "Of course he did. They're hidden in a small port on the coast of Spain. I'll give the military the exact location as soon as I leave here."

"You are indeed a hero, sir. To capture the dreaded pirate and then force him to reveal his stolen goods is a true work of valor. You will be rewarded by the Prince Regent himself, sir."

"I am but a patriot, happy to defend my country." Barrons bowed slightly and turned toward his carriage. Only then did he allow his expression of cheer to grow so that when he reached his conveyance, his smile had broadened and a burst of laughter rose from him. At last the world would be his!

Climbing up into the rig, Barrons heard what seemed like a whisper slide across the hubbub of the dispersing crowd. A single word formed and touched his ears. Barrons paused a moment, not certain of what he'd heard. Could it be someone was taunting him? Didn't they know that at the moment he was one of the most powerful men in the kingdom?

With a wave of his hand, Barrons settled back onto the plush velvet covering of his seat. It was likely nothing but some fool who'd meant to pluck his conscience. He dismissed the thought with a wave of his hand. Or he would have, except that the single word remained etched in his thoughts as solid as an epitaph carved in granite.

Vengeance.

Chapter Two

A chilly breeze stirred in the darkness. Lady Arianna Halverson shivered, pulling her wrap tighter. The only living occupant of the room, she worked to keep her attention on her ghostly visitor.

The late Edwin Carstairs III, former Duke of Savoy, sat straight-backed on the chaise in front of Arianna. His ephemeral appearance caused the temperature to plummet and the room to take on a dull, gray cast. Arianna strained her eyes in order to see him at all.

"You're not really that concerned about the money, are you, your grace? Why don't you tell me what's really bothering you?"

The duke sniffed, pulling a ragged handkerchief to dab at his eyes. "It was our last meeting, before my death. Margaret and I exchanged harsh words. I know she hasn't forgiven my poor treatment of her. I'm afraid she doesn't love me anymore."

"Your grace, if I can show you evidence of your daughter's true feelings, will you be at peace? Will you release your bonds to this life and go to your eternal rest? You seem a good soul and I'm sure nothing untoward awaits you."

He leaned forward, nodding emphatically. "If I could have proof that Margaret does yet care for her dear old father, then, yes, I believe I could give up my earthly wanderings."

"Very well, then. " Arianna reached into the pocket of her dressing gown and pulled out an object that fit in the palm of her hand. She carefully peeled back the lace wrappings to reveal a jade amulet. She held it suspended on a gold chain between them.

"Look into the center of the stone, your grace. In it you will see your daughter's true feelings for you."

In the midst of the glowing stone, a young woman was visible—Lady Margaret. She held a handkerchief to her face. Sobbing uncontrollably, she held up a cameo.

"Oh, Papa. I miss you so!"

The spirit drifted toward the amulet. His ephemeral form took shape and he leaned forward, gazing into its center.

"Margaret!" The duke moved closer still.

"Papa, is that you?" the young woman called out.

"Yes, it is I, my sweet child."

"Oh, Papa, I've missed you so."

"Have you, truly? I was so afraid that you hadn't forgiven me . . ."

"Of course I have. You were gone so quickly, I never had the chance to tell you. I'm so sorry we argued."

"As am I. 'Tis no matter now. As long as I know that you do not hate and despise me, I can finally find peace. Live well, my beloved."

As suddenly as the image appeared, it vanished and the room darkened once again.

"Oh, I do thank you, Lady Arianna," Carstairs said in a trembling voice. "You have healed my broken heart." The austere specter began to fade away.

"Then rest at last, your grace. You truly deserve it."

Exhausted, Arianna sank back in the cushion of her chair. After a moment, she held up the amulet once again.

"I wish I knew what your power was."

As she watched, the amulet began glowing once again. Inside the depths of the stone, Arianna could see a new image forming. It was a small girl with golden ringlets surrounding her heart-shaped face. Tears streaming down her face, the child stared upwards.

"No! Please, no! I want my papa!" she cried. A large man hovered near, in shadow. He reached down and grabbed the girl, jerking her forward.

"Wait!" Arianna called out, shaking the amulet. "Don't hurt her!"

The child pulled against her captor's hold and wailed. Ignoring her pleas, he threw a rough sack down over her, then hoisting her up, flung her over his shoulder.

"Wait!" Helpless, Arianna watched as the image dimmed and then disappeared.

Why was it, for all her ability to converse with the dead, she could truly make no difference for the living?

Defeat covered her like a shroud. Always she was separate from the living and only important to the dead. It was what kept her hidden away from society, unable to lead the usual life of a young lady of her status.

A loud crash of thunder shook the room. Still grasping the amulet, Arianna rose from her chair and ran to the window. She could see the storm stirring outside, its fury whipping the trees to and fro as though they had no more substance than the clouds. As she reached the sill, the window burst open.

The wind stopped and a deathly stillness fell over the room. The candle had blown out and the only sound was that of Arianna's own shallow breaths.

In the next instant, something in the room shifted and Arianna could have sworn a presence had entered. Holding up the amulet, she called out, "Who's there?"

A loud knock sounded at the library door.

"Excuse me, miss." Her butler, Henderson, appeared at the door. "Your brother has arrived."

"This late?"

Before she could say more, the door opened further and Ethan Halverson breezed through. Tall and lean, her handsome sibling waved to dismiss the butler and looked about the room.

"Have all of your 'guests' finished their business?"

"The spirits are settled tonight. We're alone, Ethan."

"I didn't think you'd mind a brief visit, since you never go to bed at an appropriate hour." Ethan was at her side, placing an affectionate kiss on her cheek.

"And you do?"

Arianna saw a shadow fall across his expression, his bright blue eyes dimming a little. He blinked it away and his face relaxed into an easy smile, but she sensed that he was keeping something from her.

"What's wrong, Ethan?"

"Nothing important, love. I stayed too long at the faro tables tonight and lost a tidy sum. Alas, I fear I'm getting too old to be burning the oil so late."

Arianna was sure there was more, but knowing how closely her brother kept his secrets, she decided not to press him.

"Nonsense. You'll be keeping your place at the tables until you're too feeble to walk."

"I hope you're right. Why don't we have a late supper together? I'll have Mrs. Mason put on some tea and set a table."

Arianna warmed to his offer. "Late supper or early breakfast? Sounds like a wonderful idea. Between your social demands and Parliament, I spend too little time with you."

After they'd settled in the dining room, Arianna poured them each a cup of tea. Ethan placed a pastry on his plate, but did not eat. An uneasy silence settled between them.

Arianna sipped her tea and watched her brother closely. They were an odd pair. She, a misunderstood young spinster, and her brother, a quiet, brooding aristocrat. No wonder they had few friends and even fewer interests.

Ethan, the fifth Earl of Castin, practiced in Parliament and kept the social agenda his status required, but had brushed off as many invitations from hopeful, doting mothers as she had handsome young suitors. A pair of deuces, they were known among the *ton*. Arianna didn't mind, but often wondered if her brother did.

"You're awfully quiet this evening, Ethan," she said as she stirred the milk into her tea.

"I'm sorry, dove. Just thoughtful, I suppose. A great deal going on at the moment."

"Anything the rest of us should be concerned about? Any new laws to yoke the aristocracy?"

"Not particularly. I'm having a nasty turn with a local merchant. He's petitioned Parliament on several issues that would be laughable if they weren't so serious. He wants to decrease the taxation on silk and other imports being brought into the country. His reasoning is that it will open trade routes once the war is over. What it will do is deplete the country's resources even more. The conflict has done enough damage as it is. We've barely enough money to support the economy now."

"Then you should vote it down."

"I would, but Lord Dennington has it in mind that this commoner is doing the government a favor, stirring up trade. He helped to put down that pirate accused of attacking the navy last spring and expects to be rewarded for his efforts. He wants to gain the title of 'Sir.' More likely, he was in league with the scoundrel. I tell you, I can't stand the man's audacity."

"Very serious. Another scheming blackguard vying to enter society." Arianna held back a smile.

"It isn't funny, Ari. Once a man like him gains a footing, there is no stopping the deterioration of the system."

"I thought you loathed society. You've said so often enough."

"I do, but you cannot replace one broken wheel with another."

"What are you going to do?"

"I've received some information about his business practices which I plan to announce in open session tomorrow. When that happens, it should be enough to damage irreparably any chance he'll be taken seriously."

"Is he a dangerous man?"

"Not particularly," Ethan answered in a level tone.

Arianna could see no hint in her brother's clouded eyes that it wasn't the truth, but still an uneasy feeling crossed her mind. Ethan was far too trusting, too certain of his immovable place in power ever to be suspicious.

"Just the same," she told him, "be careful. If he's dishonest in his business, there's no reason to think he wouldn't attempt something underhanded to take you out of the picture."

"Nonsense, Arianna. I'm safe enough. I've got my pistols."

The dreaded firearms. Arianna had no problem telling him in the past how much she detested the use of violence to solve one's problems. So many of its victims had crossed her path, the poor souls, that she hated the thought of her brother resorting to such a drastic measure. In the present circumstance, however, she almost approved of the firearms if it meant keeping him safe.

"Be careful, Ethan."

"Always." Before she had a chance to question him on just how he planned to do so, Ethan rose from his chair. "I must be off. I have a busy day tomorrow. In the evening, I've got a box at the opera. It would disappoint Lady and Lord Fennis immeasurably if I didn't show. They're launching an all-out attack on my unmarried status. Twin daughters and no good prospects on the horizon with all the younger gents gone off to war. I must plan a new strategy to avoid their efforts. Perhaps I shall drool during the intermission."

"When will you learn that even the most disgusting habits are overlooked when an aristocrat is available?"

Ethan walked to her side of the table and placed a kiss on the top of her head. Just like when they were children, she thought.

"Since when did you start accepting invitations to

the opera? Heaven knows, I haven't been able to drag you to a concert in years."

"It was a tangle I couldn't get myself out of. If you'd consider doubling with me, I might accept more social offers."

"Doubling with you? Whom would you pair me with?"

"I don't know. Lord Bradley, perhaps. He's not too objectionable despite his leg injury. They say he did terribly well on the battlefield in Spain."

"Just what I need, another man to stick his nose in my affairs."

"As if I ever did." Ethan started to leave, but as he reached the door, turned back one last time. "Please consider it, Arianna. He'd make you an awfully good match, you know."

Arianna waved him off with a show of playful aggravation. His attempts at diverting her attention hadn't been successful.

"It isn't working, Ethan. Something is wrong."

Ethan cast his eyes downward, suddenly appearing very weary. "It's nothing, really, but I am concerned for you. What if something were to happen and I could no longer take care of you?"

Arianna felt a catch in her throat. "What are you talking about? Is someone threatening you?"

"No. Nothing of the sort. I just feel that you need a husband, Arianna. A woman should be married. Think of all the things that you're missing. A home of your own, children, a life that's more than staying in dark rooms and waiting for ghosts to appear."

"I'm very happy, Ethan." Arianna knew that was no proper argument. Memories of her youthful social disasters plagued her. She alone knew that her fear of failure kept her closed in her brother's mansion, quietly hidden from society's attention.

"Are you truly? I think not, Arianna. There is an entire world outside, one that you'll never know if you don't go beyond these walls."

"I'm helping those beyond the living, Ethan. It gives me purpose."

"Yes, but those spirits of yours cannot protect you. They cannot do for you what the living can."

"Protect me? I'm safe enough here."

"For now, but if something were to happen to me, if an accident should . . ."

"Ethan, please don't say such a thing!"

"I only mean that if you've no one to watch over the estate or the finances, you could be taken advantage of. You could be swindled or worse."

"Nothing is going to happen, Ethan."

"Arianna, none of us can say what will happen in the future. I only want to see to it that you are cared for. A woman should not be alone."

"You're frightening me, Ethan."

A sad smile touched his lips. "I'm sorry, Arianna. I don't mean to. Don't fret. All will be well."

Arianna sat quietly after her brother's departure. Despite his assurances, she couldn't shake the feeling that something was wrong. Perhaps it was the storm stirring outside. Or was there trouble brewing in her own life? She rose from the table. For all her abilities as a sensitive, divining the future was not among them.

There wasn't too much about dying that Will remembered. The faces he'd seen in the crowd became stars in a midnight sky. For a moment it was as if he could hear everything at once and then nothing at all. Darkness folded around his thoughts like a velvet quilt in winter.

It would have been easy to drift off as the darkness began to overtake him, but the rage Will felt at life's injustice never lessened. Knowing that Barrons would get away with it all made him struggle against this new aspect of his existence.

In the distance, thunder rumbled ominously. It was his tempest, the storm that had pursued him to the grave still chasing after him, its rampage echoing the twisting and boiling in his soul. He was dead, he'd no doubt of it. Without looking back, Will ignored its summons and plunged toward the darkness.

Will wasn't sure how long he followed his chosen path, but before long he noticed that a small, narrow beam of light broke into the darkness.

As he watched, the luminescence took on a greenish glow, in the center of which he saw a woman. She was slight of form, with pale blond, upswept hair framing a perfect oval face. Her startling emerald gaze pensively searched the shadows. The mysterious woman trembled slightly, as if her slender frame were ready to take flight at any second.

Instantly curious about this strange creature, he followed her about the room, watching her peek into every corner and noting that she steadfastly secured the area as though she was in the habit of receiving strange visitations in the darkest hours of the night.

At first Will thought she was a dream, but as he drew closer, he felt her reality. In her hand she held the source of the light that surrounded her. The color of pale jade, the stone gleamed in the darkness and seemed to pull him toward it.

Suddenly, he was no longer just thought and bound-less energy. Looking down, Will was surprised to see his form taking shape. He now wore the outline of his earthly body but was only semisolid. He felt like half a man in a world far too real for his liking.

His reality tipped sideways and Will found himself standing in some sort of library. Expensive leather-bound books lined the shelves that covered three walls. A mahogany table and two ornately carved chairs were set in the center of the room, and a heavy desk, covered with papers and writing utensils, occupied the far cor-ner.

"Looking for someone?" a male voice said behind him.

Whirling around, Will came face to face with an-other spirit. Taking the shape of a man in his sixties, only the specter's head appeared, the rest of his body deteriorating in colorful swirls. He stared at Will.

"I am. Who are you?"

"The name's Carstairs, late Duke of Savoy. And you are?"

"An innocent man."

"I'm afraid few of us are that," the old ghost chuck-led. "What is your business here? Are you lost? I can help you get to the other side, you know. I've just re-cently been set free from the bonds that held me to my old existence. You are welcome to follow along with me, unless you have some unfinished business holding you back."

"I'm seeking a devil of a man, named Barrons. He caused my death and murdered someone very dear to me. I mean to make him pay."

"Do you? Is he among the living or the dead?"

"He is alive."

"Then you'll need help. I don't know about such things as vengeance, but the young lady there might be of help to you. She certainly was most generous in aiding me."

"Can she handle a knife or a pistol?"

"I'm not sure. Perhaps you can inquire after you've introduced yourself. Quite a lovely girl she is." He sighed. Bowing his head, the spirit winked once and then disappeared.

Will turned back to the lady holding the glowing stone. He couldn't help but be drawn to the woman's allure. Her hair shone as silver and her clear complexion seemed almost angelic in the dim light. For a moment he thought she might be the ghost and he, a witness to her haunting.

The woman moved with catlike grace across the room, her slight form and soft curves promising all the womanly delights a man could desire.

Tilting her head toward the window, she appeared to be listening for evidence of her visitor. She was the picture of a dream Will hadn't known he'd had until that moment. He couldn't help wondering if her skin would feel as soft as it appeared or if she had the scent of flowers in her hair. Deep in his soul he longed to be alive again, if only to know if his suppositions were true.

Will also sensed her aloofness, as though she wanted little enough to do with any other living creature. Indeed, he thought her very much like a rose. Not one of the deep red color that signified romantic love, but the pristine, snow-white flower of pure passion. Her very presence in the dark room seemed to cut the darkness. Drawn by her light, Will longed to get close to her, but the newness of his situation warned him to stay back.

After all, in spite of their remarkable beauty, roses had sharp thorns, too.

The door burst open and two men stood at the entrance. The glow from the stone disappeared and the candlelight flared again, flickering about the room.

He could hear the woman's voice call out and another voice answer. The gist of their words were yet indecipherable, but as time passed, it became clearer.

Feeling like an unwelcome visitor, Will faded back into the shadows, something he seemed to do easily. The tall stranger entered the room and gave the woman an affectionate kiss on the cheek. After watching the two a moment longer, Will realized it was not a lover's attention, but that of a good friend or a relative instead.

Will continued to watch as the woman turned away, but not before dropping the stone she'd held into a small jewel box that sat on the table. A few moments later the strange woman and her visitor left the room.

Will meant to follow them, but with the amulet out of sight, he found himself weaker. Odd, he thought. He must somehow be connected to the stone. Not knowing what else to do, he settled into one of the high-backed chairs and waited for the woman's return.

It was nearly dawn when the carriage rolled in to Bonhom Park. Ethan leaned toward the window, carefully checking the landscape.

"It appears we're a bit early," he told his friend.

Thomas Fielding, Viscount of Branleigh, sat back on the plush velvet seat, his hands playing at the snow-white cravat that he wore.

"I don't like this." Fielding nodded towards the horizon. The silhouette of another, less ornate carriage appeared on the road leading to the park.

"It's simple enough. Remmy made an accusation; I'm answering his call. You delivered the note. It's my reputation that's at stake here."

Fielding didn't meet his gaze, instead sniffed and twisted his tie about once again. "Yes. I saw the note."

Danver Remmington, son to the Earl of Hammond, was a young, foolish pup, just barely out of knee pants, and like a small dog, had been snapping at the heels of many of the elite. Though he'd only met the young man in passing, Ethan wasn't too surprised that the spoiled whelp had singled him out as well.

Next to him, Fielding shifted in his seat. A silence spread between them. After a few moments, Ethan cleared his throat.

"I swear, Thomas. You and I have been on at least a dozen such midnight outings. You're more nervous than a cat."

"Am I? I apologize, old man. I've not been myself lately."

"It's your gambling again, isn't it? Been doing poorly at the tables?"

The man beside him shrugged. "It's not that. I apologize. I am out of sorts. I expect that once I'm home again, this malady will pass."

"I hope so. Well then. Let's get this finished. Fortunately I've no ill will towards the pup. Don't worry, Thomas. I'll only wing the lad."

Ethan and his second climbed from the carriage. The coachman jumped down as well, reaching inside for the pistol case. Since Ethan had been the one called out, it had been his choice to choose the weapons.

When he opened the case, the pair fairly gleamed in the moonlit night.

Without further comment, Ethan and Fielding left the rig behind and walked toward the park. As they made for a small copse of trees, Ethan saw two men, but the area darkened as a cloud moved past the moon. When the dim light returned, he was surprised at the sight that met them. Remmy and his second were nowhere in sight. Instead, another more sinister figure turned to face him.

"Barrons." Even as he spoke the name, Ethan felt a twist of fear wind around his spine. "What's the meaning of this? Where's Remmington?"

Beside him, Fielding muttered. "I'm sorry, Ethan. It was a ruse." Not daring to meet Ethan's gaze, he looked toward the ground.

"Please forgive my machinations to bring you out, Lord Castin. Not being of the peerage, I know you wouldn't agree to meet with me otherwise."

"You are correct, sir. Now, if you don't mind, the hour is late and other matters require my attention." As he stepped forward, Fielding grasped his arm.

"I think you should hear him out, Ethan."

"You're mistaken, Tom. Any dealings I have with Mr. Barrons will be discussed during open session in the morning. Now, if you'll excuse me."

This time it was Barrons who stepped in his path.

"As mule-headed as ever, I see. No matter. I'd rather hoped this would be your attitude. You leave me no choice."

"What in blazes are you talking about? Do you mean to call me out? That's ridiculous. As a gentleman, I would not accept your invitation." Dismissing him with a wave, Ethan turned to his friend. "Are you coming, Tom?"

Fielding only looked away, his face pale. "I'm sorry, Ethan."

"Sorry? About what?"

Barrons laughed behind him. "He's sorry to be a party to this, Lord Castin."

"I don't understand," Ethan said in a low tone. Reaching out his hand, he brushed Fielding's sleeve. The other man flinched, jerking back from his touch.

"Perhaps I do see," Ethan whispered.

"I'm sorry, Ethan. I truly am. You were correct about my gaming debts. My father cut me off. I cannot repay Mr. Barrons the funds I borrowed in the usual manner."

"So betraying me is the price he asked?"

Fielding nodded.

Speaking with a bravado he didn't feel, Ethan turned back to Barrons and his henchman. "Very well, sir. If it's a duel you want, then you shall have it."

"How magnanimous of you, Castin." Barrons smiled, his hawklike expression narrowing.

Ethan unfastened his overcoat and proceeded to roll up his sleeves. "I'm going to give you one last chance to walk away. It's the gentlemanly thing to do since I'm the far better shot."

"So I've heard. Let me introduce my man, Elias Digby. Digby has made some arrangements, my lord."

"Arrangements? What are you talking about?"

"You've been a pebble in my boot for some time. I intend to dispense with you."

A shot rang out. Ethan whirled about. "Thomas!"

Beside him, Fielding fell forward, landing in a crumpled heap on the ground at his feet.

Digby grabbed for his coat sleeve, pistol at the ready, but Ethan was quicker. Knocking Barrons back, he managed about twenty yards before another shot exploded. Pain shattered his skull and he fell like a stone. A blanket of warm blood bathed the right side of his head.

Somehow Ethan knew the shot had been meant to kill and that he would most likely die in the next few moments. He thought he might yet try to run, but his limbs were heavy and he was barely able to move. The earl tried to cry out, but no sound came from his mouth. His only hope was that someone had heard the gunfire and would sound an alarm.

"Is he gone?" Barrons's voice sounded above him.

"Not yet, Mr. Barrons. Though I'll wager he's not far from it."

By a sharp boot to his side, Ethan was pushed over onto his back. The sudden movement sent a rush of nausea through him. Blood and bile rose up in his throat. Gurgling and sputtering, he began jerking violently.

"Can you speak, my lord?" Digby asked above him.

He grunted as his body screamed for precious air. Ethan felt himself slipping away, his spasms calming to a few seizures. A light flickered above him. Someone had brought an oil lamp.

"Eh, Mr. Barrons? Is he cold yet? The young lout at the coach was no match at all."

"No, Jacobs, he's still kicking, though just barely."

"That's a'cause he's drownin' in his own swill, sir. Do you want me to turn him over?"

Seconds passed. Knowing for certain that his death was imminent, Ethan's thoughts went to his sister. How was she to manage now?

Barrons reached down and, pulling Ethan's head upward, stared deep into his eyes.

"Can you speak, Castin?"

Another grunt was all Ethan could manage. He was so tired. Why didn't they just leave him to die?

"So that's it, eh? An invalid, are you? An idiot who can't speak. Not to worry. You might be of use to me yet, my lord."

Arianna had retired for the evening. Though she'd been exhausted, sleep refused to come. Tossing back and forth, she was assailed by an uneasiness she could not shake. Sleep was a phantom that led her on a chase. Giving up, Arianna rose from her bed, and pulling on a robe, decided to forego slumber altogether. Perhaps some reading would help to calm her nervous agitation.

A few minutes later, Arianna entered the library. Beside the door was a table and she bent down to light the oil lamp.

"Don't you think it's about time we were properly introduced?"

Arianna startled, nearly knocking over the lamp. Scanning the room, she saw nothing. Of course, that only meant one thing. Running to the table, she quickly opened her jewel box.

Instantly, the room lit up with the familiar green glow. Another spirit had come to visit.

"Go away!" she ordered the ghostly visitor. "I'll consider seeing you tomorrow after breakfast."

Only on occasion had her daily routine been breached, and then under the most harrowing circumstances. But this was an outright intrusion and she was not the least bit happy about it.

"I need your help."

Arianna whirled about, coming face to chest with

her visitor. Tall and muscular, he was mostly corporeal. She gasped. She'd never seen a spirit take such a solid form before.

Solid . . . yet not entirely of the physical realm. For a brief moment, Arianna was held in thrall by the blue eyes that stared down at her.

Well made, he appeared to have been created by an artist's hand. Dark chestnut hair framed his high forehead but was pulled back and fastened at the nape of his neck. A scar down his right cheek made him appear quite dangerous.

Impatient at her hesitation, the spirit scowled.

Arianna felt the burn of her blush as she considered that, if he were alive, how his wide, generous mouth and those white, perfect teeth would feel against her skin. A shiver passed through her and he smiled, as though he could read her thoughts.

"Well? Will you help me, or not?"

Arianna shivered as the rich baritone voice wrapped around her senses. Though a veteran of many late-night conversations with the deceased, she had never experienced more than the wispy, thready sounds of her counterparts. His voice was deep, thick, and virile. It aroused in her strange, new feelings of a very different sort.

"Well, do you have a voice, woman?"

Arianna's improper thoughts came to a crashing halt at his condescending tone.

"I believe I just told you that I don't take appointments before breakfast. Now, if you'd care to excuse yourself and come back . . ."

"Blast me timbers, woman! I have no time for such nonsense. There is vengeance to be taken. This is not a garden party."

"I realize you need intervention, but I'm afraid I

simply cannot help you right now. I need rest. Please come back in the morning."

"I'm not leaving until you do as I bid. My murderer still breathes and walks. I'll not rest until I've destroyed him. My current state of existence has somehow been tied to you. For some reason I am stranded here."

Arianna crossed her arms, tamping down her rising temper. "What do you want?"

"I need you to kill a man."

Shocked by his demand, Arianna could barely find words to argue with him. Before she had the chance, however, the door to the library burst open. Henderson entered, his sleeping shirt barely covering his knobby knees.

"I beg your pardon, Lady Halverson. You must come directly. There's a stranger at the door. He's brought Lord Halverson home. He's been shot."

Chapter Three

The young woman nearly fainted. Then, as if charged by a lightning bolt, she tore from the room, taking the amulet and by extension, the ghost, with her. The two of them raced down the stairs, through the manse, and to the front hall. She didn't stop her flight until they'd arrived at the front door.

The weather outside had progressed to a full blow, the rain coming down in thick, heavy sheets. Thunder boomed and the sky lit several times as Arianna and her butler ushered the three men inside.

Will looked them over. The man being carried by the other two had been the one who'd visited the woman earlier, but the other men Will knew well. Quite well.

The very man who had destroyed his life now stood dripping in Lady Halverson's foyer.

"Forgive the intrusion, Lady Halverson. We thought it best to come directly here."

"Ethan? What happened? Who are you?" The lady rushed forward and went to the injured man's side.

"Please bring him into the parlor." She quickly pulled the handkerchief from her sleeve and began staunching the flow of blood from his head wound.

The stranger at the rear removed his hat. "Richard Barrons, Lady Halverson. At your service." He pointed to the sagging man beside him. "Your brother has been shot, milady. It seems to be a duel gone bad. Very messy business."

"Damn and blast!" Will surged forward, his fists at the ready, but none in the room took notice of his presence.

Barrons bowed low, sweeping his arms in a wide flourish. The blackguard commanded the room as he had every other time Will had seen him. He was clothed in expensive evening attire, including a plumed hat and polished black boots. A dashing figure, the scoundrel was cloaked in a voluminous black cape with white roses embroidered along the hem.

Anger shot through Will, a dark, deadly serpent coiling in his gut, which threatened to spew forth as the heated blood sang in his veins.

For an instant he forgot everything. His weeks of imprisonment, the beatings he'd received on board the *Persuasion*—even the gallows and his own death became clouded in pure, undiluted hatred.

Barrons walked past him, oblivious to the seething emotion in the spirit's countenance. Will wanted to throttle the man where he stood, to feel his own heated hands around Barrons's neck squeezing until the man's very last breath escaped him.

Powerless, Will could do nothing but watch the interaction between Barrons and Lady Halverson. Without further discussion, the trio bustled quickly past them. Was he only visible to the woman?

After a moment's consideration, Will found that suited him. He definitely did not want to take on his enemy until he was ready. Plans had to be made and actions carefully executed. He somehow had the feeling that he would have only one chance to put Barrons down.

Forced to follow them into the next room, Will kept as much distance as the powerful stone would allow. Again sinking into the shadows, he watched the participants with increasing interest.

To her credit, Arianna expertly pulled a handkerchief from the arm of her gown and began wiping the drying blood from her brother's head. She glanced up at Henderson.

"Quick, find my mother's medicine box, heat some water, and fetch me clean cloths for bandages."

"I did all that I could, miss." One of the two attending men stepped forward. He was tall and spindly, with dark hair, black eyes, and hawklike features. Wearing an expensive coat and boots, he could have been a member of the gentry, but Arianna didn't know him.

"I thank you. What did you say your name was again?" Though she spoke, the lady didn't take her attention from her brother's injury.

"Barrons, Lady Halverson. Richard Barrons."

Without stopping her ministrations to her brother, she glanced up, her back stiffening.

Will smiled. Lady Halverson wasn't one to be easily led. Somehow, that made her even more attractive in Will's eyes.

"I don't remember my brother ever mentioning your name. How are the two of you acquainted?"

"I have a shipping business. Your brother and I had

been working on new legislation, preparing it to pass before Parliament."

"My brother told me about someone whom he was opposing in open session tomorrow. Would that be you, Mr. Barrons?"

"Oh, no, miss. Not I. In fact, we'd been discussing ways to increase his profits from foreign sales."

Will swore, his harsh words drawing a chastising glance from the woman.

"What happened? Who shot him?"

"It's not known. I'd been in a pub with business associates of mine this evening and word came to me that someone meant to kill Lord Castin. I summoned my carriage and rushed directly there, hoping to intervene, you see. Unfortunately, I was too late."

"He's lying," Will said, crossing his arms in front of him.

"Oh." Lady Halverson returned her attention to her brother, but not before giving a puzzled glance to the ghost that only she could see and hear. "I want to thank you, Mr. Barrons, for all you've done. I shall send Henderson for the physician immediately. You can see yourselves out."

Barrons hesitated. "That could get a bit sticky, if you don't mind my saying so, Lady Halverson. I mean, a doctor would ask questions. Reports will have to be made."

"I don't understand? He's been attacked. Surely whomever is responsible should be found and arrested."

Barrons smiled at her. "Ordinarily I would agree, myself being an honest citizen. However, rumors have been rampant. As a friend, I wouldn't want his lordship to be investigated."

"Investigated? For what?"

The stranger leaned closer, lowering his voice, although there were but the two of them in the room. "Surely you've heard of the pirate who was hanged today—William Markham?"

Arianna nodded, a wave of panic rising in her chest as she recalled Ethan telling her about it. "Yes, what of him?"

"There are those who say the two of them were in league. That your brother was involved in the sale of the weapons Markham was accused of stealing."

"It can't be!" Arianna glanced to where her brother lay, pale as death upon the settee.

Barrons nodded his head. "I'm afraid it is, my lady. Your brother gave me certain documents to keep safe. I would not have done it, had it been any other than Lord Castin, the two of us being such close acquaintances. Your brother trusted me to keep his secrets safe, in case anything untoward happened to him."

"What sort of documents?"

"Records of accounts and a bill of sale, a record of the secret trade routes he used to ship goods that he didn't want attention drawn to."

"Sir, what you are suggesting is unthinkable!"

"I feel quite the scoundrel to give you this harrowing information at so dire a time, but I fear the worst. The fewer who know the truth about your brother's busnisess, the better."

"Still, he needs a physician. He could die!"

"If he's found to be in league with Markham, he could be hanged."

"We'll find a way around it," she said, carefully checking her brother's eyes.

"Perhaps you might, but perhaps not."

The lady turned to him once again, her patience clearly fraying by the second. "What do you suggest, Mr. Barrons?"

"My friend here, Mr. Digby, is something of a healer. He's tended to many a sick sailor, you know. He'd be glad to look after the earl."

"I'm sure your intentions are good, but my brother is too seriously injured for me to take such a chance."

"Lady Halverson, there are other matters which require your attention."

Will stepped hastily forward. Bending over her shoulder, he muttered, "Be careful. The scoundrel wants something. It's not as if he cares whether your brother lives or dies. "

"I don't understand," she whispered back, so her living guests could not hear.

"Neither do I, but he is an evil, vile man who'll stop at nothing to get what he desires."

"Are you sure?"

"I should be. He's the scoundrel who ruined my life and many others. I mean to see him dead. Once he's like me, I can destroy him once and for all."

Before she could answer him, Henderson returned, his arms laden with clean linens, a kettle of steaming water, and a black leather case.

"Should I send Sparrows for Dr. Tumlin?"

The lady paused a moment and glanced hastily at Will and then back to Barrons who stood at the foot of the sofa, obviously feigning concern for her situation.

"Not yet, Henderson. Let's wait a moment to see if Ethan arouses first. It looks to be a flesh wound."

"As you wish." Bowing stiffly, he turned and left the room.

"A wise choice," Barrons said. "Now, perhaps we

can leave Digby here to see to your brother whilst you and I discuss matters elsewhere. The dining room, perhaps? I know it is early, but carrying your brother all this way has left me a bit sashed. Perhaps your cook could be persuaded to put together a small tray of tea and cakes?"

Lady Halverson didn't flinch. Nodding curtly, she swept up from her spot beside the injured man and motioned for Barrons to follow. It was clear by the pinning expression she gave Will that she was not at all happy with the arrangement.

"I know it's hard for you," he told her as she brushed past him, "but it's the only way. As far as he's concerned, you're the key to whatever he's after. It may be the only power you have over him, though I doubt he'll credit you with sense enough to know it. Just keep playing along the way you are. I'll do what I can to advise you."

Lady Halverson took a deep breath, but did not comment. Her face remained pensive, most likely because she wasn't particularly thrilled with dealing with him, either. Still, she took his advice and led Barrons down the narrow hall.

Unable to do anything else, Will followed close behind. The longer he stayed in her company, the stronger the tie was between them. One thing he knew for certain, she was a mystery for him to unravel, a knot that wouldn't easily come undone.

As he watched her walk in the lead to the dining room, Will decided that this was a woman of intense passion. Her devotion to her brother was immovable and her temper, though not under perfect control, showed her to be an intelligent and independent woman. While society might have frowned on such qualities in a member of the fairer sex, Will found her to be all the more appealing—and found himself wishing that he were yet alive and able to indulge in the perplexing puzzle that was Lady Arianna Halverson.

Will sighed. The reality of his situation prevented such a hope and he well knew it. He was the knight trapped in a battle to slay the evil dragon and she the fair princess locked in an ivory tower. It didn't lessen his desire for her but intensified it.

His troubled spirit's need for vengeance didn't diminish one bit, but in the depths of his heart, a new sadness grew. Lady Halverson would forever be beyond the reach of a poor dead man. And that was all he was.

Arianna was not at all pleased. Worry for her brother and fear at what this dangerous stranger, Barrons, might have planned kept her in a high state of anxiety. Add a troublesome ghost to the mix and she was sure disaster was imminent.

"Please, make yourself comfortable, Mr. Barrons. I'll summon the cook, Mrs. Mason."

"Don't be too long, Lady Halverson. It wouldn't be good to keep your dear brother waiting. Any moment might be his last, you know."

"I know."

Barely able to hold back her hysteria, Arianna quickly exited the room. Making her way to the servants' rooms she found that she was not alone in her errand. The ghost accompanied her.

"Why are you still here? Can't you see I'm busy?"

"I can. It seems, Lady Halverson, that I'm attached to you at the moment. Whither thou goest, there goest I, or some damn thing like it. I think it's your pendant."

"The amulet? It's never had that effect before."

"It does now. Which leaves us little recourse. You and I are drawn together. Like barnacles on a ship, like bees on honey . . ."

Lady Halverson quickly held up her hand. "I understand." She paused in front of a door. Knocking loudly, she called out. "Mrs. Mason. I'm sorry to wake you, but you're needed in the kitchen."

After some rumbling in the room, the door cracked open and a white-haired, disheveled servant appeared. "Yes, Lady Halverson, I'll be there directly."

"Thank you. I'm terribly sorry."

When the door had closed, Arianna turned to make her way back to her guest. Instead that damnable wall of male obstinance blocked her way. Bumping into his solid form, she stepped back, embarrassed. He shouldn't have been so well formed, she thought. Goodness, he shouldn't be there at all. What was wrong?

"I'm sorry. You must leave me be for now. When I've dealt with everything, then perhaps we can sit down . . ."

"You don't understand. I can't leave. I wouldn't if I could. I need you to slay that beast sitting at your table. He's dangerous and no one is safe until his blood is spilled."

Arianna looked up into the square features of the ghost. His eyes blazed a piercing blue and his general color wasn't difficult at all to read. Red. Deep, angry, and though she knew he was not really in this world, she could swear she saw steam rising from his brow.

"I have no one's word but yours to say otherwise. I can only hope that Ethan awakens and can tell us the truth."

"Your brother may never wake up or speak again. Barrons is quite prepared to kill him."

"So you say."

"This is ridiculous. I'll not stand here and argue with you. I don't know how else to convince you of the truth. Do you think I'm lying? Tell me, sensitive Lady Halverson, what reason would the dead have to lie?"

"Perhaps the same reason as the living. Greed, anger, hatred?"

"Greed? There is no money where I'm going. Anger? You are right about that. I see evil and I can do nothing to stop it. Hatred, without a doubt. That man stole everything from me, and I'm not speaking of mere possessions. No, something far more dear."

"Is there any point to your actions now? Will killing him retrieve what you've lost?"

"No."

"Then go and be at peace." Arianna turned away from him, expecting the apparition to return to his proper place. Strangely, despite her current worries for her brother and his dire situation, she did feel a pang of regret at the loss of her newest visitor. A part of her felt drawn to his anguish, to his pain, but more than that, to his mind. He must have been quite a man when alive, if his ghostly form was at all comparable to what his flesh had been.

"I'm not leaving. I'm not finished here." His resolute tone sounded behind her. In the next instant, the determined spirit was standing in front of her once again. His stubborn presence seemed impenetrable.

"Then stay, but go somewhere else. I must do what I can for my brother and I can't help both of you." Arianna bristled. How dare he force her attentions this way!

"I can't go."

Arianna looked up into the sea blue of his eyes. Odd . . . she'd never noticed the color of an apparition's eyes. In fact, inhaling deeply, she could smell him as well. Full male vigor was what touched her senses—that and a slight, salty flavor of the sea.

"Of course you can. All you must do is focus on where you should be."

"Where is that?" Though his statement was a question, Arianna felt the tinge of challenge in his tone.

"How am I supposed to know? It's wherever your kind goes when they are finished here."

"I'm not finished here. I feel drawn to you somehow. From the very first moment I glimpsed you in your room, it was like being on course, as if I were propelled by the wind itself."

"That's absurd. You simply had a need and it brought you here. I've conversed with the dead many times and—"

"I'm different, somehow. I don't know what it is that keeps me here, but I'm with you, tethered like a ship to an anchor."

"Fine," Arianna said with exasperation, forcing her way around him. For a vaporous spirit, he certainly took up a wide berth in the corridor.

"I must look in on Ethan."

Walking the corridors, Arianna glanced behind her, noting that the ghost had decided to stay behind after all. While she should have been glad to be rid of the troublesome spirit, at least for the present, she had to admit there was a certain emptiness with him gone.

When he was nearby, she felt his firm presence as though he were some sort of protector. Until his arrival earlier that evening, Arianna hadn't realized how alone she'd been.

Quickly she pushed away that thought. Arianna had known since her first introduction into society that she'd been meant to be alone. Even now, years later, she could still sense the harsh stares of the young ladies and gentlemen at her first soireé, feel the sting of their harsh words as they whispered behind her. A crazy girl, they'd called her. Off in her room, chattering to herself when no one else was about. Some brave man of the *ton* would soon claim her and then quickly lock her in a tower where she'd be no danger to herself or others.

From that day forth she'd decided to stay alone. Ethan had been the only one who'd understood her need for solitude. Now, with him so severely injured and possibly near death, how was she to carry on? How could she manage his estates until he was well again? She was so sick with worry that any thoughts about the troublesome ghost must instantly be put out of her mind. It was as she'd told him. Later she would try to help him. Later.

When she reached the parlor where Ethan lay, she saw that dreadful man, Digby, stretched out on the other chaise with his feet propped up on the tea service frame.

"You can go. I'll stay with him now." Not sparing Digby further attention, Arianna turned to the table beside her brother's too-still form and picked up one of the damp cloths that Henderson had brought at her urging earlier. With gentle hands, she wiped her brother's heated brow.

Digby slowly stood up behind her. Arianna could

feel the burn of his gaze on her back. She didn't care. She was lady of this house, after all. He and his master were but unwelcome guests and with every passing second, she wanted them gone all the more.

"I'll be waiting outside should you need anything, Lady Halverson."

Arianna said nothing, but let go a sigh of relief when he'd quit the room. Now she could turn her attention to Ethan.

A few seconds later, Arianna realized she was not entirely alone. She should have given the ghost a clipping for being so ill-mannered as to invade her private moments with her suffering brother, and yet it didn't feel like an invasion, really. It felt like a steel-strong presence that could very well be the structure that was holding her up, perhaps even separating her from disaster. Arianna prayed that her intuition was correct about the spirit, that he was indeed her compatriot and not the devil in disguise.

Back in the hall, Will watched her go. Waiting until she turned a corner, he realized that the reality around him began to shift. Just as before, he was to be banished to a dark shadow to wait for her return. He didn't like it one bit. He might not be alive in the physical put-your-hand-on-her-arm sense, but he *was* present and didn't care to be pushed off like a worn pair of gloves.

He went in search of her. As it happened, she wasn't that hard to locate. Whether or not it was the same magic that had pulled him to her or some mystic power that she exerted, he wasn't sure. Will had known attractions to other women in his life, but none exerted the same force upon him that she did. The tone of her voice had the soft power of the siren song that old sailors spoke of. The emerald gaze she cast upon him reminded him of a tropical sea, sparkling irresistible as she turned her eyes toward him. When he drew near to her, it was like being caught in a whirlpool, spinning out of control and threatening to overtake him.

Arianna Halverson was the brightest, most vibrant person he'd ever known. And more than just alive, he realized. Everyone else paled in her presence. A thrill stirred in him as he reached the door to the room where she knelt beside her brother.

"Ethan, please wake up. You must help me. How am I to go on without you?"

Will waited as her question went unanswered. The picture of the grieving woman sent a twinge of pain through him. Arianna Halverson presented a vision of beauty and misery. Any man of sensibility would feel the sharp edge of her pain. For Will it was much more.

None had mourned his own passing. The only other person in the world who had truly loved him had preceded him in death and try as he might, even on this side of the mortal coil, she was unreachable to him, leaving only a barren, desolate feeling in his heart.

"Have you considered he might already be gone?" Will asked gently when he could finally summon the words.

Her green eyes stared up at him. "He isn't, I tell you. I'd know," she said, tilting her head forward and giving him a pointed stare.

"Oh, that's right. You can commune with the dead."

"He's hurt. I'm sure he'll soon wake to tell me what an adventure he's had. It's always been that way with us, you know. He's the one who's gone jaunting about, living life to its fullest."

"And you've been the one to stay home and live only through the tales of his exploits."

Again she glanced up at him. "Something like that. I never needed the social whirl as Ethan did. He is the heir, you know. He always has to be in the light, to be seen and appreciated. It's the responsibility of the title."

"I wouldn't know about that. I was a common man, a merchant, and a sailor. I would have been happy to remain a simple sailor if it meant just being on the water."

"Yet you had a thriving business?"

"I did, yes. I had . . ." He paused, not quite sure how much to tell her. He still felt if anyone, her included, knew of his true need for revenge they might use it as a weapon against him. Heaven knew there had been enough blades pointed in his direction during his life. Death was no excuse for leaving oneself unguarded.

"You had what?"

"I had responsibilities. Not as many as his lordship, of course, but to me they were just as important."

"Of course," she answered, "I never intended to mean otherwise."

Will watched the way she pressed her brother's limp hand between her own. When her gaze wandered back to him, she wore an expression of pure adoration. Another pang shot through Will.

What would it be like for her to look at him that way?

The parlor door opened and Henderson entered.

"Lady Halverson, Mr. Barrons requests your presence in the main dining room."

"Tell him I cannot leave my brother."

"There's no need to worry, Lady Halverson," Digby

said, entering the room from the opposite door. "I'll be glad to stay and watch over him."

When Digby smiled, Will saw an expression of nervous fear wash over Arianna's features. She looked as though she would just as soon have her brother guarded by a pack of wolves.

"It should be all right," Will told her. "If they wanted him dead, they would have killed him by now. Let's go and see what that blackguard has to say. It's better to know the heart of your enemy when going into battle."

Arianna gave him a curious glance. "Have you fought many battles, sir?" she whispered as she pulled the quilt up around her brother's shoulders.

"Every man who makes his life on the sea fights a battle from time to time. I know what I'm talking about. Lord Castin will recover, as well as he can under the circumstances."

Arianna quickly nodded. "Very well, Henderson, let's go. The sooner we finish our dealings with these gentlemen, the sooner we can bring this unfortunate visit to an end."

When the two reached the dining room, Arianna stopped short at the door. Not yet used to his corporeal form, Will nearly careened into her. The truth of it was, he didn't feel right touching her. He didn't want to feel the softness of her skin, or be so close as to get a full breath of the wildflower scent of her hair. If he'd been among the living it might have been different, but now, when there was no hope for a future beyond his vengeance, Will didn't want to be reminded of all that he would forever miss now that he was no longer alive.

"Mr. Barrons." Arianna cleared her throat, annoyance battling with anger in her tone.

Barrons met her with an unpleasant grin. He was not an overly large man, but even seated at the high table, he looked tall. His hair was devilishly long and unrestrained, his eyes large and his mouth far too large for his narrow face. He looked like a vulture about to snap up a meal and when he stood, his gangly form towered over the delicate Arianna.

"Lady Halverson, how good of you to join me." He motioned for her to sit at a place he'd had set for her. On the opposite side of the table, the setting indicated intimacy and Arianna stiffened as she stared at the spot. Will supposed it was an arrangement she had shared with her brother not too long ago.

"I'd rather not. You asked to speak with me?"

"I did. However, I think our dealings can be dispensed with faster if you'd sit for a moment and share this fine roasted beef with me. If I must keep bobbing up and down during our conversation I fear it will but prolong matters."

Will watched a scowl cross her face. Without further argument, Arianna walked closer to her offered chair and stiffly sat down with her guest.

"What is it you want from me, Mr. Barrons? Some sort of payment, perhaps?" Arianna said in a stern voice.

Barrons's smile grew wider still. "I don't want money, Lady Halverson."

Arianna stirred at his comment. Will didn't like the way she was caught off guard. Perhaps she was no match for this scoundrel after all. What could a ghost do to save a damsel in distress? It wasn't as if he could pick up a pistol and shoot the blackguard. Making a quick decision he leaned down to mutter in Arianna's ear.

"Don't let him see your fear. If he thinks he can best you, you're done for."

Arianna met Barrons's gaze without flinching. "Then what do you want?"

"It's rather simple. I fear for your brother's life."

"You've no need to worry. He's here now. The servants and I shall do everything to keep him from further harm."

Barrons reached out to grasp her arm. "My dear lady, if only that were so. I fear that whoever tried to kill your brother may come for him again."

"Then I shall contact his man of affairs and see that guards are hired to watch the house."

Her unwelcome guest shrugged. "If only that were enough, I would agree. However, have you considered that none but your brother's closest friends knew of his whereabouts tonight? Did he tell you where he was going?"

Arianna shook her head. "There was no reason to. He said he was off to a late concert."

"Yes, but he was found in Bonhom Park. Quite a distance from the opera houses."

"What do you suggest I do?"

"I'll be putting it to the point, my lady. I believe that as an unmarried woman you are most vulnerable. With your brother so ill, anyone could try to interfere in your brother's businesses."

"Surely his staff can be trusted with that."

"One would hope so, but with so much wealth at stake—well, even the most honest men's influence could be purchased, I assure you."

"What do you propose I do?"

"What your brother would wish you to do."

"And that is?"

"Allow me to help you."

Arianna sat farther back in her chair. "Sir, I appreciate your thoughtfulness, but I've never heard Ethan say anything about you or your trustworthiness."

"I know this is a difficult circumstance for you, Lady Halverson." He reached out and took her hands in his, holding them with a firm grip. "Your not knowing me is of the utmost concern. However, I did save your brother's life this night, did I not? And I hold his most damning secrets as well. I beg you, my lady, let me do this one last service for my injured friend."

Arianna swallowed hard, her throat dry. Fear wrapped around her spine like a vine entangled around a trellis. "What would you do?"

"I propose a union between us. Allow me to do what your brother cannot."

"A business arrangement? I cannot consent to such a thing. Only Ethan can."

"I realize that. I intend a union of a different sort, Lady Halverson."

"I don't understand." Arianna leaned forward slightly, barely taking a breath. "What are you proposing?"

"Marriage."

Arrianna grasped her throat, the force of his statement knocking the air from her chest completely.

"I'm sorry," she started, her voice hardly above a hoarse whisper. "That isn't possible."

"I thought that might be your answer. But in order to protect your brother, I feel I must take the upper hand for your own good. I have told you of the damning evidence I hold—it could cause Lord Castin to be executed as a traitor. In exchange for my not turning these documents in to the authorities, Lady Halverson, I insist that you become my wife."

Chapter Four

As the carriage pulled away from the estate, Barrons leaned back and observed the landscape from his window. How delightful Lady Halverson was. He could envision long nights of her in his bed, fulfilling his every need, cowering under his touch. A good beating was what she needed, and he could hardly wait to take his strap to her.

Let the gentry have its low opinion of him. What need did he have of a title, after all? Hasn't he gathered enough wealth and power with his dealings to buy anything he desired?

And yet the very thing he desired most was out of his reach. He'd hoped that after exposing Markham as a traitor the crown might award him a peerage, but that seemed not to be the case. Very well, he thought. He did have one avenue left. He still had a plan to force another's hand. The one blood relative who remained and continued to hold back his rightful title.

It wasn't his fault his mother had been disinherited

by her grandfather, was it? No. Nor was it his concern that she'd broken her father's heart and run away with a commoner. He, Richard Barrons, still had blue blood in his veins and sooner or later, the old man would relent. And when he did, Barrons would have Arianna Halverson on his arm. Adding her brother's wealth to his own was only a matter of time.

Barrons was so lost in his thoughts that he paid no notice to the lightning that struck behind his carriage. If he had, he might have noticed that it touched very near to the Castin estate.

Arianna shivered as she watched the carriage pull away. From her bedroom window overlooking the front drive, she could make out the rambling form of the dark shape as it disappeared into the night. The irrational feeling of her life careening out of control had come again.

"You're not considering his offer, are you?"

Turning to face the apparition once more, Arianna was surprised by the increasing solidity of her specter. "I don't know what to think."

"You must refuse him."

"If I do, Ethan will be destroyed. Besides, it wouldn't be anything more than a marriage of convenience. He only wants to protect Ethan."

"Don't be a fool. Barrons is no friend of your brother's. For all you know, he might have been the one who shot him."

Arianna rubbed her eyes. "I don't know what to think. Perhaps it's just Ethan's money he's after."

"Barrons has enough money to buy and sell anything he desires, but for all he's worth, it can't buy him a seat at Almack's."

"He'll have what he wants and Ethan will be safe until he recovers."

"What if he doesn't recover? Have you considered that?"

"You're wrong. It's just a flesh wound."

"It's more than that and you know it." Will moved closer to her until they were nearly touching. "Get Barrons's blasted lackey out of here and call for a physician."

"I won't see my brother hang." Arianna ground her heels into the carpet.

"Hanging's not the worst thing that can happen to a man. Believe me, I know."

Arianna looked at him. His expression darkened. Her ghostly visitor seemed to take a deep breath, and it was the first time that Arianna even considered that the dead might still have the ability to inhale and exhale. Perhaps it was nothing but an impression left from his previous life. Whatever it was, a long silence stretched out between them.

A blast of wind rattled the window beside her. Arianna shivered again.

"I think you should rest, dear lady. You'll need to be in top form if you are to deal with Barrons."

"Whatever happens, this is my fight. I don't need your interference," she told him.

"What can I do? Rustle some draperies? Howl from the shadows? I'm no threat to Barrons. You'll have to destroy him."

"What do you want me to do? Stab him with my hat pin? Put poison in his tea?"

"Perhaps you could use those fine pistols your brother owns. I realize you've likely never fired a weapon, but accuracy won't be necessary if you don't have to aim far."

Arianna threw up her arms. "Insanity. That's what this is."

"Has your brother engaged in duels before?"

"Yes."

"Didn't he have a second?"

"Thomas Fielding, the Viscount of Branleigh— why?"

"I think you should have your man make some inquiries. Find out if Lord Fielding was with him last night and what happened to him if he was. Is he trustworthy, this fellow?"

"He wouldn't have betrayed Ethan. He was loyal to a fault."

"Perhaps the price Barrons offered was too much for him to turn away."

"Nonsense. Thomas has been friends with Ethan since they both were boys. He would have died protecting my brother."

"Perhaps the two of them were ambushed. If we find the body or any witnesses, it might be enough to convict Barrons."

"Expose Barrons and he'll use his evidence to implicate Ethan."

The ghost dismissed her concerns. "He's safe enough. Your brother has a great deal of influence, more than mere money could purchase."

"You don't care what happens to us." Arianna couldn't hold back the bite of her tone.

The specter met her gaze without flinching. "I don't

suppose I do, other than seeing Barrons pay for his crimes."

"Is that really all?" Arianna crossed her arms and awaited his answer. None came.

"I thought not. I'll make this decision myself. To be honest, I don't know who to believe. My only hope is that Ethan will awaken soon and tell me what to do."

He turned away from her, a vaporous statue standing guard over her life.

Arianna shivered again. Her brother lingering near death, a complete stranger threatening her very existence, and a troublesome spirit haunting her . . . how could her life get any worse?

The deepening shadows covered the landscape outside the lady's bedroom window. Will watched the slight movements of the trees beyond the glass, hoping that somewhere the answers he sought might appear. It was no use.

Scowling, he turned to the sleeping figure nestled amongst the linens in the ornately carved bed. The mahogany headboard was polished to show the grain of the wood and the tiny, delicate angels that watched over Lady Halverson. Angels indeed, he thought. If there were such creatures, he'd surely never seen the like. Nor did he expect to. But the devil he knew on a personal level.

Sighing deeply, he let his gaze drift about the room. From her armoire to the dressing table, everything was well appointed and highly polished. This room was the height of luxury, but then wasn't that the way of the aristocracy? All of their needs were seen to as long as they had the gold coin to see to it. It was his guess that Lord Castin had more than enough coin at his disposal.

Restlessness rose in Will like the surf at high tide. It was the worst kind of torture to be trapped between life and death, he thought. Like a hungry man gazing beyond the glass enclosing a grand dining room. He could see the luscious fare, smell its heady scent, and yet taste not the smallest morsel. Unfair indeed, he mused.

Then something caught his eye upon Lady Halverson's jewel stand. One of the drawers sat half open, a dainty gold chain hanging barely over the side of the drawer. It wasn't the chain that drew his attention, but a slight, greenish glow that seemed to be growing inside it.

Stepping closer to investigate, Will became entranced by the strange effect. Although he was nothing more than a vapor himself, he felt the confines of his skin begin to change and a burning, itching sensation covered him almost immediately. Before he knew what was happening, his hand shot out to grasp the item. When his fingers made contact, a bolt of energy struck him.

Will didn't know exactly what happened in those seconds. For a moment he lost awareness, knowing only the infinite green depths of the stone. When he came to himself again, he was seated on the floor, his legs spread out, his fist grasping the gold chain.

To his surprise, the jade stone no longer glowed. As he studied the piece, Will happened to glance at his reflection in the cheval glass across the room. For the briefest moment, he had turned the same shade, flaring up in an emerald sparkle and then just as quickly fading back to his usual ghostly shimmer. Glancing back at the stone, he saw that it had resumed its greenish tint.

Something important had obviously occurred, but unfortunately, he'd no idea what.

"Very curious," he muttered.

Arianna managed a polite smile for Lady Madeleine Tisbury, her unexpected and unwelcome visitor. She was the second cousin to Alfred Dennington, one of the men who'd been trying to thwart her brother in Parliament.

"Dear Arianna, how good of you to accept my call. I know I came on practically no notice, but since your brother didn't respond to our invitation to dinner the other night, I just had to inquire of him. Is he home?"

"Yes, but he is very ill. He, ah, ate some roast duck at the Bennerly's party the other night and has been under the weather ever since. Please forgive me for not calling him down. He's so off the trim that he cannot attend court for the rest of the week."

"Too bad! Perhaps you would allow me to send over Mr. Simons. He's the best physician on the west side, you know."

"No, thank you. Our own physician, Mr. Tumlin, has already been in. After his treatment, he thought it best for Ethan to stay in seclusion until the worst of his symptoms have abated. Please send our apologies to your husband."

"Of course, my dear. I'm so glad to hear that he wasn't involved in that other messy business."

With her tea cup half way to her mouth, Arianna could barely keep her hand from shaking. "What business?"

"You haven't heard?"

"With Ethan's condition, I've not had a chance to venture out." Arianna gently set her cup and saucer back on the tea table.

"Two bodies were found amongst the marigolds in Bonhom Park the other morning. One was none other than Lord Thomas Fielding, the other his driver, it is believed. The Bow Street runners are in hot pursuit of the scoundrels involved. Rumor has it that it was a duel gone bad. I'm sure the culprits will be caught."

Arianna bit her lip. Neither her brother's closest friend nor his driver had been seen since the night of the shooting. If it was discovered that Ethan's injuries implicated him in the deaths, it would mean even more disaster for Ethan.

"Did they leave any clues behind?"

"Not a one."

Arianna let out a slow breath. "I'm sure they'll find out who it is soon." Carefully she turned the conversation to less gruesome matters.

When Lady Tisbury had finally finished her refreshment and gone off to her next appointment, Arianna returned to her bedroom. Logically, if the amulet were put away, then there was no other way to summon the unwieldy ghost. Opening the door, she quickly found the error in her thinking. Standing beside her bureau was the form of her midnight visitor.

"Good morning, Lady Halverson." The austere figure bowed formally.

"You've come back," Arianna sighed as she went directly to her dressing table.

"You're not pleased to see me?"

"I was hoping that you might have found peace and moved on."

"Until my vengeance is complete, I shan't budge."
He shrugged, walking around the boudoir as though he
were its owner.

"Something is different about you." Arianna stepped
closer, scrutinizing his large form. "I don't know what
it is, but something has changed."

He smiled, lifting one eyebrow and tilting his head
slightly to one side. "Are you certain?"

"Yes. You're more . . . I'm not sure. More *you*."

"Am I?"

"You know, it isn't polite to visit a lady's private
quarters unannounced—and uninvited."

"No, but it is awfully interesting." He picked up
Arianna's dressing gown from the chest at the foot of
her bed.

"Here now, put that away." She moved to snatch it
from his grip, but found he'd had other intentions. With
a sharp jerk he pulled her closer. Stumbling as she
came, Arianna lost her balance, falling neatly into
his arms.

A sudden shock went through them both. She couldn't
quell the trembling that tumbled over her as she stood
motionless in his grasp.

"This isn't right," Arianna mumbled, trying desperately to make sense of this new, invigorating reality.

"Isn't it?"

"You're dead."

"I noticed that."

"But you're a ghost. You're not supposed to have
shape or solidity. It's not possible."

"I think I know why it is," he stated quietly, setting
her back on her heels. From his front vest pocket, he
pulled forth a single object.

"The amulet!" Arianna reached out to take it from

him, but her guest simply pulled up his arm, dangling it just out of her reach.

He gazed at the stone thoughtfully. "Is that what it is? A strange stone, to be sure. This morning I saw it lying there and when I leaned over it, a burning sensation passed over me. Then I found that I could touch it, pick it up and hold it in my hand." His clear blue eyes flashed back to her. "It's what drew me here, I think. What brought me to you."

"Give it back."

"I don't think so. At least not yet."

Arianna lunged again, but he pulled back. Angered beyond belief, she stepped back and crossed her arms.

"All right. What are your terms?" she said.

A smile crossed his devilishly handsome face. Devil was right, she thought. And more.

"Good. Nothing has changed. I need your help to put down Barrons. Once he is dead, I'll return your trinket."

"I am not in the business of killing people. Especially those to whom I might become betrothed."

His cheerful expression soured. "You've not accepted his proposal, have you?"

"Not yet, but I've little choice in the matter now. I fear the worst. I heard some disturbing news this morning. Thomas Fielding has been found dead. Murdered. I must do as Barrons asks or we'll all fall to ruin."

"You're set on this course?"

"I've already told you, I have no choice. You must seek your peace another way."

His solemn look bore down on her. "I don't think so." Tucking the amulet into his vest pocket once again, he turned and sat on the chaise, resolutely crossing his arms and legs.

"What are you doing?" Arianna could barely contain her upset. Things were spinning farther and farther out of her control.

"I'm waiting for you to make up your mind to help me. Until Barrons has been dealt with, I'll be shackled to you like an iron manacle on the wrist of a felon."

It was almost more than Arianna could bear. "You are the most ill-mannered, irresponsible, incredibly mule-headed man I've ever met."

"Aren't you forgetting something?" he asked, the hint of a grin playing at the sides of his mouth.

"What?" Arianna asked, her patience stretching to its uttermost boundary.

"My name. If you're going to call out a man, or rather a ghost in my case, don't you think you should at least inquire of his identity?"

"Oh, very well. What is your blasted name?"

He stood again, taking two very long steps to stand directly in front of her, leaning forward, his face less than a hair's breadth away.

Arianna knew she should have been afraid, should have been intimidated by so fearsome a specter. Instead she held her head steady and met his scathing features eye to eye.

"Yes?" she asked again, trying to make her voice as low and as threatening as he was pretending to be.

"Markham. Captain William Markham."

"The pirate Markham?" The breath left her body in one full gasp.

"The same. I was hanged on October 30th, to be exact. You may have heard of me."

Indeed she had, she thought. Of course, that was her last thought before she fell down in a faint.

*   *   *

Will watched the sleeping figure with a mixture of wry humor and concern. Of all the living souls he could haunt . . . The fates had paired him with the most unpredictable female in the world. Beautiful, unpredictable female, he corrected himself.

Indeed she was. The afternoon sunlight filtered in across the bed where he'd set her down on the quilted mattress. Now, tiny dust motes danced upon her still form, like little fairies attracted to her loveliness.

Will scoffed at himself. Romantic claptrap. A pretty face hadn't moved him in over five years, he thought. Even when his Lettie was still alive . . .

He stopped the thought. Since his late wife's death, he'd labored long to build his shipping business and be a good father to her child. He was almost at the peak of his trade when the disaster named Barrons hit. He scowled again. Damn and blast the fates that had brought him to this.

Glancing up in the cheval glass that sat beside Lady Halverson's dressing table, he took his first full look at himself since his resurrection.

Although his color was that of silver and smoke, it was indeed his own surprised expression staring back at him. That Will was now a creature that he could even see reflected in the glass was something of an amazement to him. Would others see him as well?

His question was soon answered when Henderson opened the door. Will sat quietly as the old man entered, his arms laden with fresh linens and a tray that held a crystal pitcher and a single glass. Carefully he sat the latter on the table beside Lady Halverson's bed and then he turned to place the linens inside the armoire. Turning on his heel, he left his mistress's room, with nary a glance in Will's direction.

Will turned back to the mirror. In his reflection he saw his familiar, broad-shouldered form, a body that he'd grown used to over the thirty-two years of his life. He saw the same high brow and square face. His strong nose and chin were no different, of course. Even the piercing blue of his eyes seemed to stare back with the same fierce passion that had driven him all of his life. The muscles on his arms and chest tightened as he drew a breath. The thin line of a scar ran down the side of his neck to be hidden beneath his shirt. No difference there, he thought. And yet, there was something that stood out from his appearance. He scratched his head in dismay. His thick hair was pulled back into a sailor's queue and a gold earring hung on the lobe of his right ear. It had been a small gift from the first captain he'd served under.

All of this he knew but none of it seemed out of the ordinary. Then he stepped back half a pace and saw the slight shimmer that touched upon his form. That was when the reality of his whole appearance hit him. He was dead.

"No wonder she's frightened of me."

"I'm not afraid of you, pirate," her voice said sharply as she rose from the bed. Arianna rubbed her head, as if the act could erase the circumstances that had had her collapsing like a sail on a windless night.

"I'm not a pirate."

"You were hanged as one."

"I was falsely accused. Barrons forged papers and spread vicious lies."

"I suspected he had such talents," she said absently as she straightened her gown.

"And worse," Will growled back at her.

Her piercing green eyes looked up at him. "Still, it

takes more than papers to prove such charges. What else?"

"He murdered my crew."

"According to the account I read, your crew was killed fighting the Royal Navy."

"Those were Barrons's men. Mine were already resting at the bottom of the ocean."

Arianna sighed. "I've no way of knowing whether or not you're telling the truth."

"You'd believe the word of a man who most likely has killed your brother and is forcing you to marry him?"

"I didn't say that. He alluded that it was you who were in league with Ethan. I don't see my brother as being in business with your kind. Ethan was honest to a fault."

"My kind. I see. Well, you both happen to be in league with me now. Your brother was nearly killed trying to put down Barrons. You know that much."

"I don't know for certain what happened."

"Perhaps if he doesn't die, he can tell you himself."

Will saw his words strike her as though she'd been hit by a pistol herself. "Perhaps he will," she said, her voice trembling slightly.

Feeling like a beast, Will let out a slow breath. "I apologize. I hope he does survive and not just for my own sake. If he'd intended to put down Barrons once and for all I certainly can't fault him. It takes a brave man to undertake such a thing alone."

"Ethan has always been courageous. I need to see to him now. Will you stay here, Captain?"

Will felt a small glimmer of hope. At least she wasn't calling him a pirate any longer.

"I would like to join you, if you don't mind. If he

has awakened, I need information on what happened as much as you. Planning must be done and after this incident, your brother might be able to help me."

"I don't know how, but we can ask."

As Arianna turned to leave, Will watched her. She moved with fluid grace. The straightness of her spine would make a man think twice about approaching her, and yet, Will had held her that very day. Her rigid appearance was but a ruse. He knew she was soft and well-rounded beneath her gowns. He'd felt the sweetness of her form, smelled the sweet scent of her hair. It was enough to make a man dizzy.

Except he was no longer a man, he reminded himself. As soon as his task was completed, he'd be finding his way to a grave. Better for her, he thought. A woman like Arianna needed a man alive and vibrant to care for her, not a corpse. Holding back yet another scowl, he moved to follow her. Damn and blast, he thought.

Thunder sounded in the distance. The wind blew against the side of the manse and made a howling sound. Will knew the storm was only echoing his own unrest. Yes, the tempest still waited for him. He knew he could not keep it at bay for long.

Chapter Five

Ethan Halverson lay on his own bed now. When Will entered the master bedroom, he could easily tell it was a masculine retreat. No soft curtains nor satin embroidered pillows in here. Heavy, dark furniture filled the room. One corner held a mahogany writing table and chair, the other a shelf of books. In the center of the sanctuary stood an austere four-poster bed in which the headboard was intricately carved with designs in the fashion of the far east. Arianna's brother was not a man given to frivolity, but he was a man of expensive tastes.

"He doesn't look too healthy but at least he's not dead."

Arianna was already seated beside her brother, clasping his hand in hers as though the warmth of her own spirit might pass into his.

"He's no better," she said, her voice small and trembling.

"Not yet, but that means nothing. A man with his injuries needs time to heal."

Arianna gave him a dry look. "I see, Captain. Not only are you a seaman, you are also a physician."

"I've seen plenty of men down, if that's what you mean."

"I suppose you would have, in your line of business."

"Any man would who makes his living on a ship. I apologize for not being more genteel. I realize that a man who doesn't labor at the courts or the faro tables isn't considered a gentleman at all."

It was Arianna's turn to frown. "That wasn't what I meant. I just thought that yourself being so well-traveled, you must have seen many things."

Will swallowed back his ire. "I apologize for my temper. It seems to get the better of me."

She rubbed her eyes in a single tired motion that bespoke the depth of her worry and exhaustion. "I suppose I am not in the kindest of moods myself. Have you any idea on the best way to care for him until he's recovered?"

Will took a breath. *Assuming that Ethan would recover*, he thought, but didn't voice that particular opinion.

"See that he sleeps and takes light nourishment. Some strong port, perhaps, and broth. Has your man tried to rouse him at all?"

"Just after Barrons left last night." She leaned forward and placed her hand on his cheek. "He's so cold."

"Best to have your servant maintain a good fire for him. Keep him warm and keep him covered as much as possible."

Just then the man on the bed took a long, shuddering breath.

"Ethan?" Arianna leaned closer.

Pale-faced, her brother opened his eyes, staring about. Fear crossed his expression. Weakly he struggled against her hold.

"Rest easy, man." Will knelt beside him, momentarily forgetting his current state of nonexistence. But then, he thought, if the fellow was teetering on the edge between life and death, who was to say what he actually could see? Or perhaps Ethan shared his sister's peculiar talent.

Ethan didn't respond, his eyes going wildly about the room.

"He probably doesn't see you."

"Or he's looking for the man who shot him. Tell him he's safe now."

"There, there, Ethan. There's no one here but you and I."

In response to her calming voice, Ethan settled down. In distress, he opened his mouth several times, making small, choking noises.

"I think he's trying to say something," Will observed.

Arianna leaned closer. "What is it, Ethan? What's wrong?"

Still no noise came. It was clear that whatever injuries her brother had suffered, his speech was affected. Arianna sank back in her chair.

"Oh, my darling. Rest for now. I'm sure whatever plagues you will come back when you've had a chance to recover."

* * *

It had been a long day and even longer night. Arianna was exhausted from worrying over her brother's condition. Still, she didn't leave him, but instead sent Henderson to fetch some reading material from the west wing study.

The room itself had been a mystery to Arianna and Ethan. It had been their mother's private sanctuary and they'd often been told not to enter it without her permission.

"What do you hope to find?" Will asked. He was lounging on the long sofa that Arianna had had Henderson and the groomsman, Dennehy, bring in from the main parlor. Stretching like a long-bodied cat, the spirit certainly did emulate a feline predator. His body seemed to be both at rest and ready to pounce at any moment.

Arianna swallowed hard when she thought of the strength of the arms that now lay across his broad, barely covered chest. He wore a half-opened shirt, revealing a sprinkling of dark brown hair at his chest, and almost too tight black trousers tucked into big black boots. Arianna suppressed a blush when she remembered what her mother had once hinted at concerning the size of a man's feet and other parts of his anatomy.

The captain cleared his throat and gave her a quizzical look.

"I'm hoping to find any information about you."

"About me? What makes you think I'd be in those books?"

"Not you in particular, you in general. I've been having conversations with the deceased since I was a child. My mother did before me, of course, she was also a 'sensitive.'"

"What exactly is that?"

"Someone who can hear voices from both sides of existence."

"The living and the dead."

"Exactly. Only you're different somehow."

"I am? How?"

"Well, your physical manifestation, for one. You're not completely dead, nor are you completely alive."

"No one sees or hears me except you."

"True enough, but to me, even with my heightened senses, you are much more solid than any other spirit I've seen. In fact, beyond a glimmering light, I've not seen any other spirit in the same way. I'm curious as to what makes you different."

The captain's brow furrowed. "I see. You think that book will give you answers. Could it be because I am sworn to kill the man who caused my death?"

"I doubt it. I've spoken to others who were unsettled about the circumstances of their demise. A few were even as insistent as you are. None of them compare to your presence. I have a feeling that there might be more to your being here than just your intent to seek your revenge on one evil man. Something else is at work."

"It matters not to me, as long as Barrons is destroyed. That is what we should be making plans for, not digging in a dusty tome to study the pecularities of an already impossible situation."

"You may be right," Arianna conceded, though not happily. "But I still believe that arming ourselves with as much knowledge as possible is our best gambit. It certainly won't hurt."

"Won't it? The longer we take, the more time that Barrons has to cause damage. You already said your brother meant to stop him by any means. Too bad the duel was unsuccessful. I wonder if your brother even considered the chance that he might lose."

Arianna bristled at this. "Whatever his intention, there is naught to be done about it now."

"No, I suppose not. All the more reason for you to act quickly."

"Whatever you have in mind, I won't do it."

"You may change your mind after the wedding night, you know."

"I'm sure Mr. Barrons has more interest in my bank accounts than he does my bed."

"I wouldn't put either past him. There are a few things you need to understand. Richard Barrons doesn't just love money. He adores power. I saw it in his eyes when he captured me. He so enjoyed his dominion over me that he fairly glowed from it. No one should ever have to look at the evil that lives in that man's expression."

Arianna saw the twist of pain that clenched his jaw. She meant to speak—to argue, perhaps, or even to settle his discomfort—but the look he shot her made it clear that he'd suffered at the hands of Barrons all those months before.

"You don't understand, do you?" he asked.

"I understand that you were hurt very badly."

The captain scoffed. "It wasn't about my hurt, you know. It was about my degradation. But there's little sport in torturing a grown man for a bastard like Barrons. He chooses his prey much more carefully than that."

Arianna felt her throat go dry. "What do you mean?"

"He prefers weaker subjects. Women and children are his favorite, as are the old or infirm." He looked away darkly.

Arianna didn't want to believe there was that sort of evil on the earth. The spirits she'd met in her entire life hadn't all been nice, although there had been a few who she would have called greatly misguided.

"Then what's to be done about it? I suppose if we call the authorities . . ."

"A waste of time. I'm sure he puts his money to good use. My trial and execution were an excellent example of that."

"But if we could find some damning information, something that could be brought to public attention, then that might be enough."

The captain watched her with a hooded gaze. "A knife to the throat would be quicker. I could show you how to do it. For a woman, it's all a matter of—"

Will's instruction was interrupted when the door to the chamber opened. Henderson came in carrying a very large, very cumbersome volume.

"Thank you. You may set it on the table."

When the old man had left them alone, Arianna pulled her handkerchief from her sleeve. "If I remember right, I think the reference to differential spirits is in the back."

In an instant the captain was beside her. "You don't understand. This can't be handled the honest way. You must kill him." His hand shot out to grasp hers. "Believe me, if I could do it, I would."

Arianna felt the sharp tingling of his touch. A heat was created between them, building and surging like lightning during a storm. Suddenly frightened of what their contact might mean, Arianna pulled back.

"I believe you would, Captain. However, I am the one that's alive and I'm in control of this situation."

"I still have the amulet," he stated, his eyes boring into her, his voice unflinching.

"Would you use it to force your intentions? Even if it meant hurting me?"

Arianna knew it was an unfair question and its effect on him was quick.

Stepping back a pace, the captain's face twisted with the tumultuous emotions seething inside him.

"I'm not the murderer here. I've never taken an innocent life, never wielded my sword against any but the devil's own."

"Then we do this my way," Arianna ground out. "No more talk of blades or pistols."

After a sharp nod, the captain turned away. Arianna waited for him to say more, but he remained silent. Turning back to her mother's book, she began to search in earnest.

Three hours later, Will was still scowling. Enthralled by the ancient book, Arianna had scarcely spoken. Ten minutes more and she sat back, stretching catlike and twisting her head to ease a kink in her neck.

Will found himself wanting to slip around behind her and very carefully place his hands on either side of her neck. He wanted to experience how warm and alive she would feel at his fingertips. Their brief touch before had been like the breath of air after a storm, producing sparkling little bits of lightning across the ocean surface, shimmering and full of life.

Of course she was full of life, he reminded himself. Why wouldn't she be? He was the only lost soul in the room, after all. Angry with himself for dwelling on thoughts of the glorious feel of her skin against his own, he stepped back, afraid that even his nearness might totally undo his tenuous grasp on this strange reality.

He couldn't get attached now. No, it was best to stay

away and not tempt the volatile feelings that churned within him whenever he was close to the fair Arianna Halverson.

Somehow he felt in his gut that if he fell for the flesh and blood woman before him, he would lose his hold on the hatred and anger that was the cord that held him to this life. To let go of it could only mean he'd lose his chance at destroying Richard Barrons once and for all.

"That's it. There's no reference to your condition that I can understand. Mind you, much of it is written in ancient text. Mother was going to teach me the language one day, but we never got around to it. She fell ill so swiftly. There was simply not enough time before her death for her to fully explain what exactly my gift was. Something to do with her lineage. All the women in our family have been born with some strange abilities. Mine was to be as counsel for the dead. My mother could divine future events."

"Curious. Did she predict her own death?"

Arianna shook her head. "If she did, she never told us about it. I'm not sure. I do know that my family descended from an offshoot of ancient culture, akin to fairies, she'd said. Unfortunately, I never learned much else. I suppose we could go through my mother's private journals, though."

"Then do so." Will returned to the chair he'd pulled beside the table. Sitting or standing, it made no difference to him, but he found that if he did look settled, then Arianna returned her full attention to the next object in front of her.

The lady's journal was a plain, black, leather-bound book with none of the lace trim nor delicate frippery that adorned most women's belongings. Somehow, Will thought, if he had the chance to ever meet the grand lady who had given birth to Arianna and her brother, he would have liked her very much. Although perhaps not quite as much as he found himself liking her daughter.

"There it is," Arianna said, pointing down on the open book in her lap.

"You've found the answer?"

"I have."

Will leaned over. He could see the long strokes of her mother's hand. Carefully written, noble words that spoke volumes of the woman who had penned them.

"She talks of the stone here, how it was given to her by her own mother. Known as the Joining Stone, it has been imbued with special powers that work to place together those whose souls have been matched. It states that sometimes time and circumstance separates those who were meant to be together. These joinings are required to maintain the bloodline."

"You and I are meant for each other? Preposterous." Will tamped down on the thought before it took hold in his mind. It would be too easy to let such nonsense draw him to her, to let this strange magic bind him forever with this woman of mystery—and destroy his only chance to kill Barrons.

"I'm not sure," Arianna said, though by her expression she truly did believe what she had read.

"That may pertain to the living, but what of the dead?"

She shook her head. "It simply says that it binds us together, its power lending whatever is needed to fulfill the purpose of the stone."

Just then a knock sounded at the door to the parlor.

"Lady Halverson," Henderson bowed, "Mr. Barrons has returned."

* * *

Arianna made her way to the front parlor. As she expected, Richard Barrons sat back on her fine sofa, his legs and arms crossed and an expectant expression on his hawklike face.

"The bastard doesn't even stand when you enter the room."

Arianna gave the ghost a quick glance, then looked at her visitor. "Mr. Barrons." Neither waiting for him to rise, nor paying the slightest notice to his poor manners, Arianna took the seat across from him.

"Lady Halverson. I was hoping that you might have had time to consider my offer."

"I have had time, sir."

"Time enough to inquire about your brother's recent business dealings, no doubt?"

Arianna stiffened. Of course she had sent out a query to Arthur Milkens, her brother's man of accounts. He had answered back stating that though a woman shouldn't ever worry about such complicated things, her brother had recently diversified his business interests, opening several new accounts. She knew it could have been a coincidence, that Ethan had decided to turn his business to newer, more conventional venues.

Unfortunately, she couldn't be sure. She remembered Ethan's sad countenance the last time they'd spoken. She'd sensed something very wrong. Could it be true? Was Ethan guilty of such terrible acts?

At the very least, the circumstances might give credence to Barrons's accusations. While it was near to impossible for a peer to be hanged for anything except murder or another equally gruesome crime, a nobleman could very well have his neck stretched for high treason.

"I understand the implications. Very well, Mr. Barrons. What are your terms?"

"I'm not offering terms, Lady Halverson. I am simply insisting that you and I marry as soon as possible. I've already made inquiries and we can start on the arrangements. It's to be a small wedding, very private and I've already sent round the announcements, since I'd anticipated your desire to put this nasty business behind us. I trust you accept my proposition."

Arianna swallowed the bile that rose in her throat. The thought of signing any sort of agreement with this scoundrel was beyond belief. And yet she couldn't risk Ethan. All she could do was hope that, when he recovered, her brother could defend himself against such charges and use his position in Parliament to gain her freedom from the intolerable marriage.

"I will agree to be your wife in every way but one." She slid a sideways glance at Captain Markham. He was leaning rather close, his arms crossed and a furious expression heating up his face.

"I'm sorry, Arianna, but there are no concessions to be made. You will be my wife, *in every respect*. You have only to sign the papers signifying your agreement. I've already taken care of your brother's signature."

Arianna looked down at the rough scrawl on the paper that looked so much like Ethan's. Close in appearance, but not quite. Still, she doubted whether anyone would question it.

"It's not possible." Arianna felt an ice cold chill overcome her. "That can't be Ethan's signature." She glanced up at Barrons, who only smiled back at her.

"Your brother and I spoke at length. This is for the

best. No doubt you've heard that two men were murdered in Bonhom Park. Many know of one's close acquaintance with your brother. Questions are being asked. We must act now or there will be no way to protect him."

"I must ask," she said, her voice cracking, "what it is you intend. Will you be moving into Trenton Estate, or have you another place where we will set up our home?"

Barrons smiled thinly. "Oh, I have a place for you, my sweet lady, I do indeed. Sign."

Arianna reached for the quill pen and dipped it in the inkpot. Very carefully and with a shaking hand, she signed the parchment.

"Damn and blast," Will growled behind her. "What have you done?"

"Good," Barrons said as he snatched the paper from the table and stuffed it into a leather pouch.

Arianna didn't answer for a moment. "If you don't mind, Mr. Barrons, I am very tired." She moved to stand, but he rose quickly and grabbed her arm.

"But I do mind, my sweet bride. You're coming with me."

Shocked, Arianna tried to pull away. "I need time to pack my things and to see to Ethan. Surely you don't think I'd leave him to the care of the servants?"

"I did not. I have two carriages waiting outside. You will accompany me in one and your brother is to be taken in the other. Two of my operatives will see to it you have everything you need. We'll be leaving for the coast. Once there, we shall sail to my estate, which is located on a small island off the coast of France."

"But what of the wedding? We cannot be properly married without clergy? What of our friends?" Arianna felt the blood drain from her head.

"What of them? Ah, worry not, my lovely girl. I have taken care of everything. Slipped a few coins into a clergyman's pocket, you see. The banns will be posted while you and I go on an extended holiday. For all purposes, you are my wife now and I—well, I own the two of you. In the morning one of my solicitors will be contacting your brother's estate manager. He will then take the proper paperwork to the courts and arrange to have me appointed as your brother's guardian. I've secured papers that state your brother suffered a terrible injury when he fell from his horse. Everything has been done."

His hand still grasping her arm, Barrons turned on his heel, dragging her behind him. Once she was beside him, Barrons slipped his arm around her waist.

"As soon as we reach the inn, Arianna, I will make you my wife in the true sense." His hand slipped down and gripped her bottom. Arianna was instantly repulsed at his touch and tried to pull away, but his hands were quicker and his grip tightened.

"Now, my pet, it wouldn't be wise of you to anger your new husband. With that he pulled her with him down the long corridor.

Arianna felt like a trapped animal. Fear rose in her like the evening tide. As they neared the front entrance, she saw Digby standing in the doorway, her wrap in his hand. He held it out and she barely had the garment in her hand when she was thrust out the door and pushed into the waiting carriage.

Will didn't like the cramped quarters. Not because there was barely enough room for his large frame. He found that he could easily push his shins against the wooden panel bench across from him and it would literally bend the wood out of his way. In truth, he could also spread his arms out, passing within inches of Digby's face. How he wished he could plunge the hard knuckles of his right fist into those twisted, smug features.

Worse yet was Arianna. She was seated across from them, her small frame tucked into the corner. Looking fearfully about, she'd shaken her head slightly when Will had moved to sit next to her. In the next second, Barrons had settled himself beside her, so close that he seemed to nearly smother her.

For all he couldn't do, Will scowled. How he wished to pull the pistol from the man's jacket and shoot both the blighters like the dogs they were. The answer was plain. Arianna needed to see reason. She must kill Barrons and do it soon or all would be lost.

The carriage went on through most of the night, stopping only once to change horses and to pick up a pair of prized stallions that Barrons was planning on taking with him on the voyage to his estate.

When both Barrons and Digby had exited, Will turned to Arianna. She had settled somewhat in the last few hours. Her fear for her life had been slowly replaced by a despairing resignation.

"You can't do this, you know." Will tried for the hundredth time to persuade her.

"I've no choice. I can't let them hang Ethan."

"They won't execute an injured man."

"He may recover one day. I can't take the chance that the crown may feel differently by then. Besides, you saw those papers. You know what else Barrons has against him. No, this is the only way."

"The only way to get out of this is to steal the blade

that Barrons keeps in his boot and plunge it between his ribs."

Arianna shook her head. "I won't kill a man, any man."

"If you don't kill this one, he'll very likely kill you,"—he stopped, taking a deep breath—"or worse."

Arianna closed her eyes.

Will hated himself for making her see the obvious. In a way, he thought himself little better than Barrons. It wasn't in his nature to force a woman to do anything. Not now, not ever. Will would offer no excuses, but knew what had to be done.

"Either way, if you don't do something soon, I'm sure Barrons will make good on his promise."

"I know." Arianna said nothing more, but instead turned her head toward the window. Barrons and Digby were outside talking with the stable owner.

Will scowled. "Then stop it now. You are the only one who can."

When she looked back at him, it was not as a woman facing her fate at the hands of an evil man, but that of a girl, young and vulnerable. The sight cut through Will's heart.

"I cannot."

"You must!" Will ground out the words, watching as she flinched as though he'd struck her. Taking a deep breath he tried again. "Do you want him to prevail? Do you want him to be in control of your life? Not only yours, but the earl's as well?"

"I . . ." She stopped, on the verge of tears. "I have no choice. I've told you that."

"No. I will not accept that. There are always choices."

"For you, perhaps. For a man, any man, but not a woman. There is something else to consider."

"And that is?" Will waited, his breath held back until she spoke again.

"What if Ethan does not recover? What if he remains not alive and yet not dead? Who will care for him? As a woman, I have little recourse. I will be appointed a guardian and heaven knows what will happen to him."

"Then find a husband amongst the *ton*. Surely there is someone who will . . ."

She shook her head furiously. "There is no one. Have you not noticed that I am nearly three-and-twenty and not yet betrothed? The men of our social standing have long since backed away from any possible suit."

"Surely your brother's assets would be enough to attract someone. I cannot believe that in all of the kingdom there is not one man who would offer for you."

She sighed beside him. "I'm afraid that my reputation precedes me. I've only had two gentlemen interested in marriage, both of whom met with unfortunate happenstances."

"I don't understand."

Outside a soft rain began to caress the landscape, the drops reminiscent of the gentle tears that slipped down Arianna's cheeks.

"The first, a viscount from the Lakes District, left my home in rather a rush after we sat for tea one afternoon. The authorities think he sent his horse off a bridge."

"How could you possibly be responsible for that?"

"Because during our visit, one of my family members, Aunt Lavinia, appeared and gave him a proper set-down. She felt he'd not been attentive enough to our conversation."

"And that sent him packing? Must not have been much of a man if he let an old woman furl his sails."

Arianna's cheeks flushed with embarrassment. "Aunt Lavinia had died three years before. The poor man was found, barely alive and muttering about being haunted. It was a terrible scandal."

Will drew in a deep breath. He'd known many a sailor who had tried to pitch himself overboard thinking the ship had become haunted or cursed. In fact, if he weren't a ghost himself, he would certainly empathize.

"What about the second gentleman? What happened to his proposal?"

If her first admission had made her uncomfortable, whatever story she waited to tell seemed near to un-bearable, Will thought.

"It was most regrettable. Lord Michael Calvin, the Earl of Starbury, had asked me to marry him, although we had only a short acquaintance. He was a bit brusque in his manner, some said even rude. But he quite qual-ified and after my shame with my first suitor, there was little else to be done. Half the *ton* thought me quite mad, talking to spirits and such. The rest of them were certain I'd been claimed by the devil himself."

"So, what happened?"

"Lord Starbury and I had an argument. He felt that we must be married as soon as possible and insisted my brother double my dowry. Ethan refused. He didn't believe that Starbury wanted me for any more than my lands and wealth. It was during their discussion he threw his cheroot to the floor and it caught the draperies ablaze. The entire west wing of Ethan's country house nearly burnt to the ground."

"And Starbury?"

"I believe he is probably keeping company with Aunt Lavinia. After that, no nobleman has ever come calling. So you see, Captain, Mr. Barrons's offer of marriage comes at a most opportune time. I have no choice."

Her solemn confession bit into Will's consciousness with sharp teeth.

"Damn and blast," he muttered, though the sting of his curse fell into the deep well of the silence that now lay between them.

It was near dusk when the carriage pulled into the seaside village. The inn was old and Arianna could smell the faint scent of sewage in the yard. Barrons opened the door, and, after jumping down, pulled her out, half dragging, half carrying her towards the building.

"I need a room, a private room, for my new bride and myself," he told the stocky innkeeper. The man grunted as Barrons tossed a leather pouch onto the counter. "There's extra in there for you to bring up our dinner. The lady and I will want to dine in an hour."

He turned and pulling Arianna behind him, headed for the stairs. Her fate was in Barrons's hands.

Chapter Six

Arianna wasn't allowed a moment's rest. Barrons thrust her into the narrow room, which held a bed barely large enough for two people, a small table, and a rusty oil lamp.

"Best get out of your traveling clothes, Lady Halverson," Barrons smirked.

"I didn't bring a nightdress," Arianna said in a tight voice. Her new husband left no doubt that he was not overly concerned with her appearance.

Not waiting for her to comply, he lifted his arm and struck her openhanded across the face.

When his hand connected, Arianna fell back with a small cry, landing between the table and the bed.

"If you'll not do as I say, I shall remove your clothes myself," Barrons growled.

"Wait! I'll do it."

Despite her injury, Arianna struggled to stand and began unbuttoning her traveling dress, her hands tearing at each layer of fabric, anger and fear warring within her for supremacy. When her stays were undone as best as she could manage, she stood, fists clenched and jaw set in defiance, her skirts slipping soundlessly to the floor.

"Sir, you do not know how to treat a lady." Arianna knew it would do no good to defy him, and might very likely get her killed in the process. Though her gut twisted and her breaths came in small, short bursts, she would fight him.

Barrons paused for a moment, a wicked smile crossing his face. Too late, Arianna realized that her anger only served to spark a blazing passion in her new husband. In the depths of his black eyes she could see one striking emotion rear up. Lust.

Barrons lunged forward.

Arianna struggled when he roughly pulled her into his embrace. Though she beat at him with her fists, he easily subdued her, wrapping his arms around her, his mouth grinding against hers, more an invasion than a kiss.

Arianna could feel the growling chuckle that rose within him, his breaths vibrating against her skin.

"Ah, a woman of spirit after all," he said, thrusting her back again and wiping his mouth. "I think I need to raise some color on your flesh, woman. Maybe then you'll work harder to please your husband."

Arianna didn't shrink back but met his threats straight on. As he pulled a long, leather strap from his jacket, she managed to grind out, "You never said pleasing you was part of the arrangement."

Will paused at the door to the stair which led to the sleeping areas. He wouldn't go up there. Damn her if she chose to go with that bastard. In anger, he turned to the sparsely populated taproom. It was a shame he couldn't hit someone. He felt very much like breaking a nose or bruising one of the thick, dreary faces before him.

Unleashing his frustration, Will slammed his fist on the wooden table. No one moved or otherwise acted as though aware of his outburst. Enraged that no one would hear the oaths he wanted to roar, he instead bit his tongue. It would do no good. It was Arianna's wedding night and though he knew he was a fool to care, he cared just the same.

The small inn was one that he would have frequented during his life if he'd traveled much on land. For a man as rich as Barrons, however, it was hard to imagine him spending even a farthing on it, and yet here he was with his bride.

"Did you see that chit that ol' Richie brought in, mate?"

For a moment, Will had thought the innkeeper was talking to him rather than the short, foul smelling, rat-faced man who leaned against the bar.

"Aye, I did at that. A sweet peach for the likes of him, eh?" He chuckled as he took a deep drink from his mug.

"I swear, I've seen Richard Barrons drunk to the nines and in love with every ruffled skirt from here to London, but never a lass as cheeky as that."

"True enough. If she was my daughter, I'd not let the wretch put his hands on her. Hear about Meggie Adams?"

"That I did. Cut her up something bad. So scarred she is that the only work she can find is in the dark."

"Course in the dark, it makes little difference what a girl looks like, eh?"

Both men burst into laughter. Will grimaced. Though it bothered him to think of the poor working girl so cruelly used and left without means of support, the fear in him for Arianna's safety rose even higher.

Something had to be done, he decided, but what, he wasn't sure. Seeing the two men drop into conversation, Will wished, not for the first time, that someone, anyone else could see him. Wasn't there anything he could do?

Considering the men a moment more, Will decided to try something. He walked over to them, concentrating with all of his strength. Standing behind the rat-faced man, Will took in a deep breath, and then with the full force of his being, blew it upon the back of the man's neck.

The wretch shivered as if with a sudden chill.

"What is it?" the innkeeper asked, drawing slightly back.

"I don't know, but a coldness came over me, like the dead was breathin' on me neck."

"Keep yer curses to yerself." The innkeeper grunted and turned away, crossing himself.

Will stood quietly for a moment, considering. Perhaps he could affect the living in some small way. Could the information that Arianna had located for him have been wrong? This state of separateness might well prove advantageous after all.

Suddenly, feeling that the room was too full even for the dead, Will turned and left the innkeeper and his patrons.

He'd go out where there was space to mull things over, see how far he could wander from Arianna's influence. Since he'd been carrying the stone, his freedom had increased. Not that he meant to leave her. An invisible cord still bound them together. He would not wander far.

Glancing up to the second story window, Will saw the light from a single oil lamp burning in Arianna's room. He'd had no intention of watching the bride and her groom consummate their marriage, and yet the thought of Arianna in her white lace sleeping gown made him breathe faster, his heart that was supposed to be eternally still, beating furiously within him.

"Enough of this," he muttered. As he scanned the area, he noted the two fine animals that had drawn the ornate carriage Barrons had used to carry them from the city. Damned if those weren't fine horses, too. Will, a man who'd spent little of his life on land, could recognize that.

Two stable boys led the stallions inside the barn. Curious about the stable, Will followed. Many thoughts collided in his head. What sort of catastrophe could stop the wedding night? He'd certainly been no threat to Barrons and merely an annoyance to Arianna earlier. But now, perhaps there might be something he could do.

The stallions snorted nervously. Will paused a moment, watching the animals back away from him. It seemed that the beasts knew of his presence. Will watched them a moment, a new idea forming in his mind. Perhaps something could be done after all.

It was then that the stable lad came in, hoisting a bale of hay into the manger. The horses settled somewhat and moved to investigate the hay, though still keeping a wary eye in Will's direction.

"Come on you. Eat up. Mr. Barrons will light a fire on my hide if he thinks yer not taken proper care of."

Finishing his chore, the boy turned and exited the barn. In doing so, he neglected to latch the door.

Will formed a plan and, walking to stand behind the stallions, leaned forward and estimated the distance between the stall and the barn's exit. It might work, he thought.

"Grraahh!" he yelled at the horse. The animal started upright, kicking its hooves.

"Move, you old bag of bones!" Will yelled again. The high strung stallion turned nearly in on itself and crashed into the half-open door and then went rushing out into the stable yard, followed by the other of the pair.

Seeing the valuable animals thrashing about, the groomsmen left the other horses and ran after them. The panicked stallions backed away and then turning, both of them made a mad dash for the open road. The three groomsmen and both stable boys set off in a dead run, yelling and screaming after the beasts. Will stood back and watched the chaos, pleased with himself.

It was then that someone sounded the alarm. "Mr. Barrons, come quick," a voice called out. "Your stallions have run off!"

The door to the inn burst open and several half-dressed patrons came running out. The loudest among them was none other than the partially clad Richard Barrons, his trousers clutched to his waist and his shirt tails flapping behind him.

Any other time Will would have been glad to see his enemy so distressed. For the moment, though, his thoughts were only of Arianna and what condition she might be in.

Entering the now empty taproom, Will strode to the stair, and taking the steps two at a time, he made the top floor in seconds. Only one door along the narrow hall remained shut. Immediately, Will went to it and then through it, deciding that there were times when being dead wasn't such an inconvenience after all.

The room was dark, but there was enough moonlight from the window to show there was no one present. Perplexed, Will turned to leave when the smallest of sounds caught his attention. Barely an intake of breath to even the most discerning ear, what Will heard was a silent cry. He knew the sound, having in the past held back his own anguish in just such a way.

Searching the room more thoroughly, he finally walked to the opposite side of the bed. That was when he saw her. Arianna was huddled in the corner, trying desperately to cover herself with the tattered remnants of her traveling gown.

Bending down, Will pulled back the clothing. Arianna sat with her face down, her arms thrown over her head. Despite her attempts to cover herself, he could see the bruises on her neck, arms and right leg. Her mouth was swollen and a thin trickle of blood colored her mouth and chin. The sight of her trembling form tore at his heart and another high tide of anger rose within him.

"Bastard," he growled.

Arianna's shivering worsened and she shrank away from him even more.

"Come, my lady. There's no need for you to be frightened of me," he whispered. Bending low, he gently lifted Arianna and bundled her into his arms, surprised that in his ghostly form he could actually hold her. It seemed where the two of them were concerned, his touch was as solid as the living.

"Oh," she sobbed. When he pulled her close she began to cry in earnest. Shaking violently, she clung to his shirt with fists so tight her knuckles shone white through her skin.

"Easy," he told her. "I'll take you from here."

Pulling back and standing at the same time, Will cradled her in his arms. Not knowing what else to do, he settled her gently on the bed, careful not to let her go, and let her cry until her anguish was spent.

"I'm sorry," she muttered. "I've soaked your shirt."

Will couldn't hold back the soft laugh that escaped him. "It's of no import. I'm sure it will dry well, though since I've passed on I hadn't had time to inquire about laundering. In fact, I've not even had need of a bath. It's a wonder I don't smell like the stable."

A chuckle escaped her as well. "I believe I know the answer to that," she said, her tone less shaky. "Since you aren't alive, things of this world don't adhere to you. The dust of the road, for instance. In fact,"—she drew back from him, running her hands on his arm—"that I can touch you at all is very curious."

"Don't trouble yourself about it." Will gently pulled her back into his arms. "I don't think we should examine what this is too closely at the moment." He hugged her tighter. Damned if it didn't feel good to have her so close and warm against him. He cursed himself for striving to stay so distant all this time.

"I can't," she said suddenly, pulling back again.

"Can't what?"

"I can't do this. I'm a married woman."

"Cuckolding her husband with a ghost?"

"I'm not sure that's what it is, but I don't think it's proper."

Will laughed. "The filthy blackguard half beat you to death and here you are worried about being a good wife to him?"

"Whatever he is, I am an honorable woman," she said tightly.

Will sobered. "Yes, you are. He doesn't deserve you."

"It doesn't matter." Arianna sighed.

Outside their window the commotion of the village men gathered to catch the runaways distracted them. Urgent shouts echoed beyond the yard.

"It won't be long and he'll be back," she said. Will watched her repress a shudder. "At least I know Ethan is safe for the moment." She turned toward him. "He is safe, isn't he?"

Will nodded. "What a fortunate man your brother is." He murmured as she relaxed back onto the bed, closer, but not quite touching him.

"I owe him a great deal," she said, crossing her arms in front of her. "He has taken care of me since our parents died. I don't know what would have become of me if not for Ethan."

"Nonsense. In spite of any interference with your ghostly relations or other curses, you are of impeccable lineage. Sooner or later another brave man might have come forth and given you all that you desire."

Arianna spared him a glance. "All that I desire? What do you think that might be, Captain?"

Will shrugged. "What all women want, I suppose. A fine home, children, dresses, jewels. Security, I suppose."

"I see. Everything a woman desires."

"Of course. What else is there?"

"You mean, besides marriage? We can learn to play the pianoforte and plan elaborate parties. In truth, women in our society have little use beyond being decorative cuffs for our husbands' finest suit coats."

"Hm. You don't have too high of an opinion of the male gender. Your brother is a peer and he doesn't share that view of women, surely. If he did, you would have been paired off long ago."

"My brother loves me and understands me. We are both strong personalities who don't need marriage entanglements." Will felt her stiffen in his arms. "I won't let Ethan die. I can't."

"I agree. Your brother is what is keeping the game level at the moment. As long as he draws breath, Barrons has to keep you alive."

Arianna looked at him sharply. "You mean if Ethan dies . . ."

"Barrons will very likely continue to manage the estate in hopes of your union producing a son. When and if that were to happen, he wouldn't need you. In fact, even if your brother survives, the moment Barrons is assured a place in the family lineage and inheritance, he can dispense with both of you."

Will watched a frown crease her brow.

"I never considered that." She began to tremble again.

"We won't let it happen," he said, his voice tight with determination.

"How can we prevent it?" Worry darkened the clear emerald shade of her eyes.

"There are ways."

Understanding dawned on her face. "I told you. I'm not a killer. I won't become a beast like him."

"We are all beasts, madame. Whether we like to admit it or not. Think of the unspeakable cruelties he has committed already. Think of what he can and will do in the future."

Her trembling grew more visible. "What am I to do?" she asked in a small voice.

Will relented. He was being a selfish bastard and he

knew it. Reaching out for her, he pulled her into his embrace. She relaxed this time, despair washing over her so thickly it was nearly palpable.

"Take your ease. I have set something in motion that will at least give you a short time of peace, I think."

She glanced up sharply at him. "How? What?"

A loud crash cut through the night followed by the angry shouts of Richard Barrons.

"The how I don't quite understand. The what is of little import. Your groom will be pre-occupied for a bit. Rest. You can't fight him if you're exhausted."

Arianna settled back into his arms. "How can I rest in such circumstances?"

Despite her protest, Arianna did close her eyes. In a few moments her breathing slowed and Will could feel her heart beat more softly against his chest.

In spite of her doubts—or perhaps because of them, Will wasn't sure which—he gained a new hope. If he had caused a change in the atmosphere enough to frighten the horses, could he somehow increase that power? Could he cause the wind to rise or perhaps the rain to fall? He knew one thing for certain. If he had the power, he would cause flames to fall from the sky in a lightning strike against Barrons. It would bear some consideration, Will thought.

Chapter Seven

Ethan barely knew day from night. His sleep was as uneven as his awareness. He'd been on a journey, a long one, he thought, though it was increasingly difficult for him to discern day from night, hour upon hour. Though his body grew steadily stronger, his mind did not. He was trapped somehow. Not just by those that kept him strapped to a cot in the back of a carriage, but in his head. There were times he could see and times he could not. Day and night had no governance over him, and neither did his caretakers.

Oh, they'd taken the trouble to spoon some sort of swill into him, half of it feeding him, the rest soaking his shirt and bed linens. If he hadn't still suffered from the headaches, he would have spit the offensive liquid back at them. As it was, Ethan disregarded almost everything, his soiled clothing, his detestable smell, and even the scratchy linens he was swathed in. The only thing he could feel was the blasted pressure in his head, the intense pain and nausea assailing him every waking moment.

The pain in his head was an animal of itself. It demanded all of his attention and Ethan spent his every conscious moment trying to survive it. It started with a throbbing behind his left ear and came to a full hammering at the front of his forehead. He didn't bother to try and remember where it came from or even how to resolve it. Breathing one breath upon the other had been enough.

Only one person could lessen his torture. Arianna had visited him often early on, he remembered. Her cool hand against his brow, the soft, gentle cloths she'd used to keep him clean, and her insistence to others that they move him gently had been a balm to his pain-wracked body.

That time was gone. Wherever Arianna was, wherever that fiend Barrons had taken her, Ethan suffered the pain of her absence like a gaping wound in his heart. The hope that each time he opened his eyes he'd see her there kept him from turning in on himself and letting his life energy flow away.

Ethan had known about Arianna's gift since they were children. His mother had explained it to him and then swore him to secrecy. She'd told him that if anyone ever found out about the visits or the amulet, Arianna would suffer the consequences. Stoic young man that he was, Ethan had sworn to guard her with his every breath. It was only the will to survive this ordeal and find his poor sister that kept him joining Arianna's lost souls.

If she had preceded him into death, then he survived only for vengeance against the man who'd sent her there. Of late, he'd found that it was reason enough to stay alive.

"What shall we do wi' his lordship, now, eh?" The first caretaker's voice grated on Ethan's nerves. He knew that tone, that poor pronunciation. The man had a deformity to his mouth which gave a lisping spin to his speech. He was the man who'd killed Thomas the night of the duel.

"Wrap him up well, Tuppers, nice and tight. He's going abroad with the wench. Once they get aboard the ship, they can keep each other company, though the conversation will be a bit one-sided, don't you know." The one called Digby laughed.

"Aye. Bugger hasn't spit a word for quite a while. I dunno what Old Spike's reasons are for keeping him alive, though. Bloody nuisance, if ye asks me."

"Tis his business and none of yours. Just do your job and see to it that his lordship here makes it to the island estate in one piece. Spikes says that once we're there, he'll be her problem."

Ethan hoped that the wench they referred to was Arianna, though why she'd be taking a long voyage he'd no idea. She rarely left the manse. Was she being forced against her will? What threats could Barrons possibly use against her?

Before he could consider it further, Tuppers returned, bringing a cup full of strong port filled to the brim. Ethan hated the foul liquid and its effect on him. After ten minutes of sputtering and gagging, Ethan began to drift away again. Had he been able, he would have sent curses upon the men who controlled his every bodily function. Instead, he soon calmed in response to the draft. It must have been mixed with something to make him so groggy.

"Is he asleep?" Digby asked while leaning nose to nose over Ethan, prying at his slack eyelids with grubby fingers.

"Aye, that he is. Should be out for the trip."

"Good. Keep him under the port. We don't want his grunting and moaning to make anyone suspicious. Maybe when Spikes gets what he wants, we can dispense with the both of them."

Of course, Ethan thought. He should have known it all along. He and his sister were only a means to an end. When they were no longer useful, they would be put down like draft horses at the end of their service. He railed inwardly against his affliction. Surely there must be something he could do? At least if he were dead, perhaps his spirit could warn Arianna.

Though he struggled for the last shreds of consciousness, the thoughts followed him into the darkness of slumber.

When Arianna stilled at last, Will remained awake, watching her sleep. An occasional sob escaped her and her muscles clenched accordingly. Surely she was remembering Barrons's attack earlier. Though her body rested, her hands still gripped the threadbare quilt he'd found to cover her.

Will flexed his fingers, amazed at how he could affect some things of this world and not others. It seemed whenever he was close to Arianna, his form grew stronger and when he wandered out of her scope, he weakened yet again.

Though it was tempting to curl himself around his sleeping beauty, Will knew he couldn't remain still. There was too much to be learned and perhaps in some small way, he could aid her yet again. Fortunately, the dead didn't require rest as did the living, he thought.

Before leaving, Will watched Arianna a moment more, wondering what new terrors her sleep held. The movement of her chest as she breathed in and out mesmerized him. Minutes passed as he stood enthralled by her loveliness. Then, scoffing at his own softheartedness, he turned away. After all, what did a ghost know about a woman's dreams?

Though he didn't require sleep himself, Will couldn't deny his restlessness. This must be the state of the unsettled spirits he'd always heard about. Too bad he had no chains to rattle or a storm on the horizon to carry his moans. He was in the mood to scare the bloody hell out of someone.

As he neared the stable once again, he saw the object of his anger seated on a tree stump, a short, bald, harried man leaning over him. Despite Barrons's scathing tone, the man seemed unperturbed. He continued to nod and wrap a long length of dingy cloth about the other's right hand. Barrons's left hand, Will noted, was swathed in similar fashion. It looked as though Arianna's husband had sustained some injury after all. This brightened Will's mood immeasurably.

"Hurry up, you lout! I've business to be about."

"Aye, sir. There are many requiring my service. I'll be finished shortly, to be sure if you'll just hold yer paws still. Just let me put my poultice on these scratches and you'll be fixed right away."

"Paws! I'm a man, you idiot. Why couldn't they find me a decent physician? I am one of the richest men in England! Yet all they bring me is a horse doctor?"

"Aye, and yer lucky to get me, this time a'night and all. I've told you already that the physician, Mr. Deamus, is out for the night delivering a baby. The squire's lady in Makney is fair to bustin'. It's her first babe and heaven knows they tend to take a long while."

"Never mind, you cur! The sooner I get on my way, the sooner I'll obtain true medical care."

"It's yer choice, Mr. Spikes."

Barrons drew back. "The name is Barrons, do you hear? Barrons."

"My apologies, sir, it's just that I thought I heard yer men . . ."

"Never mind. Get out of my way." He turned and bellowed, "Digby! Get your sorry arse over here this instant."

Will decided he liked the old man's spirit. Spikes was a knick-name he'd heard Barrons called when he'd been imprisoned before his hanging. Even the men of his ship had called him that—behind his back, of course.

The old man bowed once and made a quick retreat, obviously preferring to watch the rising wrath of his patient from a distance.

Will approached Barrons, still sitting on the tree stump, using his teeth and free hand to tie off the remaining bandage. His actions were clumsy and it took several attempts to manage the cloth.

Circling his enemy, Will focused all of his thoughts on the scoundrel. Would that he could throw daggers, he would strike the man dead where he sat. As it was, Will could do nothing. Anger at his own impotence stirred within him.

Leaning close, Will bent down to speak in Barrons's ear. "Vengeance," he said in an even tone, wishing with all his heart Barrons could hear his threat.

For a moment nothing moved around them. Barrons had even stopped his struggles with the cloth around his hand. Something in him raised an alarm, Will was sure.

"Yes, I mean to make you pay for your evil deeds. Make no mistake, I will have my vengeance."

The air around them sizzled with subtle electricity. A cloud covered the half moon and they were plunged in near total darkness. Perhaps he did have more an effect on the living than he'd previously thought. Will smiled.

"Who's there?" Barrons asked, his eyes now darting about.

Will laughed at the other man's mounting distress. Then, dropping his vision to the blade tucked in Barrons's trousers, Will sent all his concentration to the sharp metal. He hoped that by his will alone, he could cause the wretch to pull the knife from its trappings and then plunge it into his own heart.

To his surprise, Barrons's hand hovered a moment over the blade's handle. Seconds passed until he quickly grasped the hilt, pulling it free and brandishing it in the air around him.

Suddenly, Digby emerged from the stable.

"Aye, sir? You called for me?"

The intense moment shattered and Will watched, helpless, as Barrons lowered his knife. Across the yard, Barrons's man Digby approached.

"Where the devil have you been? How can you guard me if you're wandering about?"

"I beg your pardon, sir. I was talking to the innkeeper. It seems your animals destroyed one of the fences at the back of his property in thier haste to escape."

"I've lost two of my prized stallions. What do I care for the innkeeper's property? After all, his bumbling stable hands lost my animals in the first place."

"Not to worry, I'm sure they'll be found sooner or later. I've put out word of a reward for their safe return. Shouldn't be more than a few days at best."

Barrons spat. "We don't have that long. I have finally managed to get an appointment to meet with my uncle. I'm expected at Melbourne in less than a week. We've no time to waste. We must leave now."

"What of the girl and her brother? Are you taking them back to the city?" Digby asked.

"No. They will go on to Montclair. I'll attend to them at my leisure."

Will watched as Barrons sent a scornful glance to the second floor of the inn. At least Arianna would be spared any more of his attentions for the moment.

Arianna woke with a start. She hadn't even realized that she'd fallen asleep. The early morning sun peeked through the inn's shabby drapes and filtered down onto her bed, adding a bit of added warmth to the thin linens tucked around her.

Instantly the memories of the night before flooded her mind. Barrons's attack, the horses escape from the barn, and her time spent in the arms of Captain Markham. Well, in the arms of the ghost of Captain Markham. She shook her head. Her deluge of tears and the bruising of her body had left her mind sluggish this morning. She wished fervently for a breath of bracing cold air or perhaps some strong tea to sweep the cobwebs from her brain.

Pushing away her useless desires, Arianna scooted

from beneath the covers to stand in front of the wardrobe. She had nearly torn her traveling dress to shreds and the rest of her clothing was packed in the carriage. She decided that it could stay there. It didn't matter. It wasn't likely that any member of the *ton* would see her now.

Opening the drawer she found three faded shifts and one plain brown riding dress. It would have to do. Arianna had plenty of other worries to mull over this morning, and being a lady not given to high society fancies, she didn't mind the lack of fine attire.

Once she had changed and pulled back her hair into something of a style, she left the small bedroom and wandered into the adjoining room. What she saw peering out the window nearly took her breath away.

"Slept well, did you?"

Standing at the window, cloaked in the golden morning hue, Captain Markham—Will, as she was wont to call him in her mind—stood peering out into the main yard.

"Well enough."

"I suppose that's the best we can hope for. How are you feeling?"

"Bruised, frightened, hungry." Arianna decided there was no use to stick to parlor formalities any longer. Ye gods, the man, or his spirit rather, had lain with her the previous night. She'd found solace in his arms, and in truth, had he been a living man, she likely would have found much more, to her own chagrin.

"Good. It means you've some life left within you. Many other women in your position would cower in a corner. I can't abide a weak woman."

"I don't know what I'd be doing if things had been allowed to . . ."—she paused, swallowing hard at the realization of what Barrons had in mind—"continue."

Will turned from looking out the window to gaze at her. "This morning I am sorry to be a man. We can be such beasts."

Arianna inclined her head. "Not all men, Captain. Not you."

"True. Perhaps it's good that I am dead. If I were not I'd soon be hanging from one of those tall oaks in the yard. I'd have thought nothing about twisting Barron's head from his shoulders last night for what he'd done to you."

"Ah, a chivalrous ghost."

"A man shouldn't ever treat a woman so. You could have been my wife or sister." It was his turn to pause. He gazed back out the window, "Or my daughter." His voice dropped to nearly a whisper.

Arianna didn't know what to say to that. Somehow this stranger affected her much more deeply than any other man she'd known, save for her brother Ethan.

"What shall we do when he returns?" she asked, half expecting him to once again badger her about the knife in Barrons's boot.

"Fortunately, we won't have to face that circumstance," he said, nodding towards the window.

Arianna moved to stand beside him. In the courtyard below she saw the carriage that they'd arrived in. The last trunk was being secured on top by two stable hands.

In the next moment Barrons himself shot out of the front of the carriage. Though his words were indistinct, Arianna could make out that Barrons was shouting at his staff. As she watched, he stalked about the scene, waving his bandaged hands wildly.

The sight of him ought to have made her cringe but somehow being removed from the scene and in the presence of Captain Markham gave her strength.

"He doesn't look happy," Will said beside her.

"Hardly. What has gotten him in such a state?"

"It seems his prized stallions were accidentally set loose. He's got men searching the countryside trying to find them. It looks as though he's leaving you to the tender ministrations of Mr. Digby, who has orders to take you and your brother to the harbor and see you off. Once you've been packed off to Barrons's island estate, Mr. Digby is to return to London. They've business to see to and whatever it is, it requires them both."

"So you won't have the opportunity to kill him." Arianna turned to look at his reaction.

His face remained still. "No. Not at the present."

"You could follow him, I suppose. You caused this, didn't you?"

He turned to look at her. "Yes, but it took some doing. I had to frighten the horses near to death. It took everything I had to do that. It seems that I tend to have more of an affect on animals than I do men. I tried this morning to make my presence known to Barrons but to little avail. I could have been a block of stone for all he noticed."

"I'm sorry." Arianna meant it. It wasn't as if she hadn't agreed that Barrons needed to be dealt with.

"Are you?"

Arianna examined the questioning look he gave her. His brow wrinkled at his question.

"Of course I am. I agree that Barrons deserves punishment. I never doubted that he'd been responsible for your death and others, especially after Ethan's tragedy. My brother was right for wanting to kill him, even if his methods were wrong. After last night . . ."

"After last night you should be calling for his blood. He damn near killed you. How many deaths will it take before you act?"

His words stung her heart, hurting far worse than Barron's blows to her body had the night before.

Arianna turned away, swallowing hard.

"You don't understand."

Instantly he was at her side. "Then make me."

She turned back to look at him, defiantly lifting her chin, daring him to look away.

"It's not for me. That was made plain to me many years ago. I am to be an observer only. If I chose . . ."

"If you chose what? To dirty your hands with commoners' tasks? It's not like you're being asked to do menial labor, to clean silver or some such task that's beneath you."

"Is killing a man a high aspiration then?"

"Putting down the devil, that's what it is. A calling for someone courageous enough to do the job."

"Like you? It certainly wasn't something you could accomplish when you were alive."

Arianna watched as he flinched and the arrow of her statement found its mark. Straight through his heart, most assuredly.

He paused a moment before continuing. "It's true. I failed in my life. I was foolish and didn't see the rising cloud of evil as it was about to spread over my life. Dear God, you don't know how I wish I could go back and plunge my blade between his ribs. Not a minute passes that the wish doesn't burn inside of me." He looked away. "It's no matter. I will not ask you again. I should have known it wasn't possible. The highborn do not trouble themselves with such things. Although I will give your brother credit, he did come close."

"You don't understand," Arianna started. Her anger had fled and the desperate need to explain herself flagged high. Before she could a loud knock sounded at her door.

"Mrs. Barrons, the carriage is about ready to go," the servant's voice called out.

When Arianna turned back, she was alone. Captain Markham had quit the room, most likely escaping into the adjoining room or heaven only knew where.

For the first time in many years Arianna began to detest her solitude.

Will waited until she had gone down to breakfast before he came out of the bedroom. The corridor was busy now as travelers packed their belongings and made their way outside. The last thing he wanted was to be in a room full of people, even though they were not aware of his presence. What he needed now was to be alone, at least until the pain started to fade. Making his decision, Will navigated his way to the main door of the taproom.

Walking past the loading carriages and the hubbub of the busy village, Will made his way to a copse of trees. Although part of him ached at the distance between them, he thought it best to put some space between himself and Arianna. He needed time to think.

She would be leaving soon. Will considered staying behind, trying to make contact with another living person. But as he widened his range from Lady Halverson, the stone in his breast pocket began to falter. The steady emanating power dimmed and Will realized that the amulet by itself did not contain enough of whatever it was that allowed him to remain in this earthly realm. It must be the combination of the artifact and the lady. The fact did not make him happy.

With every passing moment he found himself becoming more dependent on the wistful smile and straightforward manner of Lady Halverson. Arianna. No, he would not permit himself to use her first name at the moment. That he had saved for when they'd been alone the night before and she'd trusted him to protect her so much that she'd relaxed in his arms.

"Damn and blast," he muttered, though his usual curse had lost some of its steam.

"You love her, don't you?"

Will whirled about when a familiar voice cut into his thoughts. It couldn't be! Could it?

"Lettie?"

At first he didn't see her and then he did. Perched upon an old wooden bench at the edge of the clearing sat the shimmering reflection of the only person with whom he'd once shared all of his secret yearnings, his hopes, and his dreams. Letitia Commons had been his confidante and his friend, his lover and his wife.

"Will. It has been a while."

A little more than five years ago their short marriage had ended when she'd died in childbirth. Even in her ghostly trappings, she smiled in that gentle way of hers. With a hand that glimmered golden in the midmorning sunlight, she tapped the seat beside her.

"Come, sit with me for a moment."

"Dear God, Lettie," he choked. "I've missed you so." He brushed forward, thinking to take her in his arms. It was the first reward for being dead that he'd yet come across. But she held up her hand in warning as he came close.

"You cannot touch me. I am no more than dust, held together by a fleeting wind."

"I don't understand." He knelt in front of her, his hands outstretched. "Aren't you a ghost as well?"

"I am. Yet I am not like you. You still have too much

life energy. I can feel it, even as distant as I am from you now. You always were the stronger one."

"I want to be like you, Lettie. I want to leave this world behind."

"No, you don't. You're just hurting, William. I'm sorry, but you must stay until your tasks are complete."

"That's not possible. I can't kill Barrons. I was a fool for even thinking I could."

"You are wrong, my love."

"No. My hands can't touch him and the only person I had hoped to persuade won't do the deed."

The woman on the bench sighed deeply. "You never did understand, Will."

He looked up at her. "Lettie, tell me everything is going to be all right. I'll believe it if you do."

She shook her head. "I wish that I could, but the fates have not determined which way it shall go."

"Then why are you here if not to council me?"

"Because you summoned me. That talisman in your pocket is very strong, though I doubt its present owner understands its power."

"On that you are correct. I can neither fathom its peculiar magic nor the woman I stole it from. She's not like you, Lettie."

"But you love her."

Will looked up into the ghostly frown on the woman's face.

"What makes you say that? I love you. I'll always love you."

"Yes, I suppose you think that it was love between us. I believe fondness might be a better description."

"Lettie?"

"It's true, though I know you don't believe it. William,

what was between us was something born out of need. Your need for love and mine for security. Don't fret so. It was an equal exchange."

"I tried to love you."

"I know. I never thought ill of you. A man needs a woman's touch, a woman's gift. I was glad to give you a child. I knew the moment I told you I was with child that your heart would never belong totally to me."

"I'm sorry, Lettie. Katherine is . . ."

"Don't." Lettie put up her hand again. "You need to go back, Will. Go back to that woman and your destiny."

"What if I fail?"

"I have faith in you, William. You'll find a way."

As he watched, Lettie began to fade away. It was true, he hadn't loved her as a husband should have loved his wife. He was younger then and she was available and willing. Her life had been a short and sad one and Will regretted that by getting her with child he'd as much as killed her. And yet, he could never regret Katherine. It would be like despising an angel.

"Captain Markham?"

Will turned to see Arianna making her way through the trees. She couldn't see him yet, but it appeared she was not turning back until she found him. Sighing deeply, Will stood up and prepared to face her once again.

Arianna knew he was close by. She could sense his presence the way she could discern when it was about to rain. *A sensitive* was what her mother had called her. It was both a gift and a curse. At the moment, Arianna couldn't quite decide which. Somehow she had to explain. She had to make the captain understand just why it was she couldn't do the violence he asked.

"Yes, my lady," he said tiredly behind her, "I'm here."

"Oh." She turned and found him just beyond the edge of the trees. "Yes. Well, I thought you'd like to know that the carriage will be leaving in a quarter hour. Will you be coming with us?"

Arianna couldn't hold back the hopefulness in her voice. The time they'd been separated she'd decided that whatever else happened, she truly did want his companionship. While she was momentarily safe from her husband, she needed to plan the best way to deal with the situation. She'd had no experience with life outside her estate and without Ethan here to counsel her, Arianna found herself at a loss.

But it was more than that, too, she realized. Arianna enjoyed William Markham's presence. His strength and intelligence were remarkable and she felt no small amount of sadness that she'd not had the opportunity to know him when he'd been alive. She knew one thing for certain, she'd miss the intriguing ghost when their time together ended. She'd miss him most fervently.

"I've decided to stay with you for the time being. I apologize for my poor behavior earlier. It seems this situation has made me intemperate."

"Oh, no, Captain. It's I who should apologize. I've no right to hold you to account for what's happened. Barrons is an evil man. You are a victim as much as I am, it seems."

"Well, Barrons has enough victims on his list. I believe that from now until the time he joins us at his estate may be enough to form an acceptable plan of action. Perhaps we can arrive at something that will help us find a weakness in his armor, so to speak."

"Perhaps." Arianna knew she wanted to believe that more than anything—that and the fact that Will wanted to stay with her. She needed all her courage to face the uncertain future before them.

Chapter Eight

When they'd left the inn a little before noon, Will had clamored aboard the gaudy carriage only to see Mr. Digby climb in behind him. As the coach pulled away from the yard, he watched the weasel of a man make a careful examination of Arianna. Will didn't care for Digby's attention to her.

When afternoon dragged on to early evening and the coach traveled down the coast to the harbor, he decided that he'd had quite enough. Arianna dozed while Barrons's henchman continued to stare. Will moved across the seat to sit very close to Digby.

"I know what you're thinking, you wretched bastard. Get your filthy eyes off of her before I pluck them from your head." Will spoke in a low and threatening tone.

Digby shuddered slightly. His eyes darted around nervously and he wore the look of a man who knew he'd just been threatened. Pulling his collar tighter around his neck, he picked up his walking stick and sharply rapped the roof of the carriage. In answer, the driver slowed the vehicle to a stop. Arianna didn't arouse, but merely shifted her position against the carriage window.

Digby quickly scrambled out.

Will leaned out the window and heard the two men's exchange of words.

"What are you about, Mr. Digby, stopping us like that? We need to get to the ship before nightfall. What if the other coach gets there first?"

"Then they'll bloody well wait for us. I don't know why ol' Spikes decided to send us separate, it's not like anyone's the wiser."

"Still, I don't like disobeying orders. Gets him awful riled."

"Just get this buggy started." He climbed up the ladder to sit beside the driver. "I've just had a feeling that someone has tramped across my grave."

Will sat back inside the coach. Satisfied that they wouldn't be bothered, he slipped over to sit close to Arianna.

"Will you be having tea, Mr. Barrons?"

Lady Jessica Flynn's voice squeaked across the small parlor. High and scratchy, it was a sound that grated on one's nervous system like broken china across a marble floor. It was too easy to read the woman's true thoughts. He watched with hooded eyes as her sour expression twisted when she asked his preferences.

"Yes. Thank you, Lady Flynn. It is such an honor to take refreshment with you today. I simply cannot believe my good fortune to happen upon you after learning of my bride's distant connection. Second cousin, did you say?"

Lady Flynn gave him a nod. "Third by marriage, but no one with breeding would keep track of such a thing, you know." She smirked sideways and then turned to the butler. "Humphries, would you be so kind as to see to Mr. Barrons's drink?"

Barrons knew he, a commoner and merchant, would never really fit in with their kind. Yet it gave him inescapable pleasure to sit in her overdecorated, stuffy parlor and trade pleasantries. A sense of power nearly overwhelmed him where he sat.

His enjoyment was made better because all of society knew what an unconscionable gossip she was. If there was the slightest hint of a scandal Lady Flynn could scent it out like a hound chasing a fox.

"Please, only half a cup. My hands are still terribly sore and managing a full cup is near to impossible."

"Yes. Damned awful accident," Martin Flynn remarked. The second Earl of Seabury was as portly as his wife was slender. Short with a nearly bald head and round, jowly cheeks, it was clear that these two were matched only in family properties and bank notes.

"I was taken completely by surprise. Two of my best stallions lost! Fortunately I've just received word that they've been located and are in relatively good condition. I could have killed the boy that left the stable door unlatched."

Both the Flynns were visibly upset by his admission. Lady Flynn was the first to comment.

"Surely a man of your age ought to forgive the clumsiness of youth."

Before Barrons could answer her charge her husband stepped in. "Nonsense, Jess. It's inexcusable. Such carelessness with prime horseflesh is completely unacceptable. If the boy survives, he should receive the harshest punishment."

"What a thing to say, Martin."

Ignoring his wife's shocked expression, Flynn leaned toward Barrons. "I know I would be inconsolable. Perhaps I could interest you in a pair from my stables. Impeccable bloodlines."

Barrons would have rubbed his hands together, except for their battered condition. This was the clinch. In short, his sources had been correct. The Earl of Seabury was near financial ruin. No true aristocrat would ever consider doing business with a commoner. Except that Barrons was no longer a commoner. His marriage into the Halverson family had been a brilliant ploy. He was mere weeks away from completing his plans for the change in taxation. Before long, he'd have the highbred dandies eating out of his hand.

"I would very much enjoy seeing your stock." Rising to leave, he paused when Lady Flynn stood and reached out to grasp his waistcoat.

"A moment, sir, before my husband steals you away?"

"Madame?" Barrons glanced over to Lord Flynn. The gentleman merely nodded to his wife, his face expressionless.

"Best to hear her out. She'll never rest until she's said her piece."

"I just wanted to say that my husband and I welcome you to our little family. It's just that I fear so for my cousins. Ethan has always been the strongest of the two. Heaven forbid anything should happen to him. Poor Arianna would be lost. It has always been my intention to take the girl to my bosom should the two of them ever become separated, you understand."

In truth, Barrons did understand. Too well, in fact.

The Halverson fortunes were vast and complex. Who wouldn't want to take over such responsibilities? He was certain the middle-aged couple had been eyeing the title and properties for some time. The woman could barely contain her glee when he'd told them of Ethan's accident.

"You can rest assured, milady, that I have long cherished an affection for Lady Arianna. She has made me the happiest man alive by accepting my offer of marriage. I can barely tolerate the miles between us. I promise to take very good care of her."

The problem with Arianna's quarters was that they were too damn small, Will decided. Pacing the floor between her bed and the door, he realized that he didn't want to leave her and yet his anxiety was growing tenfold by the moment. Damn it all! He was certain that Barrons had provided an amount to cover the cost of even a mediocre inn. Why in the blazes had his henchmen settled her here?

The Rusty Nail was just what its title insinuated. So rundown and flea-ridden that Will was certain the walls would come down at any minute from either the poor condition of the building or the vermin that clearly ruled the grounds.

Arianna muttered and turned in her sleep. She'd become more and more restless over the miles. Not a woman given to traveling. Will had noticed the deeper lines of worry that formed around her eyes with every passing hour.

Worse yet, her brother's carriage hadn't arrived when they'd stopped at the Rusty Nail and her fears were escalating. For all they knew, Ethan Halverson might have already succumbed to his injuries.

He scowled again. Wasn't it just like Barrons to hide an anchorage in the deserted cove? His smuggling ships could move in and out as easily as his honest ones moved about in the reputable trade routes.

Again Arianna twisted amongst the sheets. Then, as if answering his silent call, she slowly opened her eyes.

"Captain Markham?" She squinted through the early morning light.

"I am here, Mrs. Barrons."

"Don't call me that." She rose steadily from the bed. "I can take it from anyone except you."

He watched her pull the heavy robe about her shoulders.

"You should try to rest more. It will be a bit before you'll have your legs on land again. Not everyone takes to the water, you know."

"I'm too tired to rest."

"I am sorry for that," he told her. She then took a seat at the table by the window. The early morning dawn was struggling against the iron hold of night.

"What do you prefer I call you, milady?" Though he'd meant it in a jovial tone, Will found his words to be a shade more serious than he'd intended.

"Call me Arianna. Everyone else does."

He glanced at her, surprised.

"I'm honored. Your given name denotes a bit more familiarity."

"I don't know that I've been very familiar with anyone except for Ethan. Since you're always by my side, I think it's best."

"Perhaps. Then you should at least call me Will."

She paused a moment, pursing her lips. Will thought she might be trying out the name, sizing it up as she had done him the first night of their meeting.

"I don't think so, Captain. No. Will does not fit you at all. It's more like a name you'd give a small boy. Perhaps a mischievous child, one that's always running into trouble."

Will let loose a laugh. "Indeed? Well, then I daresay it fit me well when I was younger. Captain it is. Tell me, why so formal, Arianna?"

She smiled at him for a moment. "Because it suits you better. You're not used to taking orders and you definitely want to be the man leading the charge. When circumstances prevent it, as they do now, I think it grates on you terribly."

Her voice softened at the end of her speech. Will took in an unsteady breath then laughed at himself. It wasn't like he really needed to breathe at all, but somehow the exercise made him feel closer to being alive.

"You have read me too well, Arianna," he whispered back to her.

A knock sounded on the door. "Mrs. Barrons, yer wanted below stairs. You'd best get to it. Those gents who brought you said as you could visit your poor sick brother for only a few minutes this morning. You'd best hurry."

Arianna stood and pulled her robe tighter about her. "Yes! I'll be right down."

Will followed her out into the hall. The innkeeper's wife, a plump, gray-haired woman dressed in her nightdress and cap, waved them forward.

"He's in here, missus. Mind you, he doesn't look too well at all."

"He's been suffering several days now," Arianna explained. "I can only hope this travel has made him no worse."

True to her words, Arianna sought out her brother. He was lying in a cot and covered with a dingy, soiled sheet. Will heard her quick intake of breath at seeing him.

"May we open the window and allow some fresh air in? Ethan always deplored being shut in."

"Of course, but I'll have to get my husband up. It's fair stuck most of the time."

After she'd gone, Will moved to stand behind Arianna. "He's no better then?"

"No, but at least he's no worse." She reached over to the half full pitcher and poured the water into the washing bowl. Picking up a towel she dampened it and began to bathe her brother's face.

"There, there, Ethan. I shall just freshen you up a bit."

The man opened his eyes at the sound of her voice. His eyes wild, he formed his mouth into an *o* and struggled to say something, but a gurgling sound came out rather than words.

"It's all right now. I'm here."

Ethan turned to the sound of her voice. Only when he saw her did he start to relax. She let out a slow breath as he settled back.

"Ethan, can you nod yes or no to questions?" she asked.

He only stared at her wide-eyed. Again he struggled to speak and again only obscure sounds emanated from him.

"You'd better let him rest," Will said. "I think you're only upsetting him more."

"He needs more medicine," Mr. Digby said as he entered the room behind them.

"Medicine? What are you giving him?"

"Laudanum, ma'am. It's what's made him able to travel, you see. A healthy dose and he sleeps like a babe."

"You cannot keep drugging him, surely."

Will watched her move closer, as if she could shield her brother from the coarse man's treatments.

"Nonsense, Mrs. Barrons. If he's allowed to stay awake too long, he starts burbling and spitting something awful. Then he turns beet red in the face and sweats like a pig. No, this is what the physician ordered and this is what he shall get. Mr. Barrons's orders, you see."

Will put a hand on Arianna's shoulder. "Though I'm loathe to agree with the scoundrel, I have to say his is the best treatment for the moment. Travel is never easy on the best of us. With your brother trying to recover from such a terrible injury, it's likely needful to keep him as still as possible. Once you are settled at the estate, then you can demand they reduce the amount of the drug."

Arianna looked up at him, tears forming at the corner of her eyes.

"Very well," she said in a quivering voice. She turned to Ethan. "This will make it better, darling, you'll see. I promise we'll get through this."

Ethan began to shake his head. *No*, he seemed to be telling her, his mouth forming an oval shape once again. Whatever he was afraid of, whatever he knew must stay with him for the time being, Will realized. He just hoped, for Arianna's sake, her brother would soon come around and rescue her somehow.

* * *

Arianna watched as her brother's cot was carried onto the ship. She'd been summoned from Ethan's sickroom and informed that they must board the ship as soon as possible. The weather was ominous and threatened to get worse. Winter was not the safest time to sail as it was. Arianna occupied herself with arranging her luggage and at the same time keeping an eye on Ethan's care. As he was taken up the walkway it was clear that he had been treated passably well. She thought it must be on direct orders from her husband. Perhaps he had some use for Ethan still. That thought sent a shiver of foreboding through Arianna.

"Damn and blast," Captain Markham said behind her. It was the tone of his speech rather than his curse that drew her attention. Turning around, she found him at her side. His attention was no longer on her or her brother. He was looking up at the great vessel.

"What is it? What's the matter?"

He paused a moment before answering. Swallowing hard, he spoke, his voice hoarse with emotion.

"It's the *Persuasion*."

"I beg your pardon?"

Before he could answer, Digby waved over to them. "Hurry your skirts, missus. We've got to get underway." With that, two of the sailors approached her and giving a quick nod, began loading her bags.

Arianna turned back to the captain, but his expression remained closed. He would neither acknowledge nor answer her questions. She thought it best to leave him be.

When the last of the items were safely on board, Digby approached her. "Time to board. Up you go."

Arianna looked at the captain. His gaze flashed down at her and she could tell he was making some sort of decision.

"Are you going?" she asked in a low tone.

Bare seconds passed before he gave her a sharp nod. Arianna relaxed. She'd come to depend on Will Markham over the last few days, more than she liked to admit. Still, if he'd chosen to stay behind, she knew he would have had a very good reason.

When she turned to follow Mr. Digby, she heard the captain sigh behind her. Such a low, baleful sound it was, that a stab of pain went through her.

The missive came that afternoon. Written in Digby's long scrawl, the message read: *All are aboard, Halverson still breathing. Your lady-wife tucked away.* D.

Barrons crumpled the letter and threw it into the fireplace. He was just one step closer to success. Walking to the table, he poured himself a hefty dollop of brandy.

"So, what is your plan, Mr. Barrons?" Lord Echelby asked, himself sipping on the fine liquor.

Barrons smiled and returned to his chaise. "The same as always. I plan to petition Parliament to decrease the taxes on certain import items. That will open up the trade routes, allow for more commerce. It will be a boon to the economy."

"Don't you mean your economy? As I have read over your proposals, most of those items are ones that benefit you. You stand to make a tidy profit."

"I already am quite wealthy, though I wouldn't turn away a chance for profit. But, I am gaining something far more valuable—a chance at respectability."

"You've been pushing your way into society again, as I hear it. Very wise man, getting that chit to marry you. No doubt you have the honorable brother in your pocket as well?"

"He is in my care, the poor devil. Though I have to say, there is nothing so assuring as a well-placed bullet, you know."

"So I've heard, though I'm not a violent man myself. So, let's talk of business now. What is it you require of me? You've already got half the *ton* clamoring for your attention. Keep it up and you'll be another Beau Brummel."

"I want all of their attention. I already have two other earls doing my bidding. Lesser families, true enough, but they're in dire straits financially and so will keep my counsel."

"Let's hope they do, Richard. If you're found out, it could be you hanging from the Newgate gallows."

"I've no intention of being discovered. My ship travels to Montclair Island as we speak. The last of the goods will be stored there. With old Boney and the French out of the game now, there are smaller nations vying for position. I merely sit back and wait to see which one is willing to pay the price I'm asking."

"You are a clever fox. I'm sure they'll be knocking at your door in no time."

"It is what I hope. For the time being everything I treasure will be safely put away on that island. Winning it at cards was the best turn of events I could have hoped for."

The sway of the ship and the brisk morning breeze nearly cut Arianna into bits. Staying upright and not losing her breakfast were first and foremost on her mind. The captain remained beside her as she walked the short journey around the deck. He was quiet and subdued and she could tell that his earlier pain had now grown from a baleful ache to a grievous wound. She decided a direct course of action was the best.

"I'm sorry that you've lost your life, this life," she attempted, almost immediately sorry for the inadequate statement.

"It's nothing."

"I believe it is. You've lost everything dear to you. You are not the first of my visitors to be so stricken, but you seem especially hurt."

"Perhaps your other visitors didn't have as much to lose."

"Perhaps. And yet, we know early on that nothing in the mortal existence will really last. That's the grand joke of it all, I suppose. I tried to convince Ethan of that many times. He was too caught up in the business of being an earl to ever listen to me, though. I suppose that's the way it is with men."

"Wealthy men, anyway." The captain drew in another deep breath. "As for me, I loved this ship. I served aboard her when I was sixteen, grew to manhood and learned all I know here. All I ever wanted to do was be a sailor."

"Ah, but the confining life of the Navy was too much for you?"

"Indeed, through my predecessor, Captain Harvey, was as good a man as any I've met. He'd served in the Royal Navy and knew all about the training that good seamen required. It wasn't merely business for him."

"I suspect it wasn't for you as well."

They had reached a small patch of deck that bore a dark stain, although the rest of the ship had been scrubbed to near immaculate.

"It appears to be blood," she said, bending down to get a closer look.

"It is blood," the captain assured her, his voice dropping to almost a whisper.

"Why didn't they clean it up?"

"Because it would be bad luck. Sailors are a very superstitious lot. It's the life's blood of this ship. A life that was sacrificed so that the new owner, your husband, could take over."

Arianna glanced sharply at the ghost. "You mean someone was killed here?"

He closed his eyes for a moment. When he opened them, a dark cloud had descended over his expression.

"Not killed, cut with a sharp blade and left there to bleed. It was a long slice, down his left arm. That particular spot was chosen because it is said that the left arm is linked directly to a man's heart. Once the wood was saturated, they bandaged the poor wretch and threw him in the brig for three weeks, until the vessel limped into port."

"What happened to him then?" Arianna asked, a growing feeling of dread in the pit of her stomach.

Without speaking, Will reached down and rolled up his left sleeve, exposing the shimmering scar that ran the length of his arm.

"He was hanged."

Will could not face the pity in her eyes. More and more she stared at him, waiting for whatever details of his wretched life and death would surface. As if he could speak of such things.

Of all that he had revealed, Will had not told her the worst, and in fact hadn't intended to. But—damn those beautiful dark green eyes that pierced him with every glance—he almost couldn't help himself.

"I'm sorry," she said as he turned to stare out over the ocean.

He shrugged. "Other men have suffered far worse than I."

"I know, but to lose your ship and your life? To be branded a traitor and a pirate? How terrible it must have been."

He laughed and it was a dry, rough sound. "You'd think so, wouldn't you."

"I suspect that isn't all, is it? There's something else that's scarring you even deeper. Perhaps that's why you've come to me. To heal whatever has injured your soul."

"Nonsense. I came here to destroy Richard Barrons and nothing more."

Arianna watched as he turned away. For a moment, he looked no different than many another man she'd seen. His wide shoulders narrowed to his waist, his hips were well shaped and leading down to perfectly muscled legs. Arianna felt heat rise up her neck as she stared at him. As though there were any chance of her knowing what his strong physique would feel like under her palms. For a moment, she saw herself running her hands beneath that bleached white shirt to feel the sinewy muscle covering thick, strong bones.

What in blazes? Arianna blinked. It was as though he had filled out before her eyes. Stepping closer, she could see the fine crisscross of threads across his linen shirt, make out every detail of his musculature, and the dark brown queue of his hair hanging down the back of his neck.

"It's not possible," she muttered.

Reaching out her hand, she slowly advanced until she was mere inches from feeling the texture of his shirt. Before she could test her theory, he whirled about.

"What are you doing? Do you wish to torment me

even more? You don't have to remind me that I no longer live and breathe. Believe me, my lady, it's not necessary. I know exactly what my fate is."

"No, I hadn't meant that at all," she stammered. "I mean, it's just that . . ." Arianna paused, her gaze moving over him.

"What?"

"Sir, you are not as ephemeral as you once were."

"I beg your pardon?"

"I mean, as ghostly—well, without substance."

"I don't follow." It was clear by the twist of his mouth and the deep lines that appeared around his eyes that he truly didn't, and neither was he amused at her assertions.

"What I am trying to say is that I believe that you are changing, or rather metamorphisizing into something other than an otherworldly spirit."

"Explain." He crossed his arms, stood back on his heels, ordering her with more than the tone of his voice.

"I don't know how this could be possible, but you're becoming alive again."

Chapter Nine

Richard Barrons was at the height of his glory. It was his first ever engagement with the London *ton*. Dressed to the nines in a black velvet waistcoat, black breeches, immaculate white shirt with a deep blue cravat, he was a picture that could have made old Brummel himself jealous, right down to his expensive Hessian boots. While money could indeed purchase almost anything, it could not buy good breeding and social standing.

Richard Bartholomew Barrons, a man born to a duke's disinherited daughter and a fisherman's son, could never have hoped for anything more.

All of this had not come easy, he thought as he stood admiring his appearance in the cheval glass. It was bought at the price of another man's life, a well-placed, if not misguided bullet, and an odd little chit who couldn't wipe her own arse without direction. Barrons was now about to enter society proper.

A few quick knocks sounded on his dressing room

door. As he turned, Barrons saw that his minion, Digby, had returned at last.

"Is she aboard?" he asked, not caring to be courteous to his servant.

"Aye, she is. It took some doing. That man you hired, Captain Beaverly, was none too happy wi' taking the ship out this late in the season. Says if they go down, he'll be coming back to haunt you."

Barrons gave a rough laugh. "If such a thing were possible, I dare say he'd have to wait his turn. There would be a few more ghosts following me, I assure you."

"I think you would be correct, sir."

Turning swiftly, Barrons took two long strides and came up before him. "You will address me as 'my lord,' from now on, you uncouth lout. After the Prince Regent sees my petition, he will grant me an earldom, I'm sure. Nothing less for the brother-in-law of Ethan Halverson."

"I beg your pardon, my lord. I've been away from town." Digby gave an obligatory head bob, but his eyes never left Barrons's expression.

"See that it doesn't happen again. Young Halverson is said to be a friend to the Prince. I've spread the story that I was Ethan's rescuer and that though he lies near to death, it was his last wish for me to take over his estate. He'd even bequeathed it to me in his will should anything unfortunate happen. At the moment, the document is sitting in the courts and when I have achieved my goals, then I shall dispense with Ethan and Arianna. After I've enjoyed my wedding night pleasures, of course. I've a debt to collect from that chit." He held up his hands ruefully. "I've no way to prove it, but I think somehow her ladyship was responsible for my injuries and the loss of my prize horseflesh. Mark my words, I shall make her pay."

"Of course, Lord Barrons."

Barrons smiled to himself. Digby was jumping the gun, but *Lord Barrons* had a lovely sound to it. A decisive ring and tone that pleased him all the more.

In his imagination, Richard Barrons could see himself climbing from an even more expensive carriage and stepping down onto the street in front of Almack's. Or better yet, being presented to the Prince himself. It would be a gala affair. Young, beautiful daughters of aristocrats would be falling at his feet and their wealthy male counterparts would be hanging on to his every word. Ah, illustrious fate.

"Then will we be moving into the Halverson estate, my lord?"

Digby's question was clear enough. It was his intent that took Barrons off his guard. "I beg your pardon? Did I hear you correctly? Are you asking if *we* are to live at the estate?"

"Aye, my lord. If so, I'll need to make certain arrangements for the staff."

Barrons didn't like the tone his underling was taking with him. "I will be moving to the manor. However, such a setting is far too grand for you and your men. As it is, I shall be hiring a new staff. Of course I'll keep you and the men on retainer. You may stay at the property in Bainbridge."

For a moment a pause fell between them. A stab of alarm went through Barrons. He sharpened his eye and focused on the quiet figure behind him. For a moment, he could have sworn he'd seen the glint of a blade in the man's hands. *Ridiculous*, he thought.

"Is something the matter?" Barrons demanded, annoyed at his employee's reticence.

"Nothing, my lord." For a moment, an unreadable

expression crossed Digby's face. Then he bowed his head. "I was just wondering what would happen once your transformation is complete. I'm thinking that perhaps you will no longer need our services."

Barrons scoffed. "A man of position will always have uses for your like, Dig. What you lack in spit and polish, you more than make up for in usefulness. Every man of substance has enemies."

"Indeed, sir."

Barrons dismissed the man. Tying his cravat a final time, he surveyed himself in the looking glass. "And I am a man of substance," he told himself.

"Damn and blast." Will stood scowling at the setting sun. "You're mistaken. I'm dead."

Arianna sighed beside him. "I noticed that."

"In truth, I have no more substance than the breeze that blows across the nor'east." His thoughts traveled back to that first night at the inn when he'd taken her in his arms and carried her to the bed. He'd changed, then, too. He thought she'd been too distressed to consider the consequences. But she wasn't now.

"I noticed that. Something has happened, whether you wish to admit it or not."

"I don't want to."

He watched as Arianna surveyed him carefully. Of course, it was a lie. It had to be. It would be too cruel of a joke for fate to play on him. Not now. Not ever.

"It's not possible," he finished at last, as though the conviction of his words would truly end it all.

"It must be the stone," she said.

The two of them were now facing the sea. The ever present energy of the churning water beyond their vessel stirred endlessly, the horizon dipping and swaying with the ship's movement.

"What are you talking about?" he asked beside her. "What haven't you told me about this piece of rock?"

She glanced up, her breath quickening. For a moment, he thought she might try to grab it from him. Of course, that would be a wasted effort, as he'd already proved. Even in his present state of half-life he was more agile than she.

After a few seconds passed, her expression relaxed.

"I don't know what you mean. The stone was a gift from my mother. It has no market value. Ethan is an expert on the subject. He would have told me if it had."

"All right. What does it do for you? Does it enhance your powers?"

She chuffed. "Sir, I have no 'power.' I simply use it as a tool to help focus. My mind becomes clearer and it's almost like a mirror into another world. The world of the dead, to be exact."

"It has power, whether or not you choose to admit it."

That much was true. As he held it in his hand, the jade amulet seemed to vibrate softly. "It has energy and purpose." He quickly closed his fist around it, and lifted his eyes to meet hers.

Arianna moved closer. "That energy seems to be focused on you. It's never had that effect before. I'm not sure. I need to examine the amulet. I need to hold it in my hand."

"No." Will didn't know why he refused her. He'd felt her sympathy and respected her intelligence and yet an unreasonable fear grasped his mind.

"I won't send you away, if that's what you're thinking," she said softly.

Will could feel the caress of her breath. With a small puff of air, he felt her warmth instead of the dropping temperature of the evening. If he'd been human, he would have shivered. As it was, the chill air was something he could see, could understand as he had the substance of water and wood. But feel it, never. Nothing was as cold as the dead, he realized.

"I don't believe you would." Slowly he reached in his pocket and pulled the gem forth once more. Dangling it on its chain, he held it a few inches from her outstretched hand.

Slowly, she reached out for the treasure. Will suspected that she thought both of them might disappear at any moment. Instead of touching the stone, however, she did something completely rash. She grasped his hand.

A shock went through him, something he likened to being kissed by lightning. So complete, he shuddered at her touch and then knew that he must have her that very moment. Still holding the dangling amulet he reached out and pulled her roughly to him. Crushing her in a steel embrace, he felt the stirrings of change begin. What in blazes was happening to him?

"Oh my!" Arianna muttered. The wispy caress of dreams now turned into hard flesh and bone. Her ghost, as she now referred to the captain, was as real as the deck beneath their feet or the thick canvas that the wind pushed against to carry them farther out to sea.

"I don't know . . ." He paused, a sharp breath pulled into him. "How can this be?" he asked, shaking her.

Arianna stood unmoving as his fingers dug into her arms. His touch was strange, almost magnetic. His fingers were cool upon her sleeve and yet they seemed to be warming by the minute. It was as though the life en-

ergy of her body was flowing from her and filling him
up. Oddly enough, she felt exhilarated at the exchange.

"It must be the amulet," she whispered, drawn into
his embrace. Wonderingly, he gazed down at her, his brow
twisted in strange metamorphosis. Then he pulled her
into a full embrace, leaning closer and closer until he
leaned down, touching his lips to hers.

That was when the real explosion occurred. It wasn't
an attack from beyond the ship, but rather a burst of
energy from them both, turning inwards and lighting
the flames of passion between them.

The carriage had pulled to a stop and Barrons
grabbed for his hat on the seat beside him. With his ornate silver-headed cane and impeccable clothing he
meant to step down from his carriage and make a fine
show. The party at Lady Worther's house in Gadbury
was all the talk among the *ton*. This was to be his first
entry into the life he'd hungered for. In short, he had
arrived.

The sound of the coachman descending from his
perch atop the carriage rattled the conveyance around
him. Just as he was about to lean forward, an odd weakness overtook him. Barrons instantly felt as though the
life had been sucked out of him. He weakened and
sank back onto the seat. His body shivered and his vision blurred.

"Lord Barrons?" the coachman asked. "Sir, are you
well?"

Shakily, he lifted his hand to his brow. It was moist
and cool and for a moment, Barrons thought he might
swoon.

Not now! Not this! his mind screamed. Could it be

that on the night of his final triumph he was to be denied? Would he fall to the same apoplectic affliction that had claimed his father?

Never.

"Give me a minute," he ordered roughly, once again finding his voice. "I'll tap on the door when I'm ready."

"Yes, sir." The coachman pulled the door shut.

Reaching into his jacket pocket Barrons took out a small snuffbox. Quickly inhaling a pinch of the contents inside, he felt the rush of the powdery substance restore him. Once again his blood flowed and his skin warmed. Whatever had overcome him had now receded. Taking several deep breaths, he steeled himself. It must be a nervous affliction before his introduction. That's what it was, Barrons reassured himself. Nervous affliction.

"No," Will's rough voice said even as he leaned closer, claiming her mouth with his own. Like a drowning man he clung to her, his hands roaming all over her body, touching, needy and absorbing her very essence.

"Please," she murmured, though she wasn't really sure what she was asking him to do. They were still on deck, though out of sight of the few sailors about.

Seconds passed as his holding and touching her reached a fevered pitch. Arianna could feel the solidity of his response to her against her belly. Desire coursed through her now and she was certain she was seconds from finding out how real her ghost had truly become.

"No!" he said again, thrusting her away. His tone was thick and strained. "What kind of trick is this?" he asked between ragged breaths. "What in hell are you doing to me?"

The break in his voice nearly rent her in two. "I'm not doing anything. I told you, I think it's the stone."

He clenched his hands, breaths coming in quick, short gasps. "What can I do?"

"I'm not sure. It seems you may have been given a second chance at life."

"That's impossible."

"Be that as it may, you are real now. Whether or not you realize it, you are now more of a problem to me than ever before."

He glanced up at her, his eyes sharp and penetrating. "A problem to you? I have only one purpose, to see Richard Barrons destroyed. My purpose has not been affected. Perhaps I can wield the blade that will let his blood after all."

With that he reached forward, his hand nearly touching the railing of the ship. When he made contact with the wood, a bizarre thing happened. His hand neatly went through it.

"I don't understand," Arianna said softly. "You are real enough to me, but not to the rest of the physical world."

"Damn and blast," he repeated, stepping back. He looked as though a blow had struck him. "What in blazes is happening to me?"

Arianna considered things for a moment. "I believe the stone ties you to me, somehow. You're real enough where I'm concerned. You and I are allowed physical contact, but that is all." She looked up at him tenderly. "At least for the present."

"What good is it to me? It was torture enough to know that I have no form in this life. And now, to only be given a small measure of existence and be denied the rest? What sort of affliction is this?"

Before she could answer a man stepped across the deck. Tall and slightly bent at the shoulders, the ship's first mate spoke to her. "Eh, there, missus. Is something the matter?"

Arianna turned to him, searching his expression to see if he saw the captain standing beside her.

"No. Nothing. I'm just taking some fresh air."

"Ye must go below. There's a storm brewing in the east. We're hoping to miss the worst of it, but it may get dangerous above decks."

To prove his point, the wind picked up and sent a chilly current across the bow, rustling the sails and jarring the ship beneath them.

"Thank you, I'll go below in a moment."

"Aye." The man turned slightly, then quickly surveyed the ship around them. "I beg your pardon, Missus, but I thought I heard voices. Were you alone just now?"

"Do you see anyone, sir?" Arianna held her breath as the man swept his gaze around them.

"Nothing but the shadows, now that you mention it. But I could have sworn I heard voices."

Arianna took a deep breath. "I was talking to myself, reciting my favorite poetry. A rather long ballad by Mr. Keats. Would you like to hear it?"

The man made a wry face. "No thank you, lady. Now, I can give you another five minutes but then I must clear the deck."

Arianna let out a slow breath. Turning back to the captain, she realized he had left her, perhaps fading into the shadows again.

"It'll do you no good," she muttered to the night. "You can't hide forever."

* * *

Will groaned inwardly. Of course he could hide. Isn't that what ghosts did best? Waiting on the whim of the living. Except that he wasn't dead anymore. Yet neither was he living. A new hell had claimed him.

Satan's teeth. The woman had nearly undone him. In those fleeting moments, he'd been a man again. One whose heart beat and lungs filled with precious air. He'd touched and caressed living flesh, and God help him, he'd wanted to do more. So much more.

He'd sunk back into the darkness and watched her as she'd conversed with the first mate. Her lithe body tempted him even now. He'd wanted her then, as he did now, with an urge so powerful that it nearly undid him.

Yet he knew he couldn't have her. Not now, not ever. She was the poisoned apple, the iron wall that would keep him from achieving his goal. Even for those few seconds in her arms, he'd felt it. His sense of self had drifted off course, consumed by desire and need so great that it rivaled everything else in his existence, pale and incomplete that it was.

"Dear God," he pleaded, "this can't be happening." But then, it wasn't possible that he'd been beaten half to death, imprisoned for months, and then hanged in disgrace. It made no sense that he'd returned from the dead, or even that he stood here on the deck of his very own ship yet again. But it had happened and now he needed to keep a clear head. He could not let this slip of a woman get in the way of his vengeance. Not now.

Ethan lay in the darkness. He felt the sway of the ship around him and though he hadn't known how he'd gotten this far, or where he was headed, he knew he was on board. He also knew that Arianna wasn't far away. Even through the fog of his injury, he could feel her near. Always.

He sensed her distress. She was closer than ever. He clutched the blanket that covered him against the growing chill.

"In here, Mrs. Barrons."

"Thank you."

Seconds later, his sister's gentle, capable hands were on his forehead, caressing his brow. So badly did he want to speak with her, to tell her of the danger, that it nearly made him seize.

"Careful, Ethan. You mustn't struggle."

Opening his eyes, he saw her then. Arianna had always been a beautiful child, then a lovely woman. Although he could see the hint of worry that hung in her gaze, he could sense something else. She was slightly flushed and her breaths were quick and shallow.

"Rest easy. It's going to be all right now." Straightening his bed around him, she tucked the folds of the blanket neatly.

"I'm so grateful they allowed me to see you. I feared the worst."

Ethan closed his eyes for a moment. What could be worse than this?

"It's going to be all right," she repeated. "We're headed for France, or rather a small island just south of it. My husband owns it—imagine that. We'll be safe there, at least for awhile."

Husband? Ethan's anger swelled within him. What in blazes had happened while he'd slept? He tossed his head back and forth, grinding his teeth, yet no sound came from him.

"I know, you don't understand. He was threatening you. He has papers, Ethan. Forged papers that seem to show you were involved in illegal business dealings. I had no choice but to marry him."

Ethan swallowed. It had been all his fault after all.

Arianna watched her brother carefully for any response. Other than his choking sounds and wild movements of his eyes, he said not a word. She tried to stroke his cheek, tried to be reassuring but nothing happened. He merely closed his eyes.

"He's no better, I take it?"

Arianna turned to see her not-quite-ghost standing in the doorway. Only a few strands of light filtered through him. As much as her brother's condition troubled her, so did Markham's.

What was his curse? *Damn and blast.* Arianna only sighed. Becoming emotional now would do nothing to improve the situation. Instead she pulled the sheet up to cover her brother's chest and leaned forward to kiss him gently on the cheek. He made no attempt to respond. She swore she could feel his depression broadening beneath her fingertips.

"Let's go to my room," she said in a quiet voice as she stood to face him. "Ethan needs his rest."

"Yes, he does."

For once the captain agreed with her and moved to one side. She slipped past him and into the corridor. Though the cabin she'd been given was small, it was a haven that beckoned her now. It had been a long, exhausting day.

Once inside, she went to the small table beside the cot. Above it on the shelf sat a bottle of sherry and a single glass. Perhaps the supply master of this vessel felt a nip or two would ease the discomfort of the crossing, but she knew it would only make her stomach more unsettled. She gazed at the bottle a moment, then closed her eyes.

"Whatever it is you wish to discuss, Captain, let's be done with it. I'm tired."

He paused a moment. She glanced up to see him purse his lips, appearing deep in thought. When he glanced back up at her, his eyes had returned to a sapphire clarity. It was like gazing into clear, blue pools.

"I'm changing," he said plainly enough.

"Yes, I see." She drew in a deep breath. "I'm not sure what it means. I wasn't allowed to bring my mother's journal, not that it would have made much difference, anyway."

"This has to do with the stone and its power over me."

"Return it to me and perhaps things will change back to the way they were. The way they should be."

"No." His answer came without hesitation.

"Please, this wasn't supposed to happen. You cannot reclaim a life that is no longer yours."

"How do you know that? How do you know that this wasn't supposed to happen?"

"It just isn't done." Arianna knew that certainly wasn't reason enough, but it was all she could come up with at the moment.

"Are you sure? I think if I keep the stone long enough that I'll gain enough strength to become alive again."

She swallowed. "What will you do? Wait for Barrons to follow us and then stab him in his sleep? You've sworn to me that you are no murderer. Will you become one now?"

"He deserves to die."

"He deserves justice!" Arianna stood on her tiptoes, nose to nose with the captain. Even now, in a near fit of temper, she could feel the pull from him, the allure. By the heavens, it was growing stronger with every passing moment.

"He murdered many of my men and . . ." He stopped, his voice choked. Turning away, he paced to the end of the small room. There he stood, still except for the movement of his shoulders and he drew in several deep breaths.

Arianna shivered. He shouldn't be breathing, she thought. How long before he is strong enough to make good on his plans? How long before the rest of the living begin to see him? What would they do if they knew? Would they hang him again? Could a ghost be killed?

He turned back to her then, his face calmer, his breathing less noticeable. "He deserves to die."

"I'm not saying that he hasn't earned his place at the gallows. Help me to find a way to get him there."

"Justice will not stop him. He shot an earl, for God's sake. He has risen among the most powerful men in England because of his deep pockets and status. Do you really think any accusations would tumble him from his lofty position? He had the money to hire the men to murder my crew. He corrupted the king's own courts to judge me guilty. Don't you think he could deflect anything you or I could charge him with?"

"He's only a man," Arianna said, feeling to her marrow that what he said was true. Yet she was too stubborn to let his arguments sway her.

"He's a man with more money than the Prince Regent, is what he is. I don't know much about your rich society folk, but I can tell you they respect money."

Arianna sighed, rubbing her forehead. Her head ached

painfully, her eyes felt as if sand had been poured into them, and her heart was as heavy as the iron anchor lying on the deck above them. How could this be?

Glancing up at him she caught a glimpse of something else, the hint of a pain so deep that its depth knew no bottom. Despair.

"What did he do to you?" she asked, somehow sensing that it was more than the death of his crew or even the loss of his life that was stabbing at him.

"I've told you a dozen times."

"Yes, but not all of it," she said quietly. "There's something else. I can feel it from you. It's more than your hatred of Barrons." Arianna softened her voice, attempting to soothe him with her own inner calm. "Sooner or later he will be found out. The wealthy will use him for their own purpose and when they're done, the truth will conquer him. True, the gentry may be a greedy lot, but we're not stupid."

"No, never that." He sighed, rubbing his brow.

"Then what? What is it that makes him drive you so? Why risk everything just to spill his blood? Would it really bring back those who were lost to you? Will it return your life and liberty? I know one thing for certain. If you do not find peace, it will destroy you."

"I shall never have peace. You're correct in thinking that killing Barrons will never replace all that was taken from me. But it will make my heart less heavy if I know that he has paid for his crimes."

Arianna watched him for a moment. It wasn't true. There was still something hidden beneath his reserved manner.

"You're lying," she said simply, turning away from him, and moving to smooth down the covers on her cot.

Chapter Ten

"Damn and blast! You are the most exasperating female I have ever met."

"I may be, but at least I'm honest."

"Have you no feelings, woman?" he scoffed.

A sharp pain shot through Arianna as if he'd thrown a dagger through her heart.

"I have feelings." Stricken, Arianna couldn't help the sadness in her voice. The heat of her embarrassment and anger rushed to her face and neck.

She turned sharply from him. "This discussion isn't about me. I cannot help if you won't be honest with me." Arianna hid her shaking hands in the folds of her skirt. She waited breathlessly for the stubborn ghost to answer her. But when she turned again, he was gone.

A string of other curses burst from Will's mouth. He'd left her, turned tail and run like a raw recruit on his first voyage. Standing on the deck once more, grateful that the crew kept at a distance, preoccupied with their tasks. He watched the churning seas beyond the railing. His spirit had always had an affinity with the sea, no doubt about it.

"You can't run away from your problems," she said softly behind him.

"You've never tried, have you?" he shot back. Gripping the polished grain of the rails, he fought to find the warm touch of the wood but his hands as yet had little feeling. Still, he could feel it building within him. A powerful surge rose in him, fighting to burst forth like the waves against the horizon.

"No. But I've tried to hide from them. It isn't all that different."

Will clenched his jaw as tightly as he did the railing. He would not answer her accusations; he didn't want to think beyond his own pain. After all, it had carried him this far, hadn't it?

"I'm sorry," she murmured, now standing beside him. Together, they silently watched the horizon dip with every movement of the ship.

"You have nothing to be sorry for," he said at last. The argument had gone out of him, at least. Sighing, he turned and sank down until he was sitting on the deck, his back resting against the railing. It wasn't until he found the solid wood beneath him that he realized just how real this world was becoming. Too damn real.

A second later, she followed suit, the rustle of her skirt as soft as the sigh of an angel.

"I'm sorry you suffered so much. It's obvious that you were judged wrongly. But you must forgive the fates and Barrons himself if you are ever to get beyond this."

He sighed, suddenly remembering the great fatigue

that plagued him when he'd walked up the gallows steps. A dark cloud rolled in the sky above and he felt despair sink deep within him.

"They killed her," he heard himself say. His voice was deep and thick, laced with pain.

"Who?" Arianna asked. Coming closer, she placed her hand on his sleeve.

Will could feel the warmth emanating from her. She was a refuge, he realized. She drew him in from a stark, cold night and, desperate, pathetic thing that he was, he could not resist.

"My daughter, Katherine. She was only five years old."

"Oh."

The word came out in one anguished breath and he knew then that he must tell Arianna all of it. Willing the memory forth, he closed his eyes.

"When I signed up with Captain Ben Harvey he would bring his crew to port and treat all that wanted female companionship to a single night's sport at his favorite pub. The Dove and Tail was as raucous an establishment as ever was built." For a moment a smile came to his lips, the memories of his youth spouting forth like a spring rain.

"Ah, many a night I landed there and before long found my tastes ran to the delicious charms of one of the most beautiful women I'd ever met. Letitia Grand, they called her, though it wasn't until my wedding night that I actually knew her true name was Commons." A bitter laugh came from him then. "My wedding night, the night her daughter was born, and the night she died, all tied into one."

"Her daughter, I thought you said . . . ?"

"I did. I knew I was the babe's father, though Lettie

had never confirmed it. I realized when I first held her that she was mine, body and soul, no matter if I'd been the one who'd sired her. She opened the largest, bluest eyes I'd ever seen and looked me straight in the face with no fear, that one."

Will sighed. "I got the magistrate that very night and had him marry us. With her final breaths, Lettie agreed to marry me and make Katherine my daughter. She asked me to give her that name. It had been her own mother's, you see. Like me, Lettie'd had no living family, but when she died, she was not alone. Childbed fever took her with the hour."

Will opened his eyes and turned to the woman beside him. Arianna had remained silent and now wore a wistful expression. Her gaze had settled somewhere in the encroaching darkness of the evening.

"How sad for her to never have known her daughter or been loved by her husband."

"Lettie was a warm and wonderful woman and many of us poor sailors did love her, to be sure. Some would have married her but she'd carried a flame for one in particular who had never returned to port. I don't think he'd fathered her child—when she and I spoke late one night she'd said he'd been gone too long for that. He'd been her first and only true love. It didn't matter to me. I was honored to pay my wages just to bed her one night a year."

Arianna sighed. "The sea is a lonely place, isn't it?"

"Indeed," he chuckled. "With only the company of men it can be. But it also makes the return to port most sweet."

She nodded then. "A man has needs. I suppose it's best for you not to take a wife in the traditional sense. Too difficult."

"And yet many men do. I've never had anything to offer a woman save my name. I was glad enough to give it to Lettie, though. I have no regret for that."

"What of the child? Did you leave her behind as well?"

He drew in a sharp breath. "I couldn't. By the time I was captain of this ship, I had the means and the power to care for her. When she was weaned, we brought her on board. She was our own little mistress. Ran the bloody lot of us, she did."

"I thought a woman on board a ship was bad luck?"

"A woman, yes, but Katherine was not just female, she was an angel. We believed that it was her presence that led us to such good fortune in the trades. I know most sailors say a female on board a ship will only bring bad luck, but not my Katherine. By the gods, she was our princess."

A deep sense of misery ran through him. It clutched at his chest like some great beast, its claws closing around his heart.

"Then you were attacked," Arianna softly prompted.

"We were about fifty miles from port when we were hailed by Barrons's vessel. She limped along as though she'd been attacked. I sent orders for our ship to come about into rescue position. They were on us before we knew what was happening. The next thing I knew, my crew was dying right before my eyes. Barrons then locked me belowdecks. He killed Bart, the young lad who'd been my cabin boy and saw to the care of Katherine. Gutted him like a mackerel."

Will couldn't help the snap of emotion in his voice. In response, he felt Arianna's hand tightening on his sleeve.

"Three days they held me while they tortured and

killed my crew. Then, that final morning, they took Katherine and me above decks."

Will closed his eyes again, the memory flooding through him like the sea on high squall. . . .

It had been a morning very much like the present one in which Will found himself dragged up the stairs from the hold of his own ship. The acrid smell of smoke permeated the air—that and the all too familiar scent of decay. As he looked out on the deck for the first time in days, he saw what had taken place during the time he'd spent jailed in the hold. Death and blood tainted every surface of his once pristine vessel.

Enraged, Will struggled one final time against his captors. Kicking and biting wherever he could, he did as much injury as a man could do with his hands bound behind him.

"Bloody bastards! I'll kill you all," he ground out, when he'd been subdued at last by two of his ship's attackers. He would have continued to fight against them, but that a tall, stringy shadow fell over him. Finally seeing his enemy face to face, Will froze.

"What the devil is going on here?" Will demanded.

"Justice, Captain Markham. You're a traitor and a thief. I'm charged by His Majesty's representatives to see that his law is upheld."

"Murder is what it is. I'm no thief and I've never sailed against the royal flags."

"I have proof. Enough to fill your sea chest." Barrons waved his hand toward the officer's quarters.

"Lies. Anyone with any sense at all will see that none of this is true. What you have is nothing more than forgeries."

"Quite the contrary. I have confessions from your own crew. Everyone of them, thirty-two sailors down to a man, told us lovely stories, each one. Of course it took some convincing, but then my staff is most persuasive."

Will's stomach twisted as he looked down upon the bloodstained decking. That explained why he'd been held in a filthy cell for nearly a week. Alone with only stale bread, rotted meat and unclean water for sustenance. Yet his lot had been enjoying the height of luxury compared to the suffering inflicted on his crew. "You tortured them."

"I merely discovered the truth. Not to worry, each one has gone on to the great hereafter a redeemed man. Messy business, this carriage of justice."

"You bastard." A slow, venomous dread started to stir in Will's gut. "Why would you do this? I know we are competitors on the open sea, yes, but to murder for financial gain alone? Are you that sort, Barrons?"

"There is a question of a shipment of arms. You remember the one, about six months ago. It was headed to Spain. Enough guns and ammunition to outfit an entire regiment. Where are they, Markham?"

"I heard of the shipment, yes. Everyone from here to the Continent knew about it. I have no idea who pirated that vessel. Napoleon's forces, most likely, why?"

"I have in my possession a sworn document stating that your ship was seen in the vicinity."

"As were a dozen others. What are you getting at? Do you think I stole those weapons? That's preposterous. My hold was full of livestock for the forces in the north."

"It would not have been difficult for you to hide your cargo long enough to attack that ship and hide the guns. Where are they, Captain Markham?"

"I have no idea." Will clenched his fists. "But then, you already know that, don't you?"

"I know you are a traitor, a privateer, and a fool. Tell me where the shipment is."

"I already told you. I don't have it."

Barrons smiled broadly. "I was certain that would be your answer."

Turning to his second in command, he gave a single curt nod.

"Bring up the girl," Digby called behind him.

"No!" Will surged forward but Barrons's men held him steady. "For God's sake, let her go!"

"Tell me where the weapons are." Barrons' voice was soft against the roaring of the sea.

Will shook his head. "I don't have them."

"Then you and your daughter will pay the price of your ignorance."

The doors that led down to the hold burst open and a sailor came up with a large canvas bag tossed over his shoulder. The wiggling mass within it struggled against confinement.

"Papa!" a young girl's voice called out, muffled by the thick material.

"Katherine!" Will fought them then with every ounce of his strength. He kicked and bit the men who held him.

"Keep him steady," Barrons yelled at them over the sound of the child's crying and Will's frantic curses.

When they had him secured at last against the mast, he relented, breathless and raging.

"Let her go! Do what you will to me, but I beg you, let her go!"

In response, Barrons merely turned to his second. Digby bowed low and motioned to the man who held

Katherine. The small sack wriggled frantically when the man held it high. In the next second he pitched it out over the railing. There was a small splash and the screaming child was no more. . . .

Even now, so many months later, with the deep chasm of death separating him from that moment, Will could hear his own screams echo in his mind.

"Dear heavens," Arianna said quietly. "She was but a child."

Will could no longer hold back the torrent of emotion. He turned to her and saw the soft, glistening trail of tears on her face. She'd grieved with him as no other had. It struck a deep, resounding chord in him. He'd expected her pity, perhaps even anger, but her next words shot through him like a hot iron poker.

"I saw her."

"What? What the devil are you talking about?"

She looked away a moment. "You said she was small, only five or so?"

"Yes." He turned then, grasping her shoulders. "What is it? What do you know?"

Arianna shook her head. "What color was her hair? What did her face look like?"

"She was fair . . . like her mother. Blond curls, and a round face . . . eyes the color of the sky. Why do you ask?"

"Was her nose slightly upturned at the end? Her cheeks soft, still with a baby look about them?"

"Yes." Will could barely hold back his excitement. He searched Arianna's eyes. "Where have you seen her?"

"In a vision. I don't know where it came from. It

Take A Trip Into A Timeless World of Passion and Adventure with Kensington Choice Historical Romances! —Absolutely FREE!

Enjoy the passion and adventure of another time with Kensington Choice Historical Romances. They are the finest novels of their kind, written by today's best-selling romance authors. Each Kensington Choice Historical Romance transports you to distant lands in a bygone age. Experience the adventure and share the delight as proud men and spirited women discover the wonder and passion of true love.

Get 4 FREE Books!

We created our convenient Home Subscription Service so you'll be sure to have the hottest new romances delivered each month right to your doorstep—usually before they are available in book stores. Just to show you how convenient the Zebra Home Subscription Service is, we would like to send you 4 FREE Kensington Choice Historical Romances. The books are worth up to $24.96, but you only pay $1.99 for shipping and handling. There's no obligation to buy additional books—ever!

Save Up To 30% With Home Delivery!

Accept your FREE books and each month we'll deliver 4 brand new titles as soon as they are published. They'll be yours to examine FREE for 10 days. Then if you decide to keep the books, you'll pay the preferred subscriber's price (up to 30% off the cover price!), plus shipping and handling. Remember, you are under no obligation to buy any of these books at any time! If you are not delighted with them, simply return them and owe nothing. But if you enjoy Kensington Choice Historical Romances as much as we think you will, pay the special preferred subscriber rate and save over $8.00 off the cover price!

We have **4 FREE BOOKS** for you as your
introduction to
KENSINGTON CHOICE!
To get your FREE BOOKS, worth up to $24.96, mail
the card below or call TOLL-FREE 1-800-770-1963.
Visit our website at www.kensingtonbooks.com.

Get 4 FREE Kensington Choice Historical Romances!

YES! Please send me my 4 FREE KENSINGTON CHOICE HISTORICAL ROMANCES (without obligation to purchase other books). I only pay $1.99 for shipping and handling. Unless you hear from me after I receive my 4 FREE BOOKS, you may send me 4 new novels—as soon as they are published—to preview each month FREE for 10 days. If I am not satisfied, I may return them and owe nothing. Otherwise, I will pay the money-saving preferred subscriber's price (over $8.00 off the cover price), plus shipping and handling. I may return any shipment within 10 days and owe nothing, and I may cancel any time I wish. In any case the 4 FREE books will be mine to keep.

Name _____

Address _____ Apt. _____

City _____ State _____ Zip _____

Telephone (____) _____

Signature _____
(If under 18, parent or guardian must sign)

Offer limited to one per household and not to current subscribers. Terms, offer and prices subject to change. Orders subject to acceptance by Kensington Choice Book Club.
Offer Valid in the U.S. only.

KN094A

‖‖‖‖‖‖‖‖‖‖‖‖‖‖‖‖‖‖‖‖‖‖‖‖‖‖‖‖‖‖‖‖

KENSINGTON CHOICE

Zebra Home Subscription Service, Inc.

P.O. Box 5214

Clifton NJ 07015-5214

PLACE
STAMP
HERE

may have been in her final moments, I'm not sure. There was a man and she was crying."

Will turned her loose, then sank back onto the ship's frame. "Yes. They took her from her cell that morning. I saw them drag her out."

They were silent for a long while. Will barely had the energy to draw a breath, even though the need for breathing had long since left him.

"Perhaps when you give up your quest for vengeance you might be reunited with her."

Will shook his head, a wave of sadness rising in him. "I don't want to be. How can I? I failed her. I was a coward. I should have done everything to save her and the others. I should have kissed their boots to save her and my crew. Barrons kept asking me about that blasted shipment. I told him to go to hell." He let out a short laugh. "Imagine how surprised I was when he sent me there instead."

"This isn't eternal torment."

"It might as well be. I'm as helpless as a newborn babe. I have anger and hatred and thirst for the bastard's blood but nothing else." He held up his hand before him and made an empty fist. "I can do nothing."

"That's not true. Already you have aided Ethan and me. Together we make a formidable team, you know."

"Do we? You refuse to wield a sword and I cannot. We are as impotent as a drunkard deep in his cups. No, I fear the most we can do is continue along this path."

Arianna shook her head. "You're wrong. We will beat Barrons. There has to be something that will show him for the true blackguard that he is. We'll let justice be our blade. We'll find a way to bring forth the truth. One day he shall face his own destiny. With any luck at all it will be at the end of a noose."

At that moment, a new emotion swelled within Will. In the very next instant, he was pulling her into his arms, positioning her on his lap, pressing his lips upon hers.

From the very first second of their contact he felt himself begin to glow with their combined energies. She was strong and beautiful in his arms, and with her touch came a sort of quickening. He was filling up. He was becoming alive.

A buzz ran through his nerves, as their bodies pressed one into the other. Arianna hungrily drank from him, taking all the passion he could give her and at the same time demanding even more.

For those few moments the grief of losing his daughter passed between them, but his loss, now shared, became less of a deep well and more of a physical longing for the comfort only Arianna could give him.

"I want you," he muttered against her neck.

In answer she nodded. Her hands slid along his stomach, back and shoulders. "You're real! Dear God, you're real!"

"I want to make love to you," he said, not even knowing for sure if he could.

"Yes!" she answered breathlessly.

Like the rush of a wave crashing over him, Will could feel the heat of her excitement sweep through her. He gasped as he pulled her upward, hoisting her into his arms, rising to his feet, his lips once again finding hers. Kissing her deeply, he carried her to the stairs that led belowdecks.

Once they made it to her cabin, he thrust open the door and tossed her onto the cot. Loosening his clothes, he pulled first his shirt and then his britches off and shed the coverings. With a guttural growl, he kicked the door closed behind them and joined her on the narrow bed.

It had been years since he'd been with a woman. He didn't know how long this state would last, but it felt wonderfully surreal and he prayed to God that he would at least stay thus until they'd both been sated. To ask for more than that would have been too much, he knew. He would have to be satisfied with this moment, this blessing. It would be enough, he told himself, though not for a single instant did he believe it.

Billy Watkins had seen the woman come on board.

"She's a pretty bit o' lacin', ain't she?" Dobby said behind him.

"Aye, she's that. The cap'n says to stay away from her, though. She's the new bride of Mr. Barrons."

"He must not have much use for her, trundlin' her off to the island, eh?"

"I'm sure he has his reasons. Not for the likes of us to question 'im, though." Billy had watched as she'd walked stoically down the stair to her quarters. She'd held her chin high enough, clearly too good for the likes of them.

"I heard as she was a lady. Her brother's an earl or some such. Maybe a marquess. A high-ups, if you know what I mean." Dobby continued to swab the mop across the deck.

"Maybe. I'll bet she's had no real man. I've seen ol' Spikes himself. Only can get his willie hard on young girls, not the baby lassies, mind you, but the ones just about to bud. Naw, he likely married her for her title."

"No doubt a man like you could find his way into her skirts, though."

"No doubt. It's not like ol' Spikes will be doing much about it. He's sending her to the island. Doesn't give a whit about her."

"Mayhap you can visit her one of these nights if you get yer work done, eh?"

"Maybe," Billy said.

Now that night had come, except Billy realized too late that the lady was occupied. He stood outside her door, himself having even taken the trouble to clean up. Didn't matter, he thought. He'd wait his turn. What was it to him if she'd already taken a lover?

Slicking back his hair and straightening his britches, Billy patiently waited outside Mrs. Barrons's door. From the moaning she was doing on the other side, he thought it might yet be awhile. Pulling an apple and blade out of his pocket he began to take his evening meal. Surely it wouldn't be that long.

The feel of a man was an exquisite thing, Arianna thought. In seconds Will was upon her and she felt as though her body had never sung before. Each touch, each caress slid across her hungry flesh and left a trail of sensation in its wake.

"Kiss me," she urged and once again her ghost captain obliged, though not on her mouth. To her surprise he started at the nape of her neck and then feathered light touches down her chest, taking his time with each soft breast. His tongue teased her nipples, then moved lower towards her belly. Warm breaths blew against her navel as his hands slid around her to knead her back and then pay particular attention to the muscles of her behind.

Arianna gasped when his fingers slid luxuriously between the soft pillows of her rear, lifting her in a most erotic fashion. He didn't penetrate her, but he did caress her hips with each strong hand and when she arched her back, he slid his mouth down between her legs. His heated kiss reached her core and Arianna felt as though a fire had been set through her groin.

"Please," she whimpered, though she wasn't sure just what she was begging for. Completion, the sweet ache that soon was an all-out spasm of desire. Just as she was about to burst, he pulled back.

Looking up, Arianna saw Will's heavy-lidded gaze as he sat up and watched her. His chest heaved and a groan escaped him.

"I want you so badly" he said in a low, throaty voice that stirred her to her soul.

"Then take me." It was as simple as that. Inviting him in, Arianna spread her legs a fraction wider and watched as his eyes took on an ethereal glow. He was a hungry tiger about to pounce, a panther whose mouth watered above her. She wanted him inside her, an invading force to take her to the brink of what he'd already promised. In response to her invitation his member hardened even more, surging forward, insisting its owner go forth.

"As you wish, milady," he whispered and then lowered himself on top of her.

The moment their bodies touched, Arianna felt her senses explode. This was what she'd been made for.

Will Markham was spirit no more, she realized. He was full-bodied male. More than just the thick, sinewy muscle and hard bone, he was animal and feral and Arianna truly loved him for it.

When he entered her fully, in one forceful thrust, Arianna felt the tear of tissue inside her. It hurt for a second and then other sensations took over. Her body molded to his, her opening widening even further, and a blazing heat took hold. He was the ocean now, writhing to and fro inside of her, rocking and pushing and her body answered him in kind. Then, as if they were a ship sailing to the end of the world, the two of them tipped over the edge, their bodies tightening in unison, spasming and thrusting into orgasmic bliss.

The long and short of it was, Billy grew tired of waiting. He'd listened to the sounds of passion long enough and wanted a part of the action. Damn, but the woman's alluring sound was about to drive him mad. He'd have to interrupt them soon, or his own fittings would be in need of repair. He was so near to bursting that when Mrs. Barrons cried out her final passion it was all he could do not to explode himself.

Enough was enough. He threw his apple core under the stair and stood up to make his presence known. The unfortunate sailor on the other side of the door was about to taste Billy's wrath.

"Ahoy there! Yer time is up! Git yer britches about ye and be gone. I've a mind to meet with her ladyship now."

Pushing the door open, Billy saw what he thought was a wall. It turned out to be more than that. A solid mass of man met him and shortly thereafter a cannonball. It wasn't a cannonball, though, but when knuckle

SPIRITED AWAY   167

and bone met with the center of his face, the fist might just have well have been.

Will felt the life drain out of him. His emotion had peaked, fresh from spending himself in one long, glorious orgasm. Arianna had been every bit the woman he'd thought she was and more. She'd taken him in and no experience in his life before or after had compared to the explosive lovemaking. But even as she'd sighed beneath him, he'd felt the other's presence. Instant anger pulled him from his lover's bed to stand in the doorway. The tall, thin man, wearing seaman's clothes and a sneer met with Will's wrath and then quickly folded under the blow.

"What in blazes?" Arianna said beside him.

"Not in blazes, milady, but I've no problem sending him there if need be. What do you wish me to do?"

Arianna looked up at him, astonished. "What do I wish?"

"He was here to sample your charms, I believe. I suppose he thought that as soon as you were finished with your current paramour, that you'd be of a mind to take a second."

"Oh."

Will watched as Arianna blushed, the bright pink of her skin fairly glowing in the evening shadows. Perhaps some of his own life energy had been shared with her after all?

"I shall take care of this intruder; don't worry."

With that he stepped over the crumpled form and hoisted him onto his shoulders. With a nod he turned and headed up the stairs. He heard Arianna rushing about behind him, likely pulling her dressing gown around her. With light steps she followed him up the stairs and out onto the deck.

The moon had just began to light the evening and in the shimmering night he walked to the railing. With a heave, Will flexed his shoulder muscles and thrust the stranger upward and over into the churning sea below.

With a deep breath he then turned, smiling at his lady fair and called out, "Man overboard!"

Arianna stood stunned, her hands covering her luscious mouth in shock.

"After you, milady." Will thrust out his arm for her to take. Instead her eyes widened.

"Captain Markham, you're fading again."

Looking at his arm, Will saw the shimmery effervescence cover his flesh. It looked as though their brief encounter was not a permanent state. A wave of sadness overcame him. For in that moment, more than anything else, Will had wanted to be a real man once again.

Arianna wanted to comfort him. She watched as Will's expression changed into a myriad of emotions, anger to pain and finally to acceptance. Straightening to his full stature, he walked past her and returned to the stairs leading back to her quarters.

All around Arianna, the deck came to life. She saw men rushing forward, lowering the longboats and shouting to the man now screaming from the ocean's surface. Ignoring it all she followed her ghostly companion. She found him seated on the floor across from her cot. Cross-legged and arms folded in front of him, he had leaned his head back and now rested on the cabin wall.

"I'm sorry." Arianna stood before him, arms wrapped around herself. "If I could, I'd make you alive again."

He opened his eyes again. The deep hue of his gaze seemed to cut right through her.

"I'd almost forgotten," he said in a quiet voice.

"Forgotten what?" She tried to search his shadowy features but his face remained unmoving, expressionless.

"Why I'm here. I can't do that again. I must see Barrons destroyed. I must see him dead. What happened between you and me must not happen again."

Arianna nodded. "I'm not sure it could. But, after you . . . that is, afterwards you were very, well, very substantial."

He closed his eyes. "It didn't last. There's nothing to prove that it will even happen again." He reached inside his shirt and pulled out the amulet. The jade glow emanating from it had dimmed.

"There is no reason to doubt it," she said, though the conviction in her voice had fled.

"No, I suppose not. However, I will not allow it. While I was with you, I'd forgotten my purpose. I cannot. I must not. Else my daughter and the men who died by his hand, and even your own brother will go unavenged."

"Oh." Arianna said no more. A deep fatigue fell upon her. "When you have killed him and your purpose is met, what will happen then? Will your anger be sated? Will your soul be at rest?"

He looked at her then, a new darkness descending on his expression. "Would you care?"

Arianna rose slowly to her feet. Like a ghost herself, she went to the cot. She had no answer for him. Inside her a tumult of emotions threatened but she knew to her marrow that he must not see. She wanted him whole and real and in her arms, in her bed. She couldn't let him know that now. If she did it would be both their undoing. She could not lust after a ghost and if he did for her, then he'd fight what must be. He'd never find his way to the eternity he deserved.

"I must sleep," she answered instead. Pulling back the blankets that still held the scent of their lovemaking, she sank between the sheets, pulling them up over her once she'd settled. She heard no stirring from her companion, no sighs or even the slow, even breaths. Nothing.

Yet she knew he remained, silent as the grave and as ominous.

Chapter Eleven

The two-day journey brought them at last to the small island of Montclair. The chill winter weather had receded with the miles. The sun bathed the surf as the longboats made their way from the ship. In short order she and Ethan were unloaded. The seamen hauled out Arianna's two chests and supplies in barrels and boxes for her stay. Without a word to her, they carried Ethan's prone body on a stretcher between them.

An hour's walk found them in front of the estate mansion, a large, crumbling building. The grounds were overgrown with weeds and unkempt shrubbery.

"Inside, missus," Larken, the first mate, motioned. She nodded to him and began to climb the crumbling steps.

"Where are the servants?"

"Only one person remains, Mrs. Stanhope."

"A lone woman? How odd. No wonder the place is such a shambles. Why hasn't my husband engaged a regular staff?"

"He won it at cards—the island and the house. No time, I suppose."

"I see." She turned and toured the large foyer. The carpet at the door was tattered and the paint on the walls was chipped and flaking. The door that lead to the rest of the manor hung half off its hinges.

Arianna walked through the house, taking in the poor condition. It would take a fortune to even make the place livable, let alone restore it to its former grandeur. Finally she entered the kitchen. Larken motioned for his men to set the barrels of foodstuffs in the pantry.

"It's sealed well enough, missus. Still, ye might want to keep yer eyes open for any vermin. There won't be any supplies for two months. With just the two of you, it shouldn't be much of a concern."

"Much of a concern? Do you mean to strand us here? But who's to make the repairs?"

Larken laughed. " 'Tis not my concern, Lady Barrons. I'm a sailor, not a damned butler. The men have settled yer brother in one of the bedrooms upstairs. Mrs. Stanhope should be along. Good day."

Arianna watched the man's retreat. Walking out to the terrace she saw a familiar figure standing in the center of the garden entrance. Will Markham held the amulet once again, suspended on the gold chain, glowing against his shimmering countenance.

"What are you thinking about?" Arianna asked.

He sighed as he turned toward her. "I believe I am a fool."

Arianna cocked her head to one side. "Indeed?"

"I should go with them. I believe I can, with this." He held out the stone.

"Then you'd be stealing my property for certain. If

you did manage to kill my husband, then what would be come of it?"

He shrugged. "I've not the slightest, but that's not what's keeping me here."

"Then what? Your affection for me?"

He turned to look at her, his eyes searching her as though he were studying an exotic species of insect.

"I am fond of you, Arianna," he spoke at last.

"Oh? You've barely spoken to me since the day before yesterday. I was beginning to think that you were searching for a way to continue on without me."

"I won't lie to you. I did think about it. The truth is that, yes, I am fond of you." He sighed.

"I see. So your heart has led you here?"

He shook his head. Arianna didn't miss the expression of sadness that deepened his scowl.

"I believe that your husband will yet come for you, one final time."

"So that he can perform his husbandly duties?" Arianna couldn't hold back the shudder at the memory of the last demonstration of Barrons's "affection."

"That and the fact that he cannot claim his true inheritance unless you and your brother are disposed of."

A shot of fear went through Arianna. "How do you know that he means to kill us? Surely someone would suspect."

"You would think so, but enough money and a title would make it very difficult to prove anything. Pay off enough magistrates, line enough pockets and true justice is very hard to come by." He looked away, his voice bitter. "My own conviction should be proof of that."

"I see." Arianna gathered her skirts and sat on the stone bench. "Then we'll have to be ready for him."

"You'll have to kill him, Arianna. It'll be the only way to stop him."

Arianna shook her head. Was it possible that she could even do such a thing? Even if her and Ethan's lives depended on it?

"You don't know this for certain," she said at last. "He has control of the money and Ethan's holdings. There would be no point . . ."

Will laughed out loud. It was a dry, brittle sound. "You are naive to believe that. Barrons wants more than control. He wants total power and he doesn't give a damn whom he destroys to get it."

Ethan lay in the darkness. Awash in nausea and dizziness, he fought against the ever increasing nightmare his life had become. It had been hours since they'd arrived. Arianna had seen to washing him and spooning broth into him. The pain in his head ebbed and flowed through his consciousness like a river, at times filling up his thoughts so completely that he could hardly think of anything else. Only when they'd given him the laudanum had it abated somewhat, but the drug left his thinking muddied and thick. Now was one of those times.

In spite of his condition, Ethan had made small improvements. He could nearly make a fist with his hands and could manage the slightest movement of his toes. Still, he knew he was as weak as a kitten.

At least his condition didn't keep him from hearing his sister's voice. Like music, it drifted in and out of his hearing, ever sweet sounds echoing around him and leaving him all the more distressed at its absence. At times, he thought he'd dreamed it and others he was sure. Just now she'd been speaking with someone below his window. He decided there must be a garden there, perhaps a small orchard beyond. Arianna spoke in low, serious tones but he couldn't discern who it was she was talking to.

The deepening shadows of the evening covered Ethan's room. Within its walls he saw the etchings of the leaves from the trees outside, gently moving to and fro with the breeze.

Closing his eyes, Ethan thought he might sleep but with his injuries preventing his movement, he often drifted in and out of a dream state. There were times when he didn't know if he'd been sleeping or truly awake.

Time had passed, though he'd no way of knowing how much, when movement in the room pulled him out of his slumber. A silent shadow stood over him. Dark and foreboding, it had the shape of a man. The moonlight streamed from the window beside his bed and when the figure stepped forward, it looked as though the luminescence covered him.

It could have been real, Ethan thought. Or not. Most likely it was just another demon summoned up by his poor, drugged brain to taunt him and force the rise of panic that had assailed him in the days since his attack. Even more frightening than that was the possibility that this seeming apparition might be real, and pose an even bigger threat to him and Arianna.

"I see you're awake," the stranger said. "I wonder if you can see me?"

Ethan could not speak and wished that he could at least ask the man's identity. And yet, he wasn't quite sure it was a man at all, since the apparition seemed to blink in and out, its form nearly invisible when a cloud wandered across the moonlight.

"No, of course, you can't." The large man sighed. "It certainly makes what I have to say no less important. Still, here it is."

He moved forward and Ethan got a good glimpse of him then. Tall, with broad shoulders and a wide chest. A man who'd surely made the ladies swoon, he thought. A lady like his sister, perhaps?

"I have every intention of taking care of her," the man said. "Your sister, that is. I don't know if you are aware of it or not, but your intention of putting down Barrons backfired. Now he's used his threats against you to force her into marriage. That's why the two of you were sent here. Put away until he decides he wants you both dealt with."

Ethan blinked twice. The other man seemed to understand that he meant yes. He knew well what they were up against and it burned in his heart that he was powerless to do anything about it. Likely they would both perish beneath the vile cruelty of Richard Barrons.

The man looked at him a moment. "Perhaps you do see me after all?"

Ethan blinked two more times impatiently. He wanted more information.

"That makes two of you. Is it possible that you share your sister's gift?"

Ethan only blinked once. He'd never even attempted to understand just what it was that his sister did with that amulet of hers. It was enough that it had kept her up late at night and, in some way, feeling that her life was useful.

"Then perhaps it is the power of the stone, after all."

The man pulled out his sister's gem. "You know what this is?"

Ethan blinked twice. Of course he did. It had once belonged to his mother.

"This is what keeps me here, that and my desire to exact my revenge on Richard Barrons. I mean to see him dead."

Ethan blinked twice, again.

"I just want you to know that I will see your sister safely out of this. I don't yet know how, but I shall do all that I can."

Ethan let out a deep breath. He wanted more than anything to rise from his sickbed and face Richard Barrons one more time with pistols drawn. He would make no mistake this time.

For a moment Ethan watched the specter and then blinked twice more. They were in agreement and that was good enough. It had to be.

It wasn't until nightfall of the following day that Arianna met with the only other inhabitant of her husband's island. She'd finished cleaning up Ethan's room and was now working diligently on her own.

"Hie, who's there?" an old woman screeched from the bottom of the stairs.

Arianna put down her dust cloth and went to her bedroom door. "Hello? My name is Arianna Halv—" she paused for a moment, "Arianna Barrons. I am the new lady of the household."

At the foot of the stairs the woman stood, a ragged cloak covering her soiled dress. Her hair was white and twisted into a tight bun. A wide, wrinkled brow gave her a pensive expression.

"Mr. Barrons has married, has he?"

"Yes." Arianna descended the stairs slowly, careful not to tread on the broken planks that lay along her path.

"I see. Then you'll be expecting me to clean and cook for you, eh?"

"Not just I, my brother is an invalid. We both require your service, though I don't expect you to work as a full staff. I'll help wherever I can."

"Kind of you." The woman's tone was laced with sarcasm. Before Arianna could comment on her attitude, she crossed her arms. "And what of the girl? Who'll care for her if I'm to be tied to your muckety-muck?"

"I beg your pardon?"

"The girl? Mr. Barron's charge, or did ye not know he'd had a child?"

Arianna had made the final stair and now stood face to face with the woman.

"My husband didn't have much time to discuss the particulars of his responsibilities. You are Mrs. Stanhope?"

"Aye, that's me, yer ladyship." She gave a gross imitation of acquiescence.

"Well then, where is the child?"

"Runnin' about, I reckon. As wild as a cat, that one is. Comes and goes as she pleases. I don't do much but set out cold tea and cakes for her. Rarely ever see her."

The woman turned and began limping toward the kitchen. Arianna watched after her, curious about her new charge. At least that was how she saw it. A child amongst the wilderness of this exotic place. Clearly Mrs. Stanhope gave little care to the upbringing of this young girl. That responsibility, along with her brother and the spirit of Captain Markham, now fell to her. Suddenly exhausted beyond words, she turned to make her way back up the stairs. She'd get her cloak and begin her search for the waif.

Will watched Arianna as she wrapped her cloak around her shoulders. A thick, brown wool, it would do against the night chill. Not that he'd have any say in it. He didn't think it a good idea for her to go out this late.

"There might be wild animals out there. Did you think to guard yourself with harsh words?"

Glancing up at him, Arianna scowled. "There is only one wild animal I'm concerned with. I cannot leave her out at night in this chill. If she's not dead already, then this weather may very well do the trick."

"She? Are you referring to the housekeeper? I've gotten a good look at her and with her ill temper I doubt any sickness would dare to venture close to her."

"I'm not referring to Mrs. Stanhope, though I believe you may well be correct in your assertion. No, it seems my husband had a child somewhere along the way and neglected to mention it."

"A child?" Will felt the breath go out of him. "How is that possible?"

"My guess would be with a housemaid or some such. The usual way a beast like him acquires one." She walked past him to the hallway and then started down the rickety stairs once more.

"That's not possible."

"You of all people should know otherwise, Captain. Mrs. Stanhope told me that her charge has free run of the island. I didn't see her in the house so she must be holed up somewhere outside. I mean to find her and bring her in."

"A girl child? How old?"

"I'm not sure. Mrs. Stanhope was not very forth-coming with information. After we talked, she went to the kitchen and helped herself to a week's worth of food and then quit the house. I'm thinking she must have her own cottage somewhere on the property."

"Indeed. This changes things quite a bit, you know," Will said as they entered the front foyer.

"Really? How?"

"If Barrons has a child, then all of his holdings will go to her after his death. Unless he doesn't claim her as his own, that is."

Arianna whirled on him. "Is that all you men think about? Money and property? We are talking about a child. The girl probably hasn't ever known her father or any loving parent. She's been abandoned here to live or die. Obviously my husband has no intention of passing along any sort of inheritance to her. It's miraculous that she has survived this long."

Will stepped back a pace. "I suppose you're right. She should count herself fortunate he didn't hoist her over the bow of his ship."

He saw the immediate effect of his words on Arianna when a pained look crossed her face.

"I'm sorry. I didn't mean to be so cruel. I just cannot abide by someone suffering so. Especially a child."

"Neither can I." He motioned to the door with his hand. "Shall we get this done?"

The two of them walked the length and breadth of the island. It was near daylight when they returned to the manse.

"I don't understand it," she said as she began ascending to her room. "Where in blazes do you think she is?"

Will only shook his head. Not being alive, he was not fatigued by such activity. For the breath of a moment he wished he could gather Arianna in his arms and carry her upstairs. Unfortunately his better judgment intervened. To touch her again would invite disaster. He'd made his decision to keep his distance from her lest he become lost once again in her sweet reality.

"Did the housekeeper say how old she is? Perhaps the brat's playing some infernal game with us. I detest games."

Arianna laughed. "It's not as if we have anything better to do." She ran her hand along the length of the banister. "Other than make this terrible place livable again."

"It is a wreck, isn't it? I wish there was something I could do." He glanced around the foyer. "The roof needs repairing or you might drown in the next rain. I daresay, your brother's room is the only one that likely won't leak." A rat skittered across the floor next to the opposite wall and ducked into a small hole in the corner. "And then there is the problem of the vermin. The house is riddled with them."

"I believe I heard some mewling about half a mile from here. You know, where the path divides. There must be wild cats somewhere on this island—we might tame the kittens, if we can find them. Tomorrow when we search for Barron's child, perhaps we can coax a few out. I have plenty of cheese in the pantry."

"You won't for long if the rats get their way."

Arianna flopped down on the bottom stair, her dress billowing around her. "Is it really that hopeless, Captain? Is there nothing we can do?"

Will watched her for a moment. Even with bare feet and dirt smudged on her chin, she was truly a picture of beauty. At this hour, the growing sunlight gave her hair a fiery tint. She looked like a fairy tale princess.

No, Will decided. She was not born of a childish story. She was brave and strong and beautiful. She was every man's dream and every woman's ideal. Damn his eternal soul to hell, but he loved her in spite of it.

"Hopeless, madam? You're not going to turn into a watering pot, are you?"

"I beg your pardon?"

There it was, he thought. That unexpected streak of piss and vinegar, instant anger and puzzlement. She could take the hide off of him, were there any hide left to remove.

"No need to beg. This place just needs attention, is all. She's a ship set adrift, a barn that needs tending. Are you saying you're not up to the job?"

"In case you haven't noticed, Captain," her voice wavered, just teetering on the edge of anger, "I am a lady. Ladies do not set ships on course, nor do they clean barns."

"Of course they don't. But neither do they wallow in self-pity. There's much to do here and yours is the only body able to do it. I shall help you, of course. I shall direct and you shall perform. Simple as that."

Arianna crossed her arms. "I have never set about repairing a mansion. I wouldn't even know where to start."

"Of course not. We shall begin at the beginning."

"Where exactly is that?" A single eyebrow lifted and a sharp intake of breath hitched her bodice.

Indeed, she was every man's dream. Will smiled.

"One thing I have learned about your husband, milady, is that he is a bastard."

She blew out a puff of air. "We already knew that."

"And as such, he is also somewhat of a pirate, is he not?" Will leaned closer, his nose nearly touching hers.

"Yes, I suppose some would say so."

"So, having this island is as good a place as any to hide things. Wouldn't you agree?"

"Yes," she said slowly. "Captain Markham, what are you getting at?"

"I'm saying that Richard Barrons, scoundrel that he is, didn't get so wealthy or powerful by keeping all of his cards on the table."

Arianna gave him a questioning glance. "I never thought about it."

Motioning for her to follow him outside, Will pointed to the west. "What do you see out there?"

Crossing her arms once again, Arianna looked where he pointed. "Trees."

"Yes. And what are those trees sitting on?"

"Hills."

"Lots of hills. Where there are hills, my dear lady, there are likely to be caves. When you have distant islands, caves, and blackhearted bastards, you are likely to have something else."

Arianna licked her lips. "Hidden treasures."

"Exactly," he growled. "Arms, most likely. The very ones I was accused of stealing. Not only that, but whatever trade goods he's been hoarding. Foodstuffs, supplies, perhaps a few wanted men as well."

Will saw the streak of fear shoot through her.

"Men? You mean criminals?"

"A man such as Barrons doesn't work alone. He has

a network of thieves. Perhaps beholden to him for gambling debts, or dodging death threats, arrest warrants, and such. It would be my guess there are a few still wandering about."

Arianna shivered beside him. The urge to reach out to her was so strong that he could barely contain it. Even now the sweet temptation of reality beckoned to him. *Become a man once again*, it whispered. *Take her*.

Will's body hummed as he stood so close to her. His shaft twitched hungrily and his groin ached for the feel of her once more. Like most other men, sex had always been important to him as much as eating and breathing had been important. But this was different. This was more than a man fulfilling his needs. It was passion, white hot and wonderful.

The truth was, Will Markham wanted only to keep her to him as fast as a man would hold on to his every earthly treasure—nay, his eternal soul. Only one other thing warred for his being in that way. A black, consuming emotion battled on the grounds of his psyche and it was a formidable foe.

Revenge.

Arianna watched the horizon the following night. "There!" She pointed to a small copse of trees just beyond the trail.

Although it was completely dark, the two souls had crept along the path to the overgrown valley below the shambles of the Barrons estate.

After seeing to Ethan's care and making him as comfortable as possible, they had again spent the rest of the day searching every corner of the island for the mysterious child. Carefully following the footpaths, they'd done their best not to be seen, to cover every track, and keep a watchful eye for potential enemies. At this late hour, it was all Arianna could do to remain standing. Still, her stubborn soul would not relent. Will watched over her, amazed by her resilience. Many men would have fallen behind hours earlier.

"Do you smell it?"

Will hesitated to answer. He was supposed to be a ghost. He was supposed to be dead. He wasn't supposed to be enjoying the same sensations as the living. Yet, as before, the longer he stayed in Arianna's presence, the more human he became. It was building in him again. The need. The more he thought about her, the more his body returned to its living state. The proof of it was the scent of wood smoke that drifted lazily towards them. It meant two things, Will thought. One, that he would likely go mad, and two, that his suspicions were correct. They were not alone on the island.

Chapter Twelve

It was well past midnight when Ethan awoke the next time. He knew this because the shadows on the wall opposite his bed had climbed up the far wall, making the silhouette of the trees appear ten times larger than when he'd fallen asleep. Truth be known, Ethan was growing quite good at divining the passage of time by the movement of the sun.

In fact, as he lay there, hour after hour, he learned far more about his surroundings than he'd ever taken the time to consider. The sound of the wind moving through the trees, the incessant drip of water from the rooftop long after the rain had ceased. The hollow sound of footsteps from the men who had brought him to this strange new place. He had always been a man rushing through life and now he found himself to be still. Very still.

It wasn't the enveloping darkness that woke him this time, however. It was a sound. Small and slight, like a breath, only quiet. A sigh, perhaps.

It was no more evident than the whisper of a breeze, he thought.

Glancing to his left, he caught the barest glimpse of something. Feather light, moving like quicksilver. Frustration grew in him. First the damned ghost and now this. He didn't know what frightened him more, the thought that he'd seen Arianna's apparitions for himself or that he never had before. Did it mean that he was so close to death that the dead now came to visit him?

Sighing deeply, because it was the only action he could take, Ethan closed his eyes. Of course, he'd never really taken the time to see the spirits. He'd never stopped his business, never waited up late at night the way his sister did. He'd never summoned them and certainly never held the amulet.

For most of his life, truth be told, Ethan feared the stone. He'd seen firsthand what its power had done to his mother, her frail form diminishing day after day. He feared that most for his sister, watching her constantly for any change, any sign that the stone was bleeding life from her as it had from Lady Emma Halverson.

Only Arianna was different. She did not diminish like Emma but seemed to thrive.

That was part of the reason he'd kept Arianna so carefully ensconced at his mansion. He knew well that if good spirits could come to visit, so could the others. He knew they existed because as a small boy, he'd seen the demons himself.

Was that what this was, he asked the darkness? Or had the devil himself finally come to claim him?

That was when he felt it. Eyes. Close to him. Then, tiny breaths against his cheek. Ethan didn't blink. He didn't breathe. Seconds stretched out as the strange being leaned closer.

Ethan quickly opened his eyes and was nose to nose with what he first thought to be an angel—a smallish one. Except that she was not quite an angel. She had dirt smudged on her cheeks and thick, dirty blond curls in a riot around her cherubic face.

"Are you dead?" she asked in a small, demanding, child's tone.

Ethan blinked only once, hoping she would understand that it meant *no*. If she thought he was, she might set off in a shrieking tumult. He'd never had much to do with children in his life and clearly had no idea what the proper address was, even if he were able to talk to her. Which he wasn't.

Equally fascinated by him, the child stared back. After a few seconds she pulled away and slid her gaze down his chest to his legs and feet and then back up.

"I suppose you're still alive. You smell like medicine. Are you sick?"

Ethan blinked twice. The child tipped her head sideways.

"Does that mean yes?"

Ethan blinked twice more. It was beyond belief that this small person could possibly communicate with him when no adult had. At least no living adult.

"Did you fall down? I had a kitten once that fell from a tall tree. She didn't move either. Then she died. My da had to give her a burial at sea. That means he wrapped her in her favorite blanket and threw her off the ship. Of course he had to put her in a sack first so the sharks won't eat her. I ate a shark once . . ."

Ethan listened as the child continued to chatter. Somehow he liked the light, lyrical sound. Closing his eyes for a brief moment he wondered what it might have been like if he or Arianna had ever decided to settle and have families. They'd be enjoying spring concerts in the park and large gatherings at Christmas. Instead he was always bent on dodging the marriage mart while Ari spent all of her time with the dead. They both had missed out on life's best, it seemed.

"Maybe you're shy. Can you tell me your name?" the child asked.

Ethan blinked only once. No. He couldn't speak, couldn't move, couldn't rail against the fates that had brought him here.

"My name's Katherine. Katy Blue is what my da always called me, cause of my blue eyes. He said I look just like my mother. I don't know, because I've never seen her. He said her eyes were as blue as the sky in summer."

Ethan watched as the child looked wistfully in the distance. "I don't know what happened to my da. Those bad men came and took him away. Then they brought me here and left me with the old witch woman. I don't think she's a real witch, 'cause she doesn't have any warts or potions. But she's just awful and smells terrible. Like fish brine, you know."

Ethan blinked twice. He'd had the occasion to be visited by the wretched creature upon his arrival. When they'd unloaded him from the boat that had pulled up on shore, she'd been there. She'd looked in his eyes and with thick, dirty fingers had pinched his face painfully. Ethan hadn't been able to cry out, even when she pronounced him "as good as dead, and twice as much bother."

"You do know her? Well, I've been hiding from her for a long time now. I sneak into the pantry when she's not looking and steal biscuits and tea cakes. Sometimes, I even get butter out of the larder. That was until she found out I was taking food and locked it up. Since then I've found some really good berries not too far from here. I'm quite the smart little girl, as my da used to say. He knows such things. He's a ship captain. He should be here to get me any day, I just know it."

Ethan blinked twice for her, a new sadness creeping into his heart. He suspected who her father might be, in fact, believed he had seen his ghost just the other night. He knew also what it was like to be so young and without parents. At least he'd had Arianna to share his miseries with. What would this child do when she learned the truth?

A noise sounded in the hall, light footsteps that Ethan knew well. Arianna had returned. As she approached, he could hear the rising ire in her voice. She was yet again arguing with her spirits.

"Oh, my! The pretty lady's back. I need to go. Don't worry, though, I'll be back."

Ethan blinked at her furiously. He wanted her to know that Ari would take care of her, would love her as surely as she'd loved him. But the child took no notice of his distress and hopped off the bed and slipped down to the floor. He saw the glorious riot of curls bounce by as she scampered across the room and climbed through the window.

Ethan held his breath until he heard the old tree groan under her weight. In an instant she was gone and he'd been left alone. Tears formed in his eyes, his upset at losing his young visitor, at his sister's plight, and his own pitiful circumstances.

"It's not possible, so stop badgering me about it!" Arianna huffed as she made her way up the rickety stairs.

"You cannot survive without help. Those are two able-bodied men who can do the repairs to the manor, help you in the gardens, and protect you from any incidental marauders."

"They're cutthroats and thieves. If they learn that we're here, they'll likely come in the night and steal our food and cut our throats. I am a lady and helpless, relatively speaking, and they are not gentlemen."

"Nonsense. You are not without protection."

She rounded on him. "You're not serious? I have one pistol which is so antiquated I doubt it even shoots straight, and a sword that's so heavy that I can barely lift it. What am I supposed to do, hurl insults at them?"

The stubborn spirit crossed his arms and gave her a single-eyed glare. "You are not without protection," he stated again. "You have me."

Arianna paused. They were now standing outside of Ethan's bedroom, her hand on the knob.

"Just what do you have in mind? You're barely more than a vapor unless you and I . . ." She stopped. Well, she thought, it was embarrassing, but she'd promised herself that while having relations with a ghost might not be proper for a lady, it certainly was nothing to be ashamed of. Though technically, she wondered if it really counted. "I mean, you said it yourself, you could only raise the wind and disturb the draperies. Even your time of solidity was very limited."

He nodded. "If you're worried about your virtue, Lady Halverson, you needn't be. I shall not touch you in that way again. I agree it was a mistake. I've said it before and I'll say it again. You have something far better than those louts in the cave. You have me."

It was Arianna's turn to cross her arms. "What exactly do you propose?"

"You're Barrons's wife, are you not? You can't convince me that a man of his reputation alone wouldn't command respect. In fact, I think these men are employed by him, or were at some time, and are likely indebted to him. You could work that to your advantage."

"Very well. You think that'll be enough to convince them to work for me?"

"Not entirely. I remember a tale once about a woman who'd been a sort of witch. She'd been the wife of a pirate about ten years ago. They said that she died defending her husband against pirates. Her spirit is said to latch onto genteel ladies who travel these waters and turn them crazy. One woman, Emily Smart—Lady Drexeledge, I believe her title was—was reported to have gone mad, stabbing her husband and four of his crew members before she jumped from the yardarm of his ship. Though Emma hadn't just killed her victims. She'd cut out their tongues and hearts and then proceeded to unman them."

Arianna held her head high. "Really? That's nonsense. No woman alive would ever get away with such a thing. Besides, Ethan and I met Lady Drexeledge when we were young children. She was a bit eccentric, but her death was ruled an accident."

"I've no doubt. You and I may know the true story, but chances are these toadstools don't. A little howling from me and the proper performance from you and we could have two lackeys digging your garden before sunset tomorrow."

She chewed her lip, considering his plan. It certainly was better than living in this deteriorating estate and scavenging for food for heaven only knew how long.

"Very well. What do you propose?"

It was then that a wide grin crossed his face. His left

eyebrow raised high and Arianna felt a thrill begin to bubble within her. It reminded her of their night together on board the *Persuasion*, of the momentary promise made and a promise kept.

Barrons paced the long room for the twenty-fifth time. It wasn't fair, he thought, the duke keeping him waiting like this. He'd reached the end of the Aubusson carpet and scuffed his shoe against the marble floor when finally the long doors at the opposite end of the room opened. A tall, gangly servant stepped through.

"His grace will see you now," the man said, in a high-pitched, nasal voice.

"Indeed," Barrons huffed as he began his long trek to his appointment. "I hope Lord Melbourne isn't discomposed. Surely nothing untoward has happened to him. I know he rarely keeps his guests waiting longer than ten minutes past what is customary."

The footman only sniffed, staring down his narrow nose at Barrons as though he were the gentry and Richard was no more than riffraff.

"You will have to make your own inquiries, Mr. Barrons. However I will warn you, his lordship doesn't take well to having his behavior scrutinized. You would do well to remember that."

Barrons spun around to give the cut to the offending footman, but was met with another figure instead. Much shorter than the servant and barely within a foot of Barrons's height, the stout form of the Duke of Melbourne stood behind him.

Instantly Barrons made a low bow. "I beg your pardon, your grace. I meant no disrespect."

"For heaven's sake, Richard, get up. I know exactly

what you meant. You are as impertinent now as you were on your fifth birthday, spewing cake and watered wine like you were the King of England himself."

"Surely you cannot hold the foolish actions of a child against the stature of the man he grew into?"

"Surely not. I can, however, ask exactly why it is that you are here? You've made no move to attempt a claim on your inheritance before, why do so now?"

"There is much that has changed in my circumstances, Uncle. I wanted to sit down and discuss the situation of my mother's folly. You are without heirs and I am without family. I had hoped that the two of us could arrive at a mutual understanding."

The short, squat man looked him over carefully. The Duke of Melbourne did not give the first impression of an overly smart man. His rounded face, nearly bald head, and thick, nose made him look like one of the drawings of a court jester that Barrons had seen as a small boy. But not for one minute would he underestimate his uncle.

"Come into my parlor for a bit and we'll see what it is you think has changed and gives you the right to interfere with my day."

The older man waved him forward and then turned into the ornate room. The floor glowed with the deep, rich tone of fine, polished wood, like the tables. The furniture included a sofa and three chairs, all covered with expensive material. Along each wall hung vast, golden silk tapestries, embroidered with flower patterns along each hem. The atmosphere of the room evoked the expensive gardens of the south of France.

Richard Barrons had been a small boy when he'd last visited Melbourne, but the memory of fine silks and polished wood had never left him. Even now, if he closed his eyes, he could envision a time in the distant past before his father had died and his mother had wasted their lives on a simple merchant with dark hair and even darker eyes. To this day, Richard Barrons still cursed his stepfather.

Motioning him to a chair, the duke took his time and spread his rotund form across the chaise. At the snapping of his fingers, two finely dressed butlers entered from the side door of the parlor, carrying trays laden with a tea service and plates of sweet cakes and fruit. Without inviting his guest, the duke motioned them to the table beside his lounge and began his repast.

"Now, what has happened that has brought you yet again to my door, Richard? Be quick about it, I have an appointment to have my pedicure in fifteen minutes."

Barrons held back the rush of anger that threatened to spew forth. The last thing he needed on his campaign was to have himself thrown from the kitchen doors as though he were nothing more than the trash. No, he would keep his temper in check. He would not let the old man goad him into a fit that would yet again prove him far beneath the old duke's class.

"We've not talked in awhile. I thought perhaps we should sit down for a bit and ruminate about our lives. That's what families do, isn't it, Uncle?"

"In the first place, Richard, since your mother—my niece—behaved so badly twenty-five years ago, I've made my position on 'family' extremely clear. The papers were drawn up and have been on file for over two decades. Your mother's disregard for our good name was deplorable. Her choice was to cuckold her husband in front of all society, thus disgracing our entire family. Therefore, her bastard—you—and any other spawn from her womb have been legally separated from the Melbourne titles. You've been told this often enough, yet you persist in coming in here as if you were the heir apparent and I nothing but a doddering old fool."

"I see. It's to be like that then. Uncle, you never cease to amaze me." Barrons gave a small smile, knowing that like the great Indian tigers, he would soon be feasting on his great-uncle's life blood. "The short of it is, Melbourne, that I have become exactly what you have labored so many years to keep from me. My wealth alone places me in the upper echelon. My merchant business is among the top five in all of Europe. Not only that, but I've managed to acquire a lucrative shipping business that once belonged to you."

"Wait—are you the scoundrel that ran our company into the ground? How dare you?"

"Oh, I dare you doddering old fool. As of last Thursday, the Melbourne estates are half a million pounds in arrears. It turns out, that for once in your self-indulgent, pitiful life, you owe me. More than that, I've married a titled lady and the Prince Regent thinks highly of me. I single-handedly put down a traitorous pirate and returned an entire shipload of arms to the royal navy. You see, I really don't need you at all."

"You wretched little bastard!"

"Indeed. Despite all of your years of base treatment, I have come to do you a favor, Uncle. I will reinstate one fourth of the Melbourne shipping interests to you, in exchange for a return of my full privileges and claim to the title. It's that simple."

"Do you think there is no other who might challenge your claim?" The Duke asked, bits of berry dripping from his chin to stain his white stock.

"There was only one other and he is now dead."

"As I recall, your mother's infidelity prohibited you

from ever inheriting. All of the *ton* knew she was having an affair. It wasn't until my brother threw her down in disgrace that your true parentage was revealed. As I recall, the livery master made off not only with a fine pair of Hessians, but also your mother's virtue. Of course, she tried to please my brother by producing another child, this one from his own line. Too bad that Franklin didn't live to see his true son born."

"Lies! I am Franklin's son. As soon as I've finished with my plans, it will be you who will be living in shame."

With that, he stood, straightened his waistcoat and quit the room.

"Kennedy," the duke called after his visitor has left. The tall footman was instantly at his side.

"Yes, your grace?"

"Find a runner to keep up with Barrons. I need to know of his whereabouts at all times. There's something devious afoot and I don't plan to let a bastard great nephew get the better of me."

Arianna followed the path as it dwindled to nothing but a faint track through a narrow line of grass. The farther she went, the more the sharp branches and brambles caught her clothing, stabbing her arms and legs and snagging her clothing. By the time her husband's ship did return, she feared she'd truly look the part of the pauper he intended her to become.

"That must be it," the captain said behind her.

Arianna paused at the opening between two short hedges. Peering through the branches she could make out a small encampment. Two small lean-to's comprised the only visible shelter, and a campfire, whose flame had long since died, sat between them.

"We do have company," she whispered.

"Indeed. Then they surely have information. By the looks of it, they're guarding something."

Just beyond the trees was a large trunk. Motioning for her to stay behind him, Arianna watched as the captain sidled around the camp. At first, she was certain he would get caught. However, to her own chagrin, she remembered that it didn't really matter because he was a ghost. Besides herself, no one knew of his existence. She tried to take comfort in that.

Straining against the bushes, trying to see and at the same time not be seen, Arianna was concentrating so hard on watching her ghost, she didn't hear the soft tread of the attacker behind her until it was too late.

"Hold still, lassie," a gruff, guttural voice rumbled behind her.

Arianna didn't dare to move; she didn't dare to breathe. Only one thought scoured her mind as cold metal rested upon her neck. A man's hand placed the barrel of a pistol to catch under her chin.

Chapter Thirteen

Will had nearly finished his inspection of the campsite when he heard the shaking of the bushes. Turning, he saw the men approach Arianna long before she was aware of them. His first thought was to call out to her, to warn her of the approaching danger. His second, however, was the direct opposite.

He knew instinctively that they were capable of taking a life. That was evident by the amount of weapons he'd seen hidden among the supplies. Men didn't carry long rifles and such, and an assortment of knives and pistols unless they meant to use them. Judging by the old blood he'd seen among the weapons, used them they had.

The second reason for his not calling out to her was that he knew their "ghost" story would be more effective if there were no time for thought. Crossing his arms, he made himself go as still as stone, not wanting to draw any attention. Her worried expression deepened and puzzlement slipped across her face.

"That's a luv. Now, Herbert, check her carefully for weapons, eh?"

The man standing to Arianna's side was tall and thin, his bones barely filling out the torn and dirty uniform he sported. A French foot soldier, if Will wasn't mistaken.

The second man was somewhat larger, his frame barely fitting into the sailor's frock and paints. As tall as he was, he was also wide, though more from fat than muscle. Will knew his kind all too well, he thought, grimacing. The fellow had made his way by his mere size, likely not having the intelligence to scrape barnacles off a barge.

When he smiled, Will also noted that he'd but a single tooth sticking out at an odd angle. His large, thick fingers were filthy and the instant vision of him touching Arianna twisted Will's stomach. All too quickly, he'd measured up the two of them and he didn't like what he saw. Not at all.

"I'm not armed," Arianna said in a low voice, hands dropping to her sides, her fingers gathering in the fabric of her skirt and clenching it as though it were a lifeline in a dangerous sea and she was about to be eaten by sharks.

Will heard her trying desperately to control the tremor that was building inside her.

"O' course yer not, miss. Why would I ever think that?"

"She's right there, Gus. No gun, no blade, not even a stone."

"Indeed? Then I suppose it's up to me to ask what such a comely woman is doing on this godforsaken pile of dirt?"

Arianna chewed her lip nervously, her eyes searching the campsite, looking for Will.

"Looks to me like she might have a partner out there. Eh, miss? You have any friends that might be visiting us?"

Pausing a moment more, she widened her eyes, finally settling on his form. Will smiled, nodded to her.

"Indeed I do, sir. You will kindly direct that pistol away from my person at once."

"Will I now? What say you, Herbert? Do we dispense with pleasantries and gut her now?"

"Not wi'out any sport, Gus? Do you think it wise?"

"Ordinarily, I'd say no, but if she has an accomplice out among yonder trees, I don't think it wise to tarry."

"An excellent plan of action," Arianna said, her voice gaining strength as her eyes focused on Will, "as far as it goes."

"Eh? What have yer got boiling in that pretty head of yours?" Gus poked her cheek with the pistol none too gently. Arianna didn't blink.

"That my associate will take immediate offense if you should injure me in any way. As a matter of record, he will strip the skin from your flesh and use it to draw the wild animals of the island to feast on what's left of you. I'm afraid the captain is most determined."

The two men exchanged a quick glance of nervousness between them, obviously trying to decide whether or not she was telling the truth.

Will could have cheered. Arianna then crossed her arms and relaxed back on her heel.

"Aye, are ye not afraid of me pistols, miss?" Gus asked, brandishing said guns about her face.

"Not particularly, no. Nor am I the least bit threatened by your decision to kill me. I know there is an afterlife and I know on which side of the eternal veil my soul will fall. Tell me, gentlemen, can you say the same?"

With that she turned her lovely head and gave a look to Gus and Herbert that would have shredded them had it been a knife. Will couldn't hold back his laughter.

"I say we kill her now," Herbert said. Though scratching his head, it was clear that he had lost some of his criminal demeanor.

"Go ahead," Arianna yawned. "If you dare."

Herbert went to move forward, but Gus held up his other hand and stopped him.

"Excuse our poor manners, Miss. It appears we haven't been properly introduced. What did you say your name was again?"

Arianna gave him her brightest smile. "I dare say I can forgive your transgressions, sir. It isn't at all as my late friend Lady Drexeledge explained to me when last we met. Have you heard of her? I believe her given name was Emily Smart."

At the mention of the name, both criminals paled and quickly crossed themselves.

"You've spoken with Emily Smart? The scourge of the sailor's manhood?"

"Yes, some time ago, in fact. It's all right, though. I'm sure her ghost won't be stopping by for a visit. I do have my own spiritual companion, however. Perhaps you've heard of him? Captain William Markham? I believe he engaged in the pirate trade not too long ago."

The two men stared at her a moment, their weapons dropping low.

"Captain Markham? Will Markham who once owned the *Persuasion*?"

"That's the one. His poor soul is searching the seas for the dastardly men who caused his death." She paused. "You wouldn't know any of them, would you?"

The warm afternoon breeze had changed suddenly. Ethan sat propped against a pile of grain sacks and two of the pillows Arianna had brought from the ship that had brought them to the island. It was as close to a return to normalcy as he supposed he would ever get.

Facing the gardens, his world now consisted of four things, really. Arianna's visits were at the top of the list, although he'd felt her growing anxiety over something she'd yet to share with him. The second thing, of course, being the mysterious ghost who'd chanced to visit him only one other time since their first meeting.

The captain, as he'd heard Arianna call him in a low tone when she thought Ethan had been asleep, seemed to be his sister's constant companion now. It was a curious thing to Ethan and yet he was glad she could find solace wherever she could.

The third thing that occupied his time had been that wretch of a housekeeper, who regularly inspected his room to see if Arianna might have hidden anything of importance here. Ethan knew she was stealing from the stores left with him and Arianna, though he was unable to inform anyone. So, he continued to watch her, continued to make note of whatever she filled her pockets with. Should the day come that he could demand a return of the items, a stray comb here or there, or perhaps some bit of clothing or other, Ethan would rise to the occasion.

The fourth person that filled his daily vigil was the

small sprite who danced in and out of his presence with total abandon. She came at odd hours, chatting away and sometimes even singing to him. The last days, however, his little "Kitty," as he thought of her due to her numerous references to her shipboard pet, had begun a new mission. In short, the brazen child intended to heal him.

"Don't worry, good sir," she'd exclaimed the previous morning when she arrived in his room along with the morning sunlight. "We'll have you up and out of that hammock afore the winds kiss the sails."

Ethan knew she'd had some experience on board a ship and delighted in the way she often spoke like a seasoned sailor.

"Here, we have yer mainsail, Lieutenant Stay-in-the-bed. We'll be setting sail at day, mind you. Be ready to hoist the canvas."

Ethan blinked twice. He was anxious to see where their destination would be today. The previous afternoon they had set sail to the traitorous coast of Barbary. It had been an eventful adventure in which Kitty had sat next to him with a periscope of rolled parchment in hand and watched the horizon for any signs of pirate activity. Together they'd blown three of the "ruddy blighters" right out of the water.

Of course, their main mission was always the same. The two of them set sail on every adventure to locate Kitty's missing father. As she navigated them through the straits of her imagination, she would often regale Ethan with her father's seafaring exploits. He would listen with rapt attention and had come to enjoy her childish stories with more relish than he had any stage play or musicale he'd ever attended.

That afternoon, however, Kitty had a different objective. She meant to make him walk again. Though he knew the chance was slim that his new companion would wield some sort of otherworldly magic and return his health, in a small part of his heart Ethan began to believe that if anyone could, it would be his Kitty.

"There now, mate. First we'll start with the littlest part of you." With that she climbed up to sit in his lap, lifting up his large hand in her own small one. One at a time she wriggled his fingers. Bending them to and fro, pulling and prodding them as if he were indeed making them perform such miracles.

"We must keep them moving, you see. Ben Hardin, the oldest sailor on my da's ship, said as how you must keep the joints moving, you see. If not, they freeze up and you'll never get any use out of 'em."

Ethan blinked twice to signal his approval and Kitty proceeded. She turned and twisted, and once lifted his right arm so high that when she had held it above her head, gravity swiftly took over. His arm fell back into place beside him, completely knocking her from his lap and onto the floor.

Instant fear filled Ethan and he made a rough gurgling sound.

"Enghth?" He tried again. For a single sickening moment, no answer came from the floor. Just as he was about to think that his dastardly limb had completely killed off his new friend, her curly blond head popped up, smiling and giggling with abandon.

Ethan sighed.

"You were afraid, weren't you? I know you were, silly goose. It's okay. My da always said, 'What good is a head as what can't take a thumpin'?'" Again her laughter filled the room.

To his surprise, Ethan's eyes brimmed with tears and another, softer gurgle came from his throat.

"Did you speak to me, Lieutenant? Have you tried to talk?"

A new sadness came over Ethan as quickly as the previous moment's glee had arrived moments before. Ethan only blinked once. No, he no longer had a voice.

"Ah, I think you'll talk again one day. You just have to be patient. The same way I'm waiting for my da. You just have to wait for the words to come back."

Ethan closed his eyes, wishing with all his heart that the child was right. The dignity of his existence was gone, his connection to his life before the shooting had been severed almost completely, and now his very sanity depended on the comforting words of a child. Could his circumstances veer any farther out of control?

The evening chill of London affected him more than usual. Barrons sat in his parlor, gazing thoughtfully at the hearth. Removing his gloved hands from his pockets, he pulled them from his fingers and dropped them carelessly to the floor. He leaned forward, his frame nearing the fireplace and thrust his hands outward. Fingers barely inches from touching the flames, he grew enraged.

"What the devil?" He moved closer still, the tips of the blaze kissing his fingertips. "I can't feel the heat! Why can't I feel the heat?"

"I beg your pardon, sir." Miles Tandy edged closer to him. The newly hired valet, crisp in his fifty-pound uniform gazed down at his master as though he'd grown a second nose.

"Of course I'm fine, you idiot. But I cannot feel the blasted heat."

"Here, sir, your jacket has caught fire."

Barrons glanced down at his suit coat and realized that what his hired man said was true. He was indeed on fire. A sputtering flame had caught on his pocket and now was smoking on the damp wool. As though he were slapping at a flea, Barrons patted the fabric.

"There, it's out. What am I to do?"

"You have been a bit out of sorts, Mr. Barrons—um, Lord Barrons, that is—so I've called a physician, sir. Mr. Blevins. He comes highly recommended."

Barrons scrutinized the valet, who nearly went apoplectic at his gaze.

"A physician, you say? Really. I've not heard of him. Is he a specialist in afflictions of the circulation? That's what it must be, a problem of the fluids of the body and the nervous system, surely."

Barrons didn't wait for the man's reply, but thrust his hands once again into the hearth, this time, daring to dip his fingers into the hot coals. Unfortunately, Tandy was quicker and grasped his wrists tightly.

"Excuse me, my lord, it's just that you're about to catch your cuffs. We want to look presentable when Mr. Blevins arrives, now don't we?"

Barrons had had enough. "Let go of me, you fool. I'll tear the hide right from you, you abominable dolt."

Raising his hand to strike the valet, Barrons's arm was caught by another, stronger, gnarled fist.

"There, there, sir." Digby was now standing beside him, smiling slightly, a shimmer of mysterious intent behind his composed expression.

"Yes? Yes, what is it?" Barrons asked. "You've brought news?"

"Indeed I have, sir. Why don't we forget the fire for the moment? Please take a seat, sir. I can have this ninny bring you an extra wrap if you desire."

Barrons eyed him carefully. Of course, he knew the man was plotting against him. They all were, his uncle, his wife and her invalid brother, even the Prince himself, if Barrons knew anything. It didn't matter, he thought. He was not mad and he knew better than them all.

"Very well. Bring me a quilt, Tandy. Then ring the maid for tea. Extra hot, mind you, not that pitiful swill that she served us earlier."

As Barrons took his seat, the cushioned chair closest to the fireplace, he overheard the whispers of Digby and the servant.

"I don't know, Mr. Digby, sir. It seems he's getting worse. More distracted, you know . . . I called the doctor, as you requested. I hear he has a good reputation with the ladies of the *ton*. Especially those with *disorders of the nerves*, you know."

"Very good, Tandy. Any word from the duke's man yet?"

"Nary a word, sir."

"Thank you. Go on and fetch the maid. Here's a special note for you to dispatch. The address is on the envelope. Take it yourself and see that it makes it into this man's hands."

Digby whispered something unintelligible into the man's ear, but Barrons was no longer interested in what the men had to say. Another voice was speaking to him now. It came from the hearth. It was a word, really, only two syllables and one now that Barrons seemed to hear at every turn.

Vengeance.

* * *

"The garden is coming along nicely, don't you agree?"

Arianna was perched on the windowsill in her brother's bedroom. Ethan was dozing in his favorite chair, and though she wasn't sure just why, somehow the room seemed cozier in the last few days.

"You shouldn't be so arrogant," Will mumbled. He was leaning against the window frame, gazing down at the two men laboring over a growing pile of brush and branches.

Barebacked and sweating despite the dropping temperature, the two former pirates were debating the use of a short blade versus a pistol at being better suited to putting down a "faithless lout." Though Arianna wasn't of one mind or another on the matter, there was one thing she did know for certain. She was, for the first time since landing on this godforsaken rock, enjoying herself.

Pulling her wrap tighter about her shoulders, she breathed in the chilly afternoon air.

"For the south of France, it is a bracing climate, is it not?"

"Hrmph," Will muttered beside her. He preferred warmer places.

"Are you sorry you stayed behind with me?"

His sharp glance nearly unseated Arianna. With one eyebrow raised and the hint of a scowl at the corner of his lips, she thought he did look very much like the dreaded pirates she'd read about.

Privately, she had already imagined what his fine form might have looked like, shirtless and sweating under a warm, summer sun. How she would very much have liked to watch the muscles work beneath his golden skin, powerful muscle and perfect form combined.

Arianna's mouth went dry just thinking about it.

In truth, her heart thrummed excitedly every time he neared her. It was a constant vibration that heightened her senses and thrilled her through and through. Never in all her life had anyone ever affected her that way.

Arianna knew this condition was unacceptable. She knew that becoming enamored of a ghost was completely irrational and unacceptable. So why did she so often ache for him to come closer, for him to touch her with his broad, capable hands and bring back those few wonderful moments of bliss? Was it because for the first time in her life, she'd felt totally and completely loved? For all her high thinking and calm demeanor, he unsettled her all the more every passing minute.

Even watching him now, his brow knotted in concentration, she wondered if he had any feeling for her at all. At times she was sure of it. Especially when she'd glance up to find him watching her, a dark-eyed, hungry gaze which nearly set her off her heels. Though when she faced him, the captain's expression waned and he became as distant as the setting sun.

The real question, Arianna decided, was whether he cared for her as just a lustful distraction, or was he just more adept at fighting his true desire? If so, he was a champion at it, she thought. Especially times like now, when he daren't even look in her direction, she thought. Was it anger, lust, or something else that bothered him? Arianna wished she knew.

"I'm thinking that you shouldn't have told them your true identity."

Surprised at his statement, her mind momentarily flashed back on the conversation between herself and the two rogues who now labored in what was to be their spring garden. . . .

* * *

"Eh, miss? How are we to believe what you're spreading? Could be you're just makin' the story up, you see."

"Aye, everyone knows about Markham. He was a pirate, you see." Gus said, crossing his arms.

"Not according to him. Tell me, were you among the gents who took his ship and killed his crew?"

Both men stepped back. But Gus waved his pistol. "Nay, we was here, an' that's the truth. But we knew what our Mr. Spikes was about, you see. Wanted no part of it. That's what brought us here."

The second pirate scratched his chin. "Did you really know the pirates' scourge, that Smart woman?"

Arianna smiled. "I met Lady Smart when I was very young. Do you want me to tell you just how she killed her husband? All the details? I dare say it's not polite conversation, but if you must know . . ."

"Now, wait right there, Lady Muckety-muck." The pirate Herbert shuddered. "There's no need to be specific, you know. Besides, every sailor worth his salt knows what happened to that poor bloke."

Arianna shrugged. It was true enough. Emma Smart's legend had been much discussed, even in elite circles.

"I can prove what I say is true then, though my word alone should be enough."

"And who might you be that you are so trustworthy, aye?"

Arianna smiled. She leaned slightly inward, as if sharing a well-kept confidence.

"I am the wife of your benefactor, Richard Barrons. You do know him, do you not?"

She might have pulled pistols and shot them both, for the surprised expressions on their faces. Instantly the two glanced at each other and then back at her.

When Gus spoke, his voice filled with bravado, but his pallor betrayed his real fears.

"Just why would we believe such a claim?"

Arianna's smile widened. "Because your employer—my husband that is—had a midnight duel with my brother, shooting him and causing devastating injury. He then used my brother's presence at said illegal activity to force me to agree to marry him. After the vows, my brother and I were quickly transported here. I'm sure it was Mr. Barrons's intent to abandon us both so that we could never reveal his underhanded machinations."

"You know, it does sound a bit like our ol' Spikes, doesn't it?"

Gus only chewed his bottom lip for a moment, the implications of Arianna's admission clearly warring in his overstimulated brain.

"Aye, be dammed to a watery grave if 'tis not the truth."

"Now that we've established my identity, I think we now have to discuss the terms of your continued employment."

If her earlier statements had shocked them, this latter admission left the two scalawags completely undone.

"I beg your pardon, missus?" Gus was the first to recover from his apoplexy.

"You've no need to beg anything. Since you are in my husband's employ and we are stranded here without proper staff to care for myself, my brother, and the"—she paused, attempting to think of the best word to describe the strange old woman from the manse—"the housekeeper, it should logically fall to the two of you." Arianna paused for a beat. "Unless, of course, you wish to face my husband's anger when he finds out his wife and brother-in-law suffered from lack of proper attendance."

Gus stepped forward, his pallor now replaced by a red flush. "Now, wait just a minute! If Spikes sailed to this island, why did he not come and give us instructions himself?"

The other pirate nodded resolutely. Arianna supposed he'd completely lost his voice.

"He didn't. He was injured slightly at the inn where we'd stopped along the way. His stallions escaped and caused no end of trouble besides his injury. It's my understanding that he will come here again when his duties are discharged."

Arianna yawned demurely. The two men before her began to shuffle anxiously.

"Well then," Gus managed, his teeth and fists clenched, "what do you want of us?"

"I'm so glad you asked." Arianna stepped forward, taking the gruff man by the arm. When she allowed her attention to momentarily drift toward the captain, she saw that his demeanor had changed. She'd thought him proud of her in the first few moments she'd faced off the two blackguards. Now, however, he narrowed his eye and kept a tight-lipped expression. Clearly, he wasn't pleased.

Why? Hadn't she done exactly as he'd insisted? Captain William Markham was indeed a puzzle.

As Arianna escorted the newest members of her household staff to the manse, she could have sworn she heard the captain rumble behind her. . . .

"Why shouldn't I have been honest with them? I see no reason for lying," she said once her thoughts had returned to the present.

"You should have been more discreet, madame. It was too risky to reveal so much. Had you considered what might happen once your husband does arrive on the island?"

Arianna chewed her bottom lip. "What indeed?"

Will scowled again, turning his gaze out towards the willow tree just beyond the window. "In case you hadn't noticed, Barrons is not very fond of you. Your last encounter left him quite unsatisfied, if you'll remember. I don't believe he'll be too happy that you have usurped his authority, especially in front of his men."

Crossing her arms and kicking absently at the dust on the floor, she considered his words.

"I see your point." Sighing, she lifted her gaze. "Well, there's no point in belaboring the issue now. What's done is done. We'll just have to have another plan."

"Another plan. As I recall, the last one didn't work out too well. Never mind. It's too late for recriminations right now."

Arianna smiled, cautioning her gaze upwards. For a brief second, their eyes met.

"Something still troubles you?" she asked.

"It's nothing. I was thinking that when Barrons is dead and all is set to rights again, I shall miss this life."

"Oh." Arianna glanced out the window once again. "I shall miss you very much, Captain."

For a moment the silence stretched out between them.

"It's odd," he said after a moment, "that you and I might never have met. Do you think that stone truly does work to pull people together?"

"I know my mother believed it to be so."

"Then why didn't it do so sooner, when I was alive and there was a chance . . ."

Arianna could barely contain her smile. It meant that he was fond of her. Although their relationship was doomed from the start, the knowledge of what they might have been was a small measure of comfort.

For the moment, the two of them stood gazing into the waning afternoon. Arianna wanted to tell the captain just how she felt, but something in her breast held back the words. Perhaps they didn't need to speak of it. It was enough that they had been together, enough that they had the present. No, she told her traitorous body, she'd been fulfilled once in her life and it was enough. It had to be.

At that moment something outside the window caught her attention. It was barely a rustling of one of the bushes that lined the overgrown garden.

"What is that?"

The captain leaned out the window, his eyes sweeping the landscape. "I'm not sure. An animal, perhaps?"

"An animal, to be sure," Arianna said, grasping her skirts. "A small, clever one, who steals from our pantry and manages to keep her identity well hidden."

"The child." Will nodded. "She is a fox, isn't she?"

"We've scoped this island twice over and still not found the little scamp."

"Indeed. It would seem that she has outmaneuvered our attempts at rescue. There is only one thing left to do."

"And that is?"

"We set a trap."

Chapter Fourteen

"I really don't understand, Mr. Barrons, what you are inquiring about." Lenora Hastings stirred her afternoon tea. As Lady Houghton, the wife of Lord Marcus Houghton III, it was said among the *ton* that she was an expert on all things. Especially those facts that simmered beneath the polite conversation, such as one's sexual tastes or family inadequacies. She delighted in gossip and, as an older woman of regal bearing, was one of the most respected figures of society. Barrons, even at his level of separation from the aristocracy, knew that the main reason for such high regard was born out of a single emotion.

Fear. If you didn't conduct yourself appropriately, Lady Houghton would discover your deepest, darkest secret and expose you to public ridicule. A powerful ally and a dangerous enemy, to be sure.

Barrons gave her his best smile and tipped his teacup at her. She nodded accordingly and sipped her own.

"You see, Lady Houghton, I am newly married into society, and I have recently come across some information about my bride that I find somewhat, shall we say, disturbing."

"I see."

Barrons was more than a little afraid that she actually did see that he was not a member of her class and not permitted the privilege of hearing their secrets. He'd hoped to circumvent her dismissal in the only fashion he knew how. The only thing the titled truly respected, in his opinion, was wealth.

"Ordinarily, Mr. Barrons, I could not sit with you so openly and speak of such things. It is simply not done."

"I understand. As a common man myself, I would never dare to step across the threshold of our class separation. However, I find myself most desperate to discover the truth about my wife. I love her dearly, and though I would never break our marriage contract, I feel like I must be fully aware of any, um, irregularities of her character. It is my intention to keep her safe and away from those that would dare to trouble her fragile, emotional state."

Lady Houghton nodded. "I am prepared to believe that your intentions are honorable, sir. Indeed, the fact that you donated such a handsome sum of money to the War Casualties Fund makes it clear that, while you are not a titled gentleman, you certainly love our dear country and those who would die to defend it."

"It is my deepest hope that my small contribution might somehow ease the pain of the war effort."

Barrons sighed deeply, watching his mark out of the corner of his eye. Her hand went to her bosom and she patted her chest demurely.

"You are a fine man, Mr. Barrons. Perhaps it is a shame that you were denied your rightful place in society."

"I have been blessed in many other ways, your ladyship. For instance, the fact that Arianna accepted my proposal. Unfortunately, business keeps us apart at the moment, but she and her brother have gone to my estate for an extended stay. I simply cannot wait to return to her. She is an amazing woman."

With this, Lady Houghton nodded. "It is clear to me, sir, that you have a great affection for Arianna. This is most important since I feel you must be understanding of her peculiar condition."

"Do tell, Madame."

"She and her brother were such dear children. Their bizarre upbringing was not their fault. I personally hold their mother responsible. Filling their heads with fairy stories and such. Fortunately Ethan came to his senses and wanted nothing to do with his sister's fanciful ideas."

"Fanciful ideas, Madam?"

"Exactly. Your dear wife believes she can commune with the dead."

The trap was set. Will watched the sunset against the distant hills. He waited patiently beside the rain barrel, sitting cross-legged on the ground. Although he was a sailor at heart, he could well appreciate the sounds of nature even when on land. The sea was a mighty beast and the greatest exhilaration he had ever known came from riding her waves, and yet there was also peace to be found on land. Cricket song and the rustle of wind-blown trees made a gentle melody all by themselves, though they did not compare to the roar of the ocean.

Will thought it odd that he could feel so restful stranded on the soil and not eagerly awaiting the next ocean voyage. But perhaps it was not odd, considering the beautiful Arianna. She did more than just warm his senses, she comforted his soul. For all his life, Will had never known another who'd affected him so.

Just then a slender figure emerged from the house. Even now the gentle sway of Arianna's form was as inviting to him as the siren who calls to all sailors upon the sea. Yes, he almost believed that if he'd been alive still, she was the one woman who might be able to anchor him to the land.

"Have you seen anything yet?" Arianna asked, sitting down beside him.

"No. It's been quiet. What about you?"

She rubbed her eyes, a sigh of exhaustion escaping her. "Nothing yet. Our young friend certainly knows how to lead a merry chase."

"Don't worry. I'm sure she'll come to you eventually. That is, if she has any sense about her."

Arianna nodded. "I suppose so. Something must have frightened her very badly to cause her to stay away so. I couldn't get any more information from the housekeeper. She drained the sherry bottle while cooking dinner. I'm afraid much more of her cooking will make me dyspeptic."

"She's not much help, is she?"

Arianna gave him a dry laugh. "No. And I find that I can manage quite well on my own. For all its strangeness, this island isn't without its charms, you know."

"I was just thinking the same thing. There is a quietness here that would be difficult to find anywhere else."

"Yes. I was never much for the public life, you know. Very lucky that Ethan always looked after me. I abhor balls and society functions. I detest Almack's, long, boring entertainments, and such. Too much interesting reading to do, too much to learn about the world around me."

"Is that why you've never married?"

"Perhaps. I suppose if the right gentleman ever came along, I'd have considered it. Or, if Ethan had insisted that I wed—I'd do anything for him."

"I'm sure he's fond of you as well. It's just that it doesn't seem right for you not to have a husband."

"Now you sound like my brother. No, I'm afraid despite his good name and the substantial inheritance my spouse would control, it's the allegations of the *ton* that have kept me out of the marriage mart. Half of them believe I'm crazy."

"And the other half?"

"They believe I commune with the dead."

Will watched the playful expression cross her face. It was the dancing light that shone in her eyes, the way her dainty, slightly upturned nose twitched just a little. The laugh was not but a purr in her throat and Will found he couldn't quite resist it. He leaned forward and placed a gentle kiss on her lips.

"I have to admit," he said in a husky voice, "that if I were in other circumstances, I too might think you insane or possessed. As it is, I am most grateful for your unmarried status. That is, not counting your current husband, of course."

A giggle escaped her. Will reached out for her then,

gently taking her in his arms, he pulled her forward. Before he knew what was happening, Will kissed her long and deep. It wasn't until a shadow passed over them, that he realized what just happened.

"Papa! Is it you? Is it really you?"

The shock of the child's cry pierced Arianna to the heart! She knew that voice! She'd heard it in her vision, weeks ago. Quickly pulling away from Will, she sat back on her heels. From across the yard a small form raced toward her. Turning back to him, she saw that a cloud had passed over the moonlight and all but the faintest outline of him remained.

The child stopped ten feet from Arianna. "I thought I saw him! Where did he go? Where is he? Papa? Papa!"

Arianna jumped to her feet. "Wait! Let me help you."

The child, her blond curls shining despite her dirty, ragged clothes, backed away.

"My papa was here just a moment ago and you made him go away! Bring him back now, I say. Right now!"

Arianna shook her head. "I cannot."

"Yes, you can. You were kissing him. I want my papa! I want him now!"

Furiously, Arianna whirled around, but there was no sign of the captain. He'd completely vanished.

"Please, Captain. You cannot do this to her. At least let her know you're all right."

When Arianna turned around the child stepped back two more paces. "You don't understand. Your father is . . . well, he cannot . . ." She stopped, the words she so badly needed to say caught in her throat.

"You bring him back," the girl cried. "You bring back my papa right now."

Arianna shook her head. "I'm sorry, but I can't. Your father is dead. Only his spirit appears at times. I'm afraid that after awhile, even that will fade as well." Though she didn't know just when the captain would disappear forever, she was sure that the child must know the truth at all costs.

"That bad man killed him, didn't he? The one that threw me off the ship and left me dangling in a sack until nightfall. He threatened to feed me to the sharks but I wasn't afraid. I wasn't afraid, Papa. Do you hear me?"

With that she turned to run, heading once again for the copse of trees beyond the garden. Arianna was quicker. In seconds she reached the child and though the two struggled barely a moment, Will's daughter finally gave into the rush of tears and buried her face in Arianna's embrace.

Hidden in the shadows, Will watched them. So Katherine was alive. A moment's rush of joy swept through him, knowing that she hadn't met a horrible death at the hand of his enemy.

That thought was barely put to rights when another occurred. "Damn his black soul," Will growled. Barrons hadn't saved her life for mercy's sake. It had been but another ruse to terrify him, perhaps to threaten him with when he was in prison. Or, worse yet, he meant to use the little girl for his own purpose later on. A new anger boiled in Will's chest.

Though his hatred for Barrons didn't wane, another, older pain arose in Will. For as he stood there, hidden in darkness, he realized that the man who'd set him dangling on the end of a rope wasn't the only one guilty of horrible crimes. No, that particular bastard would spend eternity paying for his part in the tragedy of his daughter's life. Being condemned to death wasn't enough, Will thought, and then turned away.

Arianna had washed the child and put her to bed. She now lay sleeping beside her brother, the two of them side by side on the ragged bedding of the four-poster.

She thought it odd that the child had insisted upon resting with Ethan. He only gave her a blank stare, blinking several times. In the end, the little girl had taken the blanket that Arianna had offered her and climbed up beside Ethan.

Arianna now sat on the sofa beside the bed, herself wrapped in a tattered quilt. A true chill had settled on the room, and she had asked the two pirates to bring up fresh firewood. That had been hours ago. Now, she sat up, stirring the flames from time to time, trying to keep the room warm.

With all the events of the day, she knew she should have been exhausted, but a new anxiety settled in her gut. Would the captain ever return?

As if he'd been summoned from her thoughts, Will Markham emerged from the shadows.

"Thank heavens you've come back. I was beginning to worry."

The captain only shrugged. "I needed some time to think."

"Yes, I suppose you did. It's all right. I've fed and bathed her. She was completely done in, poor thing."

Will said nothing more, but instead walked to the bed and knelt beside it. Reaching out his hand, he tentatively touched her head. His caress was slow and reverent, as though his daughter might disappear at any second.

Arianna held her breath. Even without her amulet, she could feel the magic in the air. It was a warm summer breeze that dissipated the winter chill. It was the beginning of daylight after the darkest of nights. It was a father's love for his only child.

After a time, Will turned back to her and Arianna could see tiny sparkles of tears in his eyes. Until that moment, she hadn't known a ghost could cry.

"I can't believe she's really here," he said with a thick voice.

"No, it's unimaginable. Whatever was Barrons thinking, I wonder?"

Will shook his head. "A man as evil as that likely meant to keep her here until he could use her for some vile purpose. Perhaps in the future he would trade her off to a decadent aristocrat. I wonder, what does a child bride fetch for those who would exploit her?"

Arianna swallowed. Such a thing was not possible, was it? "It is a good thing then that we have found her. I will do everything to take care of Katherine. You do realize that, don't you?"

"Katherine is a very independent sort," he said with a sad smile. "Are you sure you are up to the challenge?"

It was Arianna's turn to grin. "You forget, sir, I was once a small girl myself. My parents both believed in allowing a child the freedom to grow. I was incorrigible myself, or so my tutors always thought."

Will's quiet laugh sounded like a trumpet to her ears. No matter that she'd let go of some of her own secrets. If it made his heart lighter, then any small embarrassment on her part was well worth the effort.

"Somehow, I don't find it so hard to believe. You must have given your parents apoplexy."

"Nearly. In fact the only one who could ever reason with me was Ethan. He was my hero, you know. I thought he could do no wrong. I suppose I still do believe that."

"I think your brother is a good man, Arianna. In fact, it was likely his inherent goodness that put him off his guard. Such men most often never see evil. They can't conceive of it."

Arianna watched as Will sank back on his heels. "And what of you? Did you see the face of evil when it arose before you?"

Will paused. "No. No, I didn't. I should have. I'd been on the seas for the better part of a decade. More fool I."

"You're not a fool, Will. You were a good man, I think. An honest and straightforward thinker."

"Say such things and you'll swell my head. I have my faults, you know." This he said in barely above a whisper. "I am stubborn and selfish. I have a tendency to insist on having my way most of the time. Not at all companionable."

Arianna walked to stand next to him. Placing her hand on his shoulder, she gently patted him. "I will agree that you are a most determined man. Stubborn—well, yes, beyond thinking. But selfish? Hardly that. You deserved a good life, Will. Really, you did. It's not fair that you were cheated so."

He looked up at her then, and Arianna was lost in the depths of his gaze.

"Life isn't fair, is it?" He sighed, his glance going back to the child nestled in Ethan's arms. "But then, neither is death, I think."

*   *   *

When Ethan awoke again, he could see the beginnings of daylight struggling through the cover of darkness. He didn't know when he had fallen asleep, only that it had been sometime earlier and when his room had been completely empty. Now, however, it was quite the opposite.

Curled in the crook of his left arm, Kitty, his elfin child visitor, had made her bed. Like her namesake, she was soft and warm and making the most pleasant little noises while she slept. A quiet whistling through her half-parted lips.

It was the picture beyond his bed that made Ethan take notice. Arianna lay huddled in the sofa, her knees drawn up, sleeping and finally content. Ethan had seen the pirate ghost once before. Kitty's father, he'd thought.

If he looked hard enough, Ethan imagined that he could see the ghost now. He was sprawled upon the tiny sofa, his legs spread out before him and his head thrown back in a sleep so deep that even his dreams were beyond his reach.

Ethan sighed. Did the specter keep Arianna company as he'd thought? How awful that his sister could not find comfort among the living. Would that he could somehow turn back the days and find the soul of her companion when he'd been alive. That way the two of them might have followed different paths and he could now go on to his own eternal rest.

Weeks before, such a thought would have been completely out of the question, Ethan thought. But now, when he was no more than a useless shell, the child had become a lifeline for him. A flesh and blood tether to a world that was denied to him, and wretched soul that he was, he held to it with all of his might.

At that moment the child beside him stirred. She

must have sensed his unease. Rubbing her eyes and stretching, she looked up at him. It was after a wide-mouthed yawn that she reached out her small hand and caressed his cheek.

"You must promise me something, Lieutenant-stay-in-the-bed. You must never leave me. My papa left me, but it was because that other awful man took him, I think." Her eyes grew moist and she sniffled. "I don't want to lose you as well."

Ethan blinked several times but he felt the warm track of a single tear glide down his cheek.

"It's all right," she told him, settling further into the crook of his arm. "I know you wouldn't leave me on purpose."

Suddenly Ethan felt a heavy veil lift from his life. For all that he wanted to speak and walk again, an incredible gift had been given to him and he was not fool enough to regret it.

The heavy pounding on the front door split through Digby's gin-soaked brain. Of course he'd drank too much the night before. It had been the only way to fight off the paralyzing cold of a winter's evening. He'd been chilled to the bone because Barrons had made him wait outside the Houghton estate for hours the night before, and then, after a sparse few hours of sleep, had dragged him out into the early morning to travel to his wife's home. As the sun was rising above the London tree-tops, the two of them shivered awaiting the ancient butler to open the door.

"Hurry up, you dolt! I've no time to waste!" Barrons yelled for the fifth time.

"Perhaps we should just shoot the door handle, sir."

Digby yawned, wrapping his arms around his chest and hoping the fool would give up this particular scheme.

"Nonsense. These are my servants now; they'd best learn how to snap to, or I will dispense with the lot of them."

After another barrage of banging, the door finally creaked open. Henderson, tall, spindly man that he was, bent his white head forward.

"Yes?"

"I am the master here! What took you so damn long to answer my call?"

"I beg your pardon, Mr. Barrons. I was otherwise engaged."

"Sleeping, you mean. I'll have you sacked for laziness, see if I don't."

Without waiting for further comment, Barrons pushed himself past the ancient servant.

"As you wish, sir." His expression hadn't changed one bit, Digby thought. If it had been him, he'd have given Barrons a piece of his mind, to be sure. But then, Digby had been biting his own tongue often enough of late, so perhaps not. Nodding to Henderson, he walked past. If the old fellow found himself unemployed, Digby decided that he'd write the man a reference himself. Better yet, if things went according to plan, perhaps Henderson would be in his employ one day.

Barrons wasted no time getting down the hall and to the main parlor.

"Where the devil is it?" he demanded as he went through the room and into the library.

"Please forgive me, Mr. Barrons. Where is what?" Henderson stood stiffly in attendance. Was that a bit of distaste that had crept into his voice?

"My wife's private rooms! I need her journal, if you please. Don't all the titled women keep journals? Anything . . ." Barrons continued to mutter to himself, berating the aristocracy, his wife, and women in general. His usually impeccable attire sagged, his shirt coming out in disarray from his trousers, his jacket, too hurriedly adjusted and twisted at one side. His dark hair sprouted about in a most undignified manner.

It was clear to Digby that his employer was beginning to fray at the edges. He didn't know for sure what was bothering the aggressive, ruthless man who'd single-handedly procured enough wealth to rival the richest peers of the realm.

"Here," he said at last. "This is it."

From the books strewn about the table in the library he picked up a plain, black book, its pages covered in a neat, tilted, script.

"Is that the lady's journal?"

"No. It's even better. The scribe is none other than the first Lady Halverson, Arianna's mother."

With that, Barrons settled himself at the table, his shoulders hunched over the tome, his nose inches from the yellowed text.

Digby looked about and found the most inviting spot in the room, the velvet covered chaise longue. Smiling and humming a lively tune to himself, he reverently lowered himself on the soft cushions, thinking it was far, far better than shivering in the cold drizzle that soaked the countryside.

"I'll be damned to the eternal fires of hell!"

Digby looked up from his slumber to see his employer sitting rod straight in his chair, his eyes staring off into a darkened corner of the room.

The sun had risen outside, though with the overcast sky and the continuous rain, one might not have noticed.

"What is it, sir?" Digby asked, rubbing the sleep from his eyes. The hint of a headache still plagued him, and surely he could have used a few more hours of sleep, but he fared much better now than the night before.

"It's here, my man! It's all here. I've learned the chit's every secret now. I know what must be done."

"What is that?"

Digby held his breath, wondering what in blazes the old buzzard was prattling on about.

"My wife taunts me, Digby, far away though she may be. She's summoned from the grave and sent it hence. Somehow she knows of our actions against Markham and she wishes to destroy me."

"Ah, sir, you've been hours without food or drink. What say we go back to your house and tip up a few? Mr. Beckons has acquired a few new lassies to his trade. I've heard they're ripe for the picking."

Barrons slammed the cover of the book shut, making a noise that cut through the room like a knife through cloth.

"I've no time for such idiocy! I must make arrangements. It's time to visit my lady wife."

Digby was certain that it would be no pleasant visit, and were he a man who felt pity for others, this would certainly be the time to feel it. Unfortunately, he had other concerns.

"But, sir, what about the duke? He expects you to close on his properties within the week."

"I've no time for such trivial things."

"If you abandon your plans now, then you'll lose the footing that you've worked so hard to gain."

For a moment, indecision warred on Barrons's face. It was true. Only when he had completely ruined his uncle would he have the chance to plead his case against the crown. It was all set. And yet, if he didn't, Digby knew Barrons thought his wife might yet be able to thwart him.

Inwardly, Digby smiled. He knew Richard Barrons would never allow himself to be put down by a woman. His thoughts were proved correct a moment later when Barrons turned to him.

"Here's what must be done. I shall write a letter. You will deliver it to the duke. I will give him one month to come around to my thinking or I will ruin him."

"But he's not budged in the last two weeks. What makes you think he will do so now?" Digby pressed.

"Because you are going to go to the docks and gain entry into his warehouse. When you are there, you will set fire to it and send his business straight to hell."

Digby nodded. "As you wish, Mr. Barrons."

Chapter Fifteen

Arianna stretched luxuriously. It had been two weeks since Katherine had been found and brought into the house. The child, though truly heartbroken at the news of her father's death, had Arianna and now seemed somewhat happy. She chatted on and on about their days at sea and frequently asked if her father was in the room.

As much as Arianna would have liked to tell the child that the captain did indeed stay close, he had strictly forbidden it.

"No good will come of her thinking that I'll stay in this world indefinitely," he'd said the morning after her reappearance. "No, let her believe that I am dead and gone. When the time comes and I accomplish Barrons's destruction, there will be no time for farewells. It is best this way."

It was all he'd had to say about the matter, though he watched her constantly, and only after she'd fallen asleep at night, did he dare to come out of the shadows. Although she knew he'd been devastated at the thought of his little daughter's death, a new sadness had taken hold when he'd discovered her alive. It was a heavier yoke he now bore, Arianna thought.

She'd also found that it was no use talking about it. More than once he'd used his ghostly powers to disappear when a subject came up between them that he didn't want to discuss, making Arianna near to bursting with frustration. How was one to argue with a stubborn ghost?

But this morning in particular, Arianna put away thoughts of her spectral companion, of her continued worry for Ethan, and even the constant reminder of the uncertain future before them. No, today was Christmas Eve, and she was determined to celebrate the holiday to the fullest.

The island didn't know the season, the temperature had fallen, but only to a brisk chill. There was none of the gentle snow she'd known during her childhood in the country. No, the sky was a near perfect blue and though no flowers bloomed, there was still a fragrance in the air.

Rising before everyone else, Arianna set about to finish the fanciful tea cakes she'd iced with sugar snowflakes. She had spent the last few days gathering small items to give as gifts, and asked Gus and Herbert to procure two wild ducks from the other side of the island. The two were roasting nicely and the wild strawberries had now been made into a nice sauce, meant to be spooned liberally over a plain cake, made especially for her by Mrs. Stanhope, who, bribed with of a bottle of sherry, had been more than willing to comply.

She'd prepared gifts for each as well. To Mrs. Stanhope, she would give a fine handkerchief and a pair of her silk stockings, a royal purple color. What the strangely dressed housekeeper would make of such a present, Arianna could not say. For Herbert and Gus, she'd managed to produce two pair of riding gloves that had belonged to Ethan. Thinking that it would be a while before her brother would be riding again she'd thought it wise to ensure what goodwill she could from the two pirates.

A gift for Katherine had posed a problem. As she worked in the garden, she come upon quite a few weatherbeaten stones. They were rough but nicely colored and in her spare moments Arianna worked hard polishing them to a shining finish. This was not the most important gift she could produce for the child. She also decided to pass along a cloth doll that had been hers as a child. Despite the worn, frayed seams and tattered lace, she had cherished the doll well into her teen years. It was her hope that the comfort she'd received from her mother's gift would be sufficient for Katherine as well. At least until they returned to civilization once again.

Even with those gifts, Arianna felt compelled to add one more. In her mind, nothing was more painful than a child robbed of her childhood. That's why the final gift she'd chosen for Katherine she thought the most important of all.

"Does Katherine favor her mother all that much?" Arianna asked one afternoon as she'd sat sipping her tea and watching the child play with a wild kitten she'd found wandering amongst the wildflowers.

"No artist could have drawn her closer. Why?" The captain had decided to come out of hiding on that particular morning. He often did when Katherine was about her business of being a child. Playing in the marigolds, or sketching her own version of Ethan's portrait, Arianna would often see the child's father hovering just at the edge of the glade. It heartened her to see him, still so obviously full of love for the girl, yet not able to bring himself to come close enough for his presence to be known.

Not that anyone but her could sense him, she thought. Only one other time had another come close, or at least she had thought so at the time. Ethan was sitting in his chair on the balcony outside his room and his eyes had been gazing at the very spot where the captain had hovered.

A shiver passed over Arianna. Sometimes she did wonder if Ethan were entirely among the living. Could he be teetering on the very same threshold as the captain?

She dismissed the thought and returned her attention to the captain.

"I was just wondering. She is such a pretty child. I should like to do her portrait one day."

Will looked at her sharply. "Can you do such a thing?"

"Oh, yes. I'm a dab hand with the charcoals. It was part of my training as a young girl. My mother insisted on it. Like her, I was always the odd one out. I didn't have any playmates other than Ethan and she thought such a talent might bring me closer to other children." Arianna sighed. "She put a stop to it, though, when she realized that the faces I was drawing were those of some of our deceased relatives."

Glancing up, she saw the hint of a smile playing at his lips.

"Do you find that amusing, Captain?"

He chuckled. "No. Not particularly."

"Then what?"

"I find it all the more charming. More human of you, really."

"How is that?"

"You have an artist's eye. You can only create what is in your heart. I'll wager those faces you'd fashioned were spirits that were dear to you."

Arianna looked away a moment, her discomfort growing with his consternation. "One drawing was of a favorite aunt and her second husband. When I was a child Dorothea and Edgar would visit me frequently. They were my playmates whenever Ethan was otherwise occupied with his scholarly duties."

"I see. When did they stop visiting?"

"When I was thirteen. I knew I had outgrown them, you see. I was supposed to be a young lady and they . . ." She paused. How could she make him understand? "They were not serious enough."

"I see. So you sent them away." His voice had grown quiet, distant.

"Yes. There's been plenty of times I've regretted it, though. Until recently, I could have used the company."

His smile grew wider at that. "You mean since a bastard pirate came to occupy all your time?"

"Yes, as a matter of fact. He and his unruly daughter, that is."

The captain's smile faded. For a moment quiet stretched between them like a fine lace cloth.

"You will take care of her, won't you?" Will's voice was strained, barely cracking, but with enough conviction to convince her that the child was indeed his true heart's desire.

"As if she were my own," Arianna said. "I can never be her father or mother, but I can be her friend and protector."

He nodded, crossing his arms and settling back into his chair.

In those moments Arianna felt as if something had been settled between them. That was when she began to see him dull just around the edges, as though he were a painting left out too long in the sunlight. She could sense their time together was indeed growing shorter.

The very next morning, Arianna rose to find him keeping vigil over Katherine and Ethan, since the child had insisted on making her bed beside Arianna's brother.

Not wanting to disturb the quiet of their slumber or Will, she'd excused herself quietly and gone into the spare room where her yet unpacked luggage remained. After locating her pad and charcoal, she'd begun to fashion what she hoped would be the best gift of all.

Now, it was Christmas morning and she'd put on her finest dress, a green silk gown. It had always been her favorite. Though most women of her station busied themselves with acquiring every new and costly garment, Arianna was happy with her few favored items.

"I swear to heaven above, Ari, you should have been born a pauper." Ethan had joked one early morning as she was setting out for yet another boring round of visits with her few acquaintances among the *ton*.

"It would be much simpler, I assure you. No, I prefer to leave all the finery and pomp to you, dear brother. I am a simple woman at heart."

Arianna chuckled at the memory. She practically

lived on those catches of her past. In truth, if it hadn't been for her brother, the captain and Katherine, she knew she would have drifted into melancholia long ago. As it was, the trio of her "family" gave her sense and purpose every day, and she thanked God for it.

As she filled her arms with the assorted gifts, Arianna took one last look in the mirror. The sadness of the last few weeks had faded from her cheeks and she was glad of it.

Of course, she had no real gift for Ethan, save that she'd ordered Gus and Herbert to bring him below stairs in his chair. She thought it might be good for his spirits to have him at the head of the table, cracked and warped though the seat was. She'd planned to also serve up a bottle of wine she'd found buried in the dust in the mansion's cellar. It wasn't a particularly fine wine, as she recalled, but after cleaning the bottle and finding two unchipped glasses, she thought it might add a refined touch to the evening.

Last but not least came the captain. What could one give a ghost? She'd no idea. But since he couldn't participate in the celebration in any real sense, she thought instead to give him something better. A reading.

In one of her chests she'd tucked away a book of poems, "The Sailor's Life," an obscure collection that had been given to her by one of her more awkward beaus. It was all she had for Will and she hoped that he would like it. Arianna turned to speak to him.

"You will come to dine with us tonight, won't you, Captain?"

Will watched the dawn of hope in her eyes. How could he deny this woman anything?

"Yes, because you wish it, but you must know that a

ghost has no place at such a gathering. Such a celebration is for the living."

"It is a time for family and friends to band together. Do you mean to tell me that you don't believe in the season? A time of hope, faith, and love?"

Will sighed even as he tried desperately not to show the chasm that separated him from such notions. "As a matter of fact, I do," he told her, unable to keep the exhaustion from his voice. "Those may be the only things holding me here. Any hope I had of punishing Barrons seems to have drifted out to sea along with the tides."

She looked away a moment, her eyes blinking furiously. "I am sorry that you cannot find peace, Captain."

"Nonsense. I've come to think that I've no need of it anyway. Perhaps time and fate will catch up with the scoundrel."

"You are giving up your quest, then?"

Will couldn't miss the mixed tone of her question. Would she be happy if he did? Or would she be saddened if he let loose of that final tether that kept him tied so closely to her?

"I am coming to believe more and more that it may not even be my own will that makes the choice. Perhaps there is another who has made it for me." He chanced a glance at Katherine, so pretty in her patched clothing and dull ribbons.

"Oh."

Though she'd said only the one word, Will realized she had said much. He watched as her hopeful look faded away.

"No tears for me, Arianna. Strangely enough, I begin to find myself content. As it happens, I am a bit fatigued by it all, yes, but not quite ready to give up the ghost, if you'll pardon the expression."

A faint smile rose in her eyes. "I am glad of that, Captain. Perhaps we should look upon this as the blessing it seems to be."

"My thoughts exactly."

After the last of the duck had been cleared, and the participants enjoyed their dessert, Will watched as Arianna began to clear the dishes. He was amazed at how a young woman who'd been waited on all her life now busied herself with such menial tasks. He'd thought that all of the titled were nothing more than selfish, boorish, layabouts. Arianna had taught him differently. Although she'd been born to a high station, she'd not asked for it, and she didn't impose her status on those around her. Her courtesy extended to Mrs. Stanhope and the two pirates, whom she treated as though they were gentry, as high on the social ladder as she.

More than that, Will couldn't help admiring the way she handled Katherine. Treating her as though she were precious, rather than the child of a prostitute and a wayward sailor, Arianna embraced the six-year-old. She considered her an equal part of the family, asking her opinions on every thing from china patterns to the state of the garden. Other times, when she cradled the little girl in her arms and recited bedtime stories, Will thought she loved Katherine just as if the child were from her very own womb.

"Ah, Letitia," he whispered to himself, "we couldn't have asked for better."

A distant wind whistled outside the house. An answer to his statement, perhaps?

"You've done a fair job of it, missus," Mrs. Stanhope

whimpered, clutching the embroidered handkerchief to her face. Will recognized it as one of Arianna's own. "These is as lovely a thing as I've ever had." The house-keeper then proceeded to cry into the cloth. It was as though heaven itself had opened up and bestowed the gifts upon her.

"I'm glad you like it, Mary-Margaret." Arianna patted the woman's arm affectionately.

"M'am, these gloves are as fine as ever has been made," Gus said, the hint of emotion riding high on his voice as well.

"They'll do," Herbert echoed behind him.

Will knew that was as good as an endorsement as Arianna was going to get from that corner.

Ethan sat back in his chair, arms and feet propped up comfortably, watching the activities as though he were a king holding court. Will noticed how carefully his sister had tied his cravat and the now dried trail of a tear that had slipped down Ethan's face when Arianna had wished him a merry holiday and presented him with his boots, now shining with a fresh polish. Ethan now sat dozing, cracking open his eyes every once in a while as if keeping abreast of the situation.

The true wonder of the evening, however, was ruled upon by the smallest member of the gathering.

"Oh, Arianna, she's beautiful!"

Katherine was seated in the midst of the parlor floor with her new treasures spread out in front of her. The brightly colored stones, or jewels from the sea, as Arianna had called them, reflected the candlelight beautifully.

Katherine clutched the ragtag doll as though it were made of the finest silks ever to arrive from the far east. Happy tears glistened in the little girl's eyes.

"I'm glad you like her. Fanny Flatham has ever been my best companion. I hope you'll get as much joy from her as I have."

"I know I shall," Katherine said seriously.

"I do have one more small gift for you, precious."

"Another gift? For me?"

"Yes, for you. It isn't much, certainly not as lovely as the treasures you've already amassed. Still, I hope you like them."

From beneath her cushion, Arianna pulled out two parchments, both rolled up neatly and tied with a tattered pink bow.

"Let me see!" Katherine demanded, her voice high-pitched with excitement.

Carefully undoing the ribbon, Katherine reverently revealed the picture within. The first one was a charcoal sketch of a man, who at first glance looked a fearsome beast. His forehead was high, and his jaw set into a hard line. In one ear he wore a ring, and his scowling expression managed to hold a bit of softness just about the eyes. It looked as though he was concentrating very hard on something extremely important.

"It's my papa!" Katherine squealed with joy. "Oh, thank you, Arianna!" She instantly jumped from the floor and Arianna barely had time to open her arms to catch her.

"Wait! Wait! There's one more!"

"You've made another picture of my papa?"

"No, I haven't. Believe me, capturing him just once was difficult enough. No, this is someone else."

"Who?"

Will, though still suffering a shock at the revelation of the first picture, leaned forward attentively.

"Yes, who is it?" he asked.

Arianna gave him a wink, then turned to her young charge.

"I know you may not recognize her, since you were so small . . . but I've done my best to capture what I thought she might have looked like. I mean, taking into account your own features . . ."

"Damn and blast, woman, out with it!" Will exploded beside her.

Arianna was noticeably unruffled by his outburst. "No matter, I suppose. Katherine, I would like you to meet someone very important. May I introduce you to Letitia Markham. Your mother."

For all her life, Arianna would remember many things. The pitch of the ship beneath her feet the first time she boarded the *Persuasion*, for one thing, or the image of the sunset on this island prison she'd been banished to. But more than that, she would always remember the anguished sound of one Captain William Markham that was followed by the ghostly whoosh as he fell to the floor, cold as a fish.

Smiling sweetly to her guests, she made no mention of the sudden thud that shook the room. "It must be a distant storm," she told those gathered with her.

"Must be an awful blow, don't you think, Arianna?" Katherine asked, her wide eyes searching the room.

"Yes, indeed. A huge squall."

"That wasn't very kind of you," Will muttered when he sat back up, staring around the now empty parlor.

Arianna was snuffing the last of the candles and smiled over at him. "You don't approve of Katherine's gifts?" She smiled at him, her expression that of a mischievous kitten caught with its paw in the milk jug.

"As a matter of record, I believe that is one of the nicest gestures I've ever seen. You give me hope, Arianna."

Arianna stopped for a moment, casting a careful eye at him. "I'm glad there is room for such things in your heart, Will."

"If there is, it's because of you."

Her smile widened, lighting up her face as if the sun had risen inside her eyes.

"Thank you."

"You're welcome," she said softly. Putting down the single burning candle, she gathered her skirt and made her way to him. Sitting on the sofa, curling herself into him, Will wrapped his arms around her, pulling her ever closer.

"I'm glad we've had this time. And I'm sorry that I've nothing to give you."

"You've given me more than you know," she said, her voice slightly muffled as she rubbed her face into his shirt. "You've given me Katherine. She's worth more than all the riches in the world."

"I'm glad you think so."

"I do."

For a moment they held each other, the shadows of the candle flame dancing around the room like little Christmas fairies spreading their sprightly magic.

Will wanted more than anything to hold onto this moment forever. The truth was, he no longer regretted the loss of his life. Only one thing still hung heavy on his soul, one final debt that had to be settled before he could move on.

Arianna moved beside him, glancing up as though she felt his thoughts.

"What is it, darling?"

He searched her face a moment, deciding on the best way to reveal what yet needed to be done.

Taking a breath and very sorry for spoiling their time together, he began telling her of the difficult task ahead of them.

The duke stirred his chocolate thoughtfully. A new wrinkle had arisen and he was not a man given to dealing with such a distressing turn of events.

Ever since his brother had dispatched his only living daughter into the world of poverty, he had been certain of a wrong that lived among the family. It wasn't because of that bastard, Barrons, either. That blighter could rot in hell for all he cared. No, there was something else, something that had taken away the sweetness from their lives, and damned he was if he could figure out what it was.

Now, another challenge sat before him.

"What did you say your name was again?"

"Digby. Elias Digby. I'm an associate of your nephew."

"In case he's forgotten to tell you, by law we are no longer related. That devil has had the audacity to darken my door one time too many. If he shows again, I shall have the footman remove him at the point of a pistol. Unless you want the same fate, I suggest you make haste to leave."

The man didn't budge. Hawklike and cunning, Digby stared squarely in the duke's eyes. Damn the soul of him to be so bold!

"I have a proposition for you, your grace. As it happens, I've decided that it is no longer profitable for me to continue with Mr. Barrons."

"And why is that?"

"Let's just say that my employer's sound judgment has been slipping of late. He's on a path that will end at the Newgate gallows."

"And you don't wish to join him there. Very well, then. Don't."

"I wish that it were that simple, your grace. I have managed to put by a bit of gold from our dealings, but once your nephew is found out, my involvement with him will come to light. We are unfortunately tied together."

"I sense a proposal in the air. Very well, what do you want?"

"In exchange for my revealing the dealings of Mr. Barrons, I want two things. Immunity from prosecution, for one."

"I would think that goes without speaking. And the other?"

The duke's drink was growing cold, but the discussion was heating up nicely.

"The other is a small sum of money and a small entitlement—nothing fancy, a viscountcy, perhaps. Of course, my name must be erased from any incriminating documents to avoid a subsequent chase and hanging. Gruesome business, hanging."

"I see. What do you have to offer me that is so important it will essentially absolve you of all your sins?"

"I can prove once and for all that Richard Barrons did the deed for which an innocent man was hanged, several weeks ago. Further more, there are records of illicit dealings that bankrupted several companies, up to and including those of the crown."

The duke paused, his hands settling on the embroidered tablecloth. If the information this man held were true, it could result in more than just the demise of Richard Barrons. It could mean the reinstatement of his own financial and social status.

"Very well, Mr. Digby. Let's get to the particulars."

Chapter Sixteen

"Will? What is it?"

Searching her face, Will paused a moment. How he wished he could somehow stop the moment, remain in this room, in her embrace forever. That could never be and, too well, he knew it.

"You know there will come a time when Barrons returns to the island."

He watched the fine muscles of her throat move as she swallowed back her fear, like velvet rustling beneath silk.

"Yes. I know that."

"Then you must arm yourself. You have too much here to protect, my love. If you don't, he will surely destroy everything."

Arianna looked away a moment. His words, no longer couched in anger and hatred, rang true.

"I know."

"I'm not asking you to kill him unless you must. You were right what you said before, that justice will eventually catch up with him. I know it now."

She looked up at him, her face pensive, her eyes watching him for any revelation of facts.

"What then?"

"Do you remember the night we found Gus and Herbert?"

"Yes."

"I found something else."

The silence between them opened like a deep well, full only with possibilities and regrets.

"What did you find?"

Will searched her face. Was she ready for the truth? All the truth, he wondered? Even the lie that he had kept so well hidden in his heart that for a long time he hadn't recognized the face of it?

Will knew he should have told her everything that was in his heart that night, but he also knew of the betrayal that shimmered just beneath the surface of that knowledge, and to save his very soul he could not tell it. Soon, but not quite yet.

Taking a deep breath, he began.

"That night, while you were scaring the daylights out of our resident pirates, I was doing a bit of searching on my own."

"You found something?"

Will could hardly bear the hope and excitement rising in her expression.

"Yes. I found two chests. One was out by the campfire. It holds several weapons. Two short-bladed knives, a host of pistols, ammunition and so forth, and two long-barreled rifles with bayonets. The very same that were headed to Spain. Part of those shipped that I was accused of stealing, I imagine."

"Then that will prove your innocence?"

"Perhaps, but that doesn't matter now. What does

matter is that you have the means to protect yourself against Barrons."

"Oh. There is that."

"I'm not asking you to kill him outright. I know now that it was wrong of me to ask such a dreadful thing of you."

She shook her head. "No. I've been a stubborn fool, Will. I was so high and mighty that I didn't see the necessity of it. Things are different now. You were right. Evil like that must be put down."

Will reached out and took her face in his hands. "Listen to me, beloved. I was wrong to ask. You are too beautiful and too perfect—I beg your forgiveness for ever even considering such a thing. Please, don't stain your soul because of the imperfection of mine. I beg you."

"But—"

"I know I'm right in this, now. You've helped me to see that. I don't know how or when, but you have. There is something else . . ."

Will held his breath. He would tell her one other thing now, saving the very worst of it for another time. *Yes,* he thought, *that's how it has to be.*

"What?"

"I found another chest. It was half buried in a cave about a hundred yards from their campsite. The evidence against Barrons has been there all along."

Arianna swallowed again. "You knew this? Since that first night?"

He nodded solemnly. "I know I was wrong for keeping it from you. I wanted him destroyed no matter what, no matter the cost to you. I was wrong. You taught me that. When I first saw Katherine, I understood completely how wrong it would be."

"But he killed you! He tortured your crew. He threw a little girl from a ship, frightening her beyond belief! For heaven's sake, Will. He took the only person she ever loved away from her and stranded her in this wilderness with no one to care whether she lived or died! For that alone he should suffer!"

Tears flowed freely from her now, spilling onto her bodice, onto his hands as he cupped her face.

"Yes, he should, but my love, it's not up to us to make him." His voice was soft, broken by her distress. "Don't you see, we've been spared. It doesn't matter what happened before. The past is in the past and it should stay there. This is your chance, yours and Katherine's, to have a good life."

"What are you saying?" she sobbed openly.

"I'm saying that you need only defend yourself. Take the knowledge of what's in that cave back to England with you, if at all possible. Let the courts have him. That's as it should be. Do this, Arianna. Do it for me. But more than that, do it for Katherine and yourself. That alone will ensure my life and death will have some meaning after all."

Arianna lunged forward, burying her face in his shirt. With all of the love in his heart, Will wrapped his arms around her, pulling her vibrant warmth to him. For the first time in his pitiful existence, he felt more alive than he ever thought possible.

Arianna awoke some time later. The day had not yet dawned and the fire had gone out in the hearth. She felt chilled, but not from the cool air in the room, for Will had placed a ragged wool blanket over her.

No, she felt the sort of cold that went clear to the

soul. Last night she had learned the truth of it. She would somehow find a way to get herself and Katherine back to England. She knew now that she could kill Barrons if she had to. Perhaps she'd known that all along.

For the moment, though, the day needed to be started. There were meals to prepare, baths to give, a garden to be tended, even though it was only to prepare it for a spring planting. She must embrace this life somehow.

This was how it was to be, she thought as she looked around the room. Her alone. Only with her own death would she find her true love and if there were any real justice to this existence, then she would be allowed to share it with Will.

The ship's deck rattled underneath him, but Barrons took no notice of it. He'd enough to do to keep himself upright as a gale threatened to push them all to the bottom of the sea.

"This is madness, I tell you!" Captain Davis shouted behind him.

Barrons gave no notice to the barrel-chested foghorn. The man had been badgering him for two days now, telling him how impossible it was to skirt the storm and make landfall. He didn't care. He had to return to Montclair. He had to kill his wife.

"Please, sir," Davis begged behind him. "Have a heart. Let us put into port in France."

"Get out of my way!" Barrons shouted over the roar of the approaching storm. "You accepted your pay right enough. Just steer this ship close enough to my shore and you can navigate it all the way to hell, for all I care!"

Barrons shoved the man back and made his way to

the stairs. Descending to his cabin, he barely even heard the curses thrown after him. It didn't matter. He'd long since lost his sense of feeling, both in his fingers and his heart. He was no better than a dead man. What did the cares of the living matter to him?

"Let the blasted ship go down. I'll walk the bottom of the sea to get to her if I have to!"

The fire in the hearth was burning low. Ethan yawned, strangely content. He'd been put back to bed, with the assistance of Herbert and Gus. The two were jovial enough after the events of the evening. Being so, the two chatted on about the various strains of living their enforced exile, waiting for Barrons to return and forgive whatever transgression it was that left them stranded here.

"I tells ya, the missus is one fine lady, that she is," Gus said as he pulled the covers up from the foot of the bed, tucking them roughly about Ethan's shoulders.

"Quit yer moonin', you fool. The likes of her ain't got no thoughts for a lout such as yourself," Herbert answered as he struggled to relight the fire. "I mean, look at you, for the dev'l's sake."

"But she treated us right fairly tonight, you know, acting like we wuz close family and all."

"You're a bigger jugbrain than I thought. She ain't got no thoughts for us at all, except to carry his lordship about, wiping his arse and his drool."

"Now, that's where we're different," Gus informed him. "I rather prefer doin' this task. Makes me feel like an uppity-up valet, you know. All I need is a right nice jacket wif brass buttons and instruction as to proper manners. I could be as good as any of them blighters."

Gus patted Ethan on the top of his head, in what he meant to be an affectionate gesture. "Aye, and I could be the Prince of Wales, meself."

"Mebbe you are, you never know. Stranger things have happened."

Herbert threw down the last of the matchsticks. "You are either the stupidest beast ever born or . . ."— he paused, racking his limited mind—"or I don't know what. You silly goose, have you ever given any thought to what Ol' Spikes has planned fer yer little hatchlings?"

"What d'ya mean, Bert? I never heard of no plan."

"Of course ya din't. You and I don't need to know the minds of our betters."

"What d'you suppose he's going to do with them?" Gus pulled a soiled handkerchief and began wiping Ethan's chin.

Ethan was no fool, even if his caretakers weren't the brightest lamps on the post. He'd known full well what Barrons intended for them from the beginning. The only hope he, Arianna, and little Kitty had was to convince the pirates to help them. Only that or an act of God could stop Ol' Spikes.

"He's going to carve them up like a Christmas goose, no doubt. Toss them into the sea, or shoot 'em square and plant them in that frozen garden we've been digging."

Gus drew back, a sad expression crossing his dull features. "Do you think so? The missus is quite a nice bit of muslin. I can't see him casting her off."

"Not right away, to be sure. No, he'll probably take his pleasure with her. Maybe even leave Lord High-n-Mighty over there to fend for himself. That would be a fine kettle of fish."

"Well, it's not very nice, now is it? Let me ask you this, old thing, what's to happen to us then, eh? Like when he's through having us do his dirty work and all. Think we'll be walking on the sea bottom, ourselves?"

Ethan noted the silence that fell between them. Clearly these two were at least considering the very possibility that Montclair Island might prove to be their last resting place as well. Somehow that made him feel a bit brighter, despite their dire circumstances.

Will sat beside his daughter's bed. She had fallen asleep playing with her doll in the little room just across the hall from Ethan's. Surely as soon as she awoke, she would burn a trail to his side and climb in bed beside him. It nearly broke Will's heart to see the child cuddle in the arms of another the very same way she used to do with him.

That was when he first noticed it. The sensation of fading. Now, that he knew his daughter was safe, or at least relatively so for the moment, Will knew the force of his anger had fallen like a full sail on a windless night.

He hated Barrons for what he'd done. Surely he, more than anyone else, deserved to burn in the fires of hell. With what Will had discovered, then at least the villain would hang. Will was almost content to let a higher power decide his enemy's punishment from there.

As he watched his daughter's slow, gentle breaths, Will's heart began to heal just a bit. Only a single thread of guilt ran through him now. It was a singular pain that would never go away, he was sure.

It was at that moment that Arianna entered the room. Searching the darkness, her hair in disarray and her fine silk dress rumpled, Will swore she was the most beautiful woman he'd ever seen.

Arianna was aristocratic by birth, but the heart and soul of her was both enticing woman and mystical goddess. Sun-kissed tresses trailed down her neck from the knot she had fastened in her hair earlier in the day. Her neck was long and luxurious and her form slender and graceful. Arianna was a woman to be desired, to be held and adored, and to be loved as she loved others.

It was that love, and that of his daughter, that pushed away everything dark and blighted in his soul. In the winter of his existence, two perfect roses had sprung from the dust, and damn his life and death, if he deserved either one.

Yes, Will thought, they were roses. The sturdiest of flowers if given a chance to take root and grow. Blooms that could withstand a winter and come back, alive and whole in the spring. Thorns to put off predators and the ability to remain upright on a strong stem when the winds of troubled times came to beat it down.

Ah, Katherine was a white rose, pure and lovely, no doubt. Despite the terror of the last months she remained a child who, when grown into a woman full, would truly be one to be reckoned with.

Arianna. Will had realized that she was the blood-red rose, full of passion and life, with the tips of her petals dipped in a bit of violet perhaps, denoting her noble lineage. But it was her center that showed her to be the true person she was. A soft pink lingered there, for she was a woman given to compassion, her insistence of caring for others shown time and again for all the responsibility she'd taken on. Katherine, Ethan, even the servants. And him. She'd taken him in and tried to repair his very soul.

What she didn't know was that some wounds are never intended to heal.

Will knew the truth. Though his time here seemed to linger on, the substance of him was slowly seeping into that other realm. The one where dust and destiny combined and a man's soul must go to reside. Would he meet with heaven's grace? Or would a fiery hell await him? Will realized that the only thing he really wanted was to wait at that place where one day Arianna would join him, hoping beyond hope that he could yet linger at the edge of eternity.

Arianna turned. "Oh, there you are. I'd wondered where you'd gotten to."

"I wanted to watch Katherine for awhile."

Arianna nodded. She understood what he was about. She could feel the tether that bound him stretch farther still.

"Are you all right?" she asked, half afraid of the answer he might give.

Will looked up at her, his eyes glowing now with a low flame, replacing the burning anger she'd seen there before.

"I'm better than I thought I'd ever be again," he answered in a slow, relaxed tone.

"Yes. I can see that now." Arianna took a deep breath. "I want you to stay," she blurted out. "That is, I think that having you around is all right. You cannot pass into eternity just yet. Stay with me awhile longer."

She saw his eyes drift upwards as though he was searching the heavens for some sort of answer.

"I don't know that I have any say in the matter, Arianna. I wish I did. I wish that I had the chance to live my life over again. There are so many things I would have done differently."

"Really?" Arianna knelt down in front of him. "Like what?"

He shrugged. "Just small things, really. I would have risen a little earlier each morning, perhaps stayed awake a bit longer. I would have settled Katherine into a better life. I would have sought you out, I think."

"How would you have done that? We never had the chance to meet when you were alive."

He smiled. "I think that my heart would know better where to look."

Arianna nodded. "Whatever happens, I'm glad you came."

"I am, too. Now, go put Katherine to bed. We can watch the sunrise together if you'd like."

"I'd like that very much."

Captain Alms was a stiff man, rock hard, and straight as an arrow. His imposing figure stood watch on the deck of the naval ship *Elkhurst*, his eyes sweeping the miles of ocean beyond them. Taking out his spyglass, he examined the horizon further.

"There it is, Mr. Digby. That would be your employer's ship?" he said, holding the instrument for Digby to peer through it.

"That would be the one, sir. Doesn't look too good, though, does she? Listing to the side a bit, two sails torn."

"Indeed. My guess is she encountered bad weather. Makes it all the better to catch up with her."

"Is there no danger from the weather for us?" Digby held tight to the railing. He didn't like it one bit, this was the wrong time of year to go so far from home. No one could tell what might crop up from the winter climate.

"We've skirted most of the bad storms, I'd think. Didn't sail as direct a course as Mr. Barrons. We're not in as big a hurry."

"No. His reasons for haste won't affect us, sure enough."

"Unfortunate for his wife and her brother, though, isn't it? I know of the former Lady Halverson. My cousin, Lord Bradley, is a friend of Lord Castin, her brother. Said that she was prime for the marriage market but had no desire to tie herself to anyone at the present. Damned peculiar, is what it was."

"I've heard she has strange ideas, thinks she can talk with the dead."

"Nonsense. No one of any breeding would ever consider such a thing. Unless, of course, they were mentally unstable. I could see how Lord Castin would want to keep such a thing below stairs, though."

Digby didn't comment further. He'd seen the very same journal that Barrons had and while he never set much store in the supernatural, he certainly didn't discount it entirely. In this instance, whatever means Arianna Barrons had summoned the malady that affected her husband had very well had its effect. For the moment, at least, Richard Barrons was as mad as an inmate of Bedlam.

In an odd sort of way, Digby found himself wishing that Barrons's wife would manage to thwart the old devil. It would certainly make things simpler. He himself could tell Captain Alms the location of the ledgers and weapons, collect his ransom once they pulled into port and never be the wiser. He'd made a deal to keep himself from Newgate, true enough, but one never knew when something might come out that would threaten his safety.

Digby pulled at his shirt collar, feeling the same tightness that came over him whenever he thought about paying for his crimes. He never let himself think about any punishment he might have coming after his life was through. No, better to concentrate on the here and now. Here was on board a ship that would alter the course of his life forever and now he was safe from the long arm of the law as well as his employer's vengeance.

Digby found himself extremely pleased at his current circumstances.

"Don't know why you want us to be dragging these cumbersome crates all over the island. It's not like there's anyone who knows where they are, or what's in 'em," Herbert complained.

"True enough," Arianna said as she led the way down the path back to the mansion. "However, that cave is fairly damp, especially since all the rain the last few days. I'm afraid something will happen to my husband's property. More than that, he'd think me responsible and I'd surely have to suffer the consequences of his temper."

She glanced back and saw the exchange of understanding expressions between the two men. Just as she'd thought, they'd likely been on the receiving end of Barrons's rage. Surely it was an experience none of them wanted to repeat.

"Aye, there is that. No need to upset Ol' Spikes." Gus grunted.

"Exactly. We'll just store them upstairs, then. In Ethan's room. It seems to be the driest of the lot."

"Oh, aye," Herbert grumbled, "and perhaps you would like us to work on repairing the roof as soon the bad weather clears?"

"What a marvelous idea, Mr. Herbert. You are such a generous man. I'm sure my husband will reward both of you when he returns."

Gus coughed, quickly glancing about. "Gawd save us from Mr. Barrons's rewards."

Arianna turned back to the path and did not reply.

Chapter Seventeen

After Gus and Herbert brought the chests into Ethan's bedroom, she and Gus helped Ethan from bed and, propping him in his favorite sitting chair, positioned him to look out into the gardens. Beyond the wall, they could see Katherine playing with her kitten, her sing-song voice drifting in with the noontime breezes.

Although he had not said a word, and seemed to drift in and out of consciousness, these last few days Arianna had detected a calmness in her brother's manner. Not that he'd been able to communicate it, though. She thought perhaps it was just in the expression he wore. She knew Katherine was a huge help to his spirits. If she hadn't already loved the child before learning of their closeness, she certainly would now.

Chores done, she reminded Gus and Herbert of Herbert's suggestion to repair the roof. Both men grumbled, but a quick reminder of her husband's insistance on comfort and his possible displeasure at not seeing any improvements on the estate sent them scrambling to get hammers and nails.

The entire rest of the afternoon was spent unpacking the chests. Will had informed her that because the locks were so rusty, it would take little effort to break the corroded metal. With a piece of iron, she managed to wedge it under and snap both of the mechanisms.

"For all his vast wealth, you'd think Barrons might spend some of it on a safe."

Will chuckled. "He didn't have to. With his reputation, no one who really knew him would ever brave going into his private business."

"Still, not very wise."

Will shrugged. "I imagine that he meant for those two jackanapes to find a better hiding place for them. It's our good fortune that they fell quite short of his expectations."

"Indeed."

Arianna opened the first chest. It was filled with plain, leather-bound books. Pulling off the string that tied one set, she opened the first book.

"Look at this. It's a record of movement of various shipments of items, canons, ammunition—large and small caliber guns, pistols, knives, swords . . . My goodness, he certainly was thorough."

"Probably supplied half of Napoleon's forces, damn him."

Arianna sank back on her feet. "And all the while, our brave men were being wounded or killed on the battlefield."

"Indeed. What else?"

Arianna went through the remaining volumes. There were twenty-five in all, detailed as to amount, cost to him, dates of shipments and receipt of payments, and the profit made.

"No wonder he's wealthy. I wonder what's in the second chest?"

Their curiosity was soon satisfied when the last of the rusted hinges gave way. Opening it and brushing away the dust, she dug through the layers of clothing and jewelry and soon discovered a treasure of a different sort.

"I think these are personal journals." She opened three of the five books and flipped through the pages. Long, tilted lines of script filled every page, top to bottom.

"He must have been keeping them a long time," Will said, motioning to another three at the bottom of the crate.

"Truly. Perhaps something in here will indicate just why he has chosen the path that brought him to us."

Will grumbled, "I'm not so sure I want to know."

"Oh," she said, flipping through one. "Wait, here's something." She quickly turned the page, her eyes following the text.

With Will leaning over her shoulder, she began to read aloud.

1 December,

I have finally achieved victory. My one, most dangerous opponent is put down. This morning, I attended the hanging of the man who kept me tethered to this objectionable state. He alone, had he known the truth of his lineage, could have cut me to the quick, reduced my empire to rubble. The threat is no more. This morning at dawn, William

Markham was hanged. My victory will soon be complete . . .

Arianna sat back. "What does he mean? Were you his enemy?"

When she turned to look at the captain, she had a moment's problem finding him. For some reason, his countenance had faded somewhat. "Will? Are you there?"

A few seconds passed before an answer came.

"I was not the enemy he imagined. Why my existence should bother him so, I have no idea."

"I see. You think him a madman, then?"

"I do. One who is not mentally stable cannot be held accountable for their actions."

At last he said in a whisper, "How terrible to imagine your enemy is always lurking."

"The man is disturbed, that's true enough. Whatever he saw in you had tragic consequences. But I have a difficult time having pity on him, considering his cruelty to you, Katherine, and the crew of your ship."

"Perhaps."

Will looked away from her for a moment, toward the balcony where Ethan now dozed.

"I'm tired, Arianna."

"Oh. Well, perhaps this has all been too much. I think we should retire for the evening."

She quickly closed the book in her lap and began replacing the things in the chest.

"It's not that sort of exhaustion, my love."

Arianna glanced up at him. This time merely the outline of him remained.

"Will, where is the amulet?" she asked, her fear mounting with every second.

Without answering, he reached inside his shirt and pulled out the leather string which tied it to him and held it suspended in front of his eyes.

The jade stone barely gleamed.

"It's grown weaker." She nearly choked on the words. How could this be? Now, when he'd found his daughter, when there was so much more for them to share . . .

"I think it's nearly time for me to go."

His words echoing in her ear, Arianna ran to him. "Please! You must fight it! You must try for me and for Katherine."

In the mist that had nearly overtaken him, Arianna saw two silvery streaks fall from his eyes, as otherworldly tears fell, one by one.

"I think it's not up to you or me, but perhaps time. Or is it that I can no longer hold on to my anger? It's a strange thing, this place between life and death."

"No!" She went to him, reaching out her hand, but could not grasp him, instead going through him as though he were but a shadow. "You can't leave me now. What if Barrons returns? How will I fight him?"

"You have the weapons, Arianna. You have your wits. You have the advantage."

"Oh, no!" She sobbed openly, her hands dropping to her side.

"Please, don't cry. Let my last sight of you be of that dear, beautiful woman who tried so hard to be one with an unruly ghost."

Arianna cried a few moments more, struggling to silence her sobs, to stem the flow of her tears.

"I shall try," she said at last, stiffening her spine and lifting her gaze to meet his.

"There is a place on the island," he told her, his gaze

locked with hers, "where there are still a few beautiful shrubs, where the trees are yet green and a cliff that drops off into the sea. The view is breathtaking. Would you go there with me now? I would like to have a memory of you by the sea, I think."

Arianna nodded, her chest tight with pain, her heart breaking.

As she turned to go, Katherine arrived at the bedroom door. Her face flushed from playing, her breaths coming in short, quick bursts.

"Arianna? What's wrong? Are you sick?" she asked, rushing forward.

Sniffing and wiping her face desperately, Arianna shook her head. "No. Sometimes a lady needs a good cry. It helps to clear the melancholia."

"Really? Do you think I should cry? I shouldn't want to be cluttered up with melanch—what did you call it?"

"Never mind, dove. Would you sit awhile with Ethan? I have a small errand and I don't want him to awaken and find himself alone."

"I will. Then I shall tell him of our newest friend, Tabitha. She's the kitten I've been coaxing today. I think we shall be great friends."

Arianna nodded and, gathering her wrap, left the two of them alone. When she arrived at the bedroom door, she took one look back at the two of them. Katherine had settled herself on Ethan's lap. She heard her brother sigh and knew that they would do well, the two of them. She only wished the same for her and Will.

The trip to the island had been eventful and at last Barrons stood on the shore, the two sailors who'd come with him pulling in the long boats.

He could have taken any number of men, but decided against it. The acts he was about to commit should have no witnesses, to be sure. No one would be left to testify against him. It had to be that way.

Walking up the path toward the house, Barrons had worked it all out in his mind. He knew exactly which of the six he would approach first. As he neared the main house he saw a most peculiar sight. Two men were busy hammering on the rooftop. Every so often a piece of wood would slide down the surface of the roof and fall to earth, landing with a dull thud.

Barrons surveyed the ground in front of the house. It was littered with various pieces of wood, nails, and repair supplies.

"Ahoy up there, you swabbies!" he called up.

Instantly the two men turned to his summons, Gustavson nearly slipping and falling down. Herbert merely watched him, seeming not at all bothered at his clumsiness. It wasn't until the two men recognized just who had interrupted their work that they made a mad scramble down the rickety ladder at the front of the building.

"Oh, aye, sir!" Gus wheezed, nervously straightening his shirt. Barrons noted that the buttons were fastened unevenly, leaving a gap at the center of his round belly.

Herbert, though out of breath as well, was less outwardly bothered. In fact, he gave Barrons a cool look, his eyes measuring and weighing the danger to himself. He was very likely considering the two pistols that Barrons had strapped to his sides and the wickedly long blade that hung from his belt.

"What in blazes were you doing? Explain."

The two men exchanged a glance, Herbert stepping forward, a scowl growing on his scarred face.

"We was doin' as yer missus ordered us, that's what."

"Repairing the roof. So she wouldn't get wet, you see, when it rains," Gus added, twisting his shirttails in both hands.

"I'm aware of what you were doing. Why were you doing it? Did I give you those orders?" Barrons began to pace in front of them, his hands lighting on the pistols. He was pleased to see the alarm in their eyes.

"Oh, no, sir. You did not." Herbert clenched his fists. "You also did not inform us that there was to be others on this pile of dirt. That yer lady-wife and that brat would be running the island."

"I see. Is that what she told you?"

"Aye, that and more. We were only trying to do as you might wish," Gus added, nodding quickly.

"Indeed? Men who can think for themselves. 'Tis a good thing, I think. Or it would be, did I not give you orders to stand guard over my belongings on the other side of the island. Tell me, do you even know what's become of my things?"

"Oh, aye, we do," Herbert answered. "We've brought them into the house, safe and sound."

Barrons nodded. Perhaps it was a good idea, he thought. And the chests had been secured, so even his bride would not have access to the contents. His anger receded a notch.

"What of the earl? Is he still alive?"

"Aye, if yer want to call it that. Can't move a muscle, can't sputter a word. Just sits in his chair of a day, drools on himself, and then back to bed at night. Pitiful thing, he is. Much rather be dead than like that, meself."

"Really. And the others?"

"Yer missus has headed toward the other side of the island. Said she wanted to look at the view from the cliffs for one of her drawings. The child is with his lordship. Mrs. Stanhope is in the kitchens drinkin' her sherry and watching the wild pig roast, I imagine."

"Very well. All accounted for, then. I have a few tasks for the both of you."

"Aye? We'll be glad of it. Get us off this damned rock. We wants to be back on ship, working the sails," Herbert said.

"Of course you do. Now, here's what I want."

What he didn't tell them was that he never intended for them to return to the ship. Indeed, when they'd finished killing the earl, the child, and the housekeeper, Barrons would use at least two of his bullets to put them down as well. No witnesses, that was his motto.

That would leave one person left to deal with: his lovely wife.

Barrons had thought long and hard how he would destroy her. Would he use a knife or a pistol? Would he drag her to the sea and hold her under the cold waters until she breathed no more? No, he'd told himself. None of that. What he really wanted was to feel the last of her pulse as it faded beneath his fingertips. He wanted her to struggle and clutch at his hands as they closed around her long, elegant, lovely neck. Yes. Strangling it would be.

He turned once again to Gus and Herbert. Giving them a thin grin, he admonished them in a calm tone to set aside their repair work. He reveled at their nervous reaction to the new smoothness of his manner. It gave him no end of glee to watch the two bumblers make their way up to the mansion and then, check anxiously behind them to see if he still stood watching them. He widened his smile and saw them hurriedly duck inside.

Now to the business at hand.

The path to the cliff was an overgrown mixture of beauty and danger. A misstep might lead one to trip into the tangle of bushes, or take a turn deeper into the wilderness. But the golden glow of the afternoon sun against high trees and doppled shadows more than made up for any uncertainty lurking there.

Arianna knew none of this. All she was aware of was the wide shouldered stance of Will as he ducked between the branches. At that moment, more than any other, Arianna began to realize how deeply she'd come to desire him, not just on the level of a woman sated by an experience of lovemaking, exquisite though it had been.

Indeed, she realized sadly as the two continued their upward journey, he was her soul mate, the other half that made her whole. Losing him now could be no more divisive than death.

Arianna held back her tears, taking short, shallow breaths. She'd be strong for him, she resolved. She had to, lest it not be her own physical existence that faded into eternal twilight.

"Here, this is where I want to see you," he said, suddenly stopping in front of her. They had reached the outcropping where the wilderness opened into a panoramic view of the vastness of the sea beyond the land.

Arianna held back a sob. "It's beautiful." She didn't look at him then, turning instead to the view of the ocean beyond and below them.

A new thought struck her. Could she do it? Could she turn away and resign herself to never seeing him again? Could she leave this man who over the last few weeks had come to mean so much to her?

For a second she was tempted. Tempted to abandon the remainder of this life, to fling herself from the edge and go with him into the uncertain future that no living being understood.

"Don't," he said behind her now. Rising up like a falcon, his wispy shadow cast over her. "You've too much life to live to throw it away."

"It's mine to do with as I please." Though the words sprang from her heart, she was surprised to hear them just the same.

In that instant he became solid once again. Arianna gasped as his thick hands took form, grabbing her shoulders, spinning her around to face him.

"Please, Arianna. Don't even think it! Your life is too precious, too important to cast away."

"What of yours? Yours was stolen and because of it we can never be together. Never truly together." Arianna couldn't help the high pitch of her voice or the catch in her throat when she spoke. "I'm angry! So much was taken from you, from us! It isn't fair!"

In one blind moment she threw herself forward into his embrace. She felt him surround her, his shape changing and reforming even with her touch. Then, as if a candle had been put out, she felt him change again. He could not hold to physical form any longer.

"I can't go on like this," he choked. "I am neither living nor dead. I want to hold you in my arms, I want to feel your touch on my skin, I want to be full and alive for you and I cannot. It is such exquisite torture, both a promise of heaven and evidence of hell. I cannot remain in both worlds. I see that now. Much longer between the two and I shall go mad."

Arianna felt the stab of his words. "I'm sorry. I hadn't realized what it must be like for you." She choked over the words, the pain of losing him binding around her like a great snake coiling and readying itself to take its prey.

"No. Don't blame yourself. I was a fool for thinking I could use my anger and pain to fashion myself back into life. I have achieved neither and caused you even more hurt in the doing. I am sorry, Arianna. Sorry for putting you through this, though I'm not a bit regretful of having the chance to know you. If it were in my power, I'd turn back the days and find a way to prevent my death. I'd have promised them anything if it meant getting back to you and Katherine."

"Dear God!" Arianna sobbed openly now, her hands clenching, twisting in each other. She knew to her very soul that she was powerless to keep him with her.

"There is one thing left for me to do, beloved." He stepped closer. "One truth remains. When I tell it to you, I fear the final thread that holds me here will disappear once and for all. I'm sorry, Arianna. More sorry than you know."

Folding her arms, Arianna stepped back. The realization came to her that by denying him his final words, she was inflicting even more distress on him. Nodding her head resolutely, she took a deep breath, wiped her hands raggedly across her drenched face and raised her eyes to meet his.

An expression of understanding passed between them.

"I wasn't completely honest when I said that Barrons was responsible for everything that happened to me. Hell, I didn't even realize it myself until a few days ago."

"Realize what?"

Arianna watched him pause a moment, the words gathering in him like energy in the air before a storm. "That I am at least partly at fault. There would have been one life saved, had I not been the selfish bastard that I am."

"I don't understand? To whom are you referring?"

"Katherine. I could have spared her so much if only I had taken the good advice offered me when she was born."

"Advice?"

"Yes. One of the barmaids who was present when Katherine was born told me I was a fool for taking a child on board a ship. She belonged on land, in a good home, with a real family. Not rattling around a merchant ship with disreputable sailors. No. I couldn't let her stay! I had to have her with me."

"You loved her very much," Arianna said in a soft tone, though in her heart, she knew he spoke the truth. A ship was no place to raise a child.

"I'd never known love, a family. I just wanted to have her near, to watch her grow. You see, I knew her from the first. I had no money to stay on land myself. I was nothing then. It was the help of the crew that kept her safe. An old sailor who'd raised six of his own children taught the rest of us. But it was wrong. She would have been spared so much . . ."

Arianna stepped forward again. "Don't blame yourself for wanting to be loved. Katherine loves you so much and the life you gave her. No one could have foreseen what happened. Barrons is the one to blame, not you. Never you."

He shook his head. "I wish I could believe you. I

wish I could change what has happened. I look at her now, so small and vulnerable."

"I hardly agree with you there. Think about it! She's a survivor just like you. She fought the elements and outfoxed us all for awhile. What a child she is! What a woman she will become. That's all because of you, Will. Yes, what happened was unfortunate, devastating at the least. But none of it your fault. Do you think she would have been happier never knowing you, never having the love and devotion of an entire crew? No. No regrets, Will. Not now. Not after so much has happened."

A slight breeze rustled through the trees about them and Will looked off in the direction from where it came.

"I hope that you're right," he said, his voice less certain than before, "but I fear there is naught to be done about it now."

Reaching into his shirt, Will pulled forth the amulet. It no longer glowed, nor did the energy that seemed to live in its depths remain. It was dull and dead, and Arianna felt her heart crumble at the sight. It was true; their time was at an end.

"Oh, God."

"I'm sorry, Arianna," he said quietly. Moving to take it off, he pulled the string upwards, when Arianna held up her hand.

"No. Don't take it off. I can't bear it."

"It's yours. I promised I'd return it."

"It will remain after you've gone. Just keep it a little longer. I promise I'll come back for it later." She sobbed again. "I want to look out over this scene and remember you."

"Please," his voice broke, "don't mourn me. I don't think I could take that."

"What am I to do?"

"Go on living," he said at last. "Go back to your life, only this time leave behind the dead, Arianna. You have so much to give to those around you. You must find a good husband, raise a house full of children, and live your life to the fullest. I promise to be waiting for you when your end comes."

She looked up at him through damp eyes. "You promise?"

"I do." With that he leaned forward and placed a feathery kiss upon her brow. "Now go. I want my last memory to be of you walking down that path. I want to rest knowing that you will go on where I cannot."

After a moment, Arianna gave him a jerky nod. "Yes. I promise, too."

Turning away from him had been the hardest thing she'd ever done and yet, doing just that seemed right. That she should turn away from him now. The promise of their love was locked in her heart. She would honor his wishes, though it would be the most painful thing she'd ever attempted.

Those were her final thoughts as she stumbled down the path.

Katherine crept around the base of the door on hands and knees. Peering cautiously into the room, she caught the voices of the two pirates.

"You take the child, I'll take the invalid," Herbert ordered, dispensing the pistol to Gus without even lifting his gaze. The tattered chest lay open with much of its contents strewn about the room.

"It's not right, killing a child like that, Herb. And look at his lordship," he said, pointing to the balcony where the outline of the Earl's shape could be seen. His chair had been turned partially around so that he faced the west side of the garden and the door to the house.

"What about him?"

"He can't hurt a fly. He's been like this for weeks. It's not like he'll ever be a threat to Ol' Spikes. What say we just lock up the house and leave 'em? We'll tell the boss that we've done put them down. He'll not know any different."

"And do what? Leave them here to die? Who'll feed them? Who'll care for him when he needs to be cleaned or moved from the chair, eh? Naw. It's more humane just to put the poor soul down now, like a horse that's broke its leg. Besides, if Spikes was to find out we disobeyed orders, it'd be our heads on the pole, if you get my drift. Mark Benjamin Herbert don't put his neck out for nobody."

"You're wrong, and so's Spikes, if he thinks this is the best thing to do. Lady Arianna has been more than kind to us. Sure, she made us dig in the dirt and put tar on the roof, but it ain't no worse than swabbing the deck of a ship, aye? And she paid us rightly by sharing her larder and givin' us these nice presents. What has Spikes done but give us more threats and empty promises?"

"Och! You talk too damn much. We're criminals, you dolt! We're not nursemaids to kiddies or the infirm. We do what we do. Now, no more talking! Look in that chest to see if there's more ammunition. I could have bloody swore this is where we put it."

Laying two primed pistols on the bench, he turned to rifle through the remaining weapons.

Her eyes wide with fear, Katherine crawled on hands and knees to the bench. With a quick hand she grabbed one of the guns and then took off at a dead run for the balcony.

"Here now! What in the blazes . . ." Herbert shouted as he dove for the child. He tripped forward, falling short of grasping the hem of her skirt.

"What the devil?" Gus began, himself turning and taking in the scene.

"The little hellion has taken me pistol! Grab her!"

Before either man could reach her, Katherine had bounded out onto the balcony and run the short distance to Ethan's chair. Startled out of a doze, he blinked his eyes furiously at her.

"Don't worry, Lieutenant! I'll save us!" With a bounding leap, she landed, skirts all a tangle, head first into Ethan's middle.

An "Omph!" escaped his lips and his chair tipped precariously backwards. Prevented from falling back entirely, it stopped as the frame touched the railing.

Herbert reached the door first, with stalwart Gus behind him, craning his neck and peering over at the scene.

Whirling around, Katherine faced them in an instant, the pistol pointed at the dead center of Herbert's chest.

The two pirates and Ethan had no chance to take more than a breath when the child squeezed the trigger. A loud report rang out. Their eyes incredulous, Herbert and Gus looked down their fronts. Herbert, seeing the hole in him, turned instantly and saw a similar one in Gus's shirt. The two men spared each other a surprised glance and then both fell to the floor, dead.

Before Katherine could react to the scene, something on the old railing gave a loud snap. Before she knew what was happening, the two of them tilted even farther back, hung suspended for a bare second and then with a great whoosh, plummeted backwards, falling in a single motion, Ethan, Katherine, blankets and chair toward the tangle of bushes at the base of the manse.

Arianna had made her way halfway back through the path, navigating her way by means of instinct and a veil of continuos tears. More than once, she had to stop herself from running back to the overhang and begging Will to return. It wasn't until she was nearly at the bottom when an all too familiar figure stepped out.

"There you are, my lady wife."

A chill ran through Arianna when she'd heard these words.

"Barrons!"

"Indeed. I had thought perhaps you might have forgotten our agreement."

"I've forgotten nothing. What did you expect from me after you'd stranded us here, leaving us to die? It's not as if I've been building a ship to escape, is it?"

"No, your conjuring has managed to procure something else. Something far more heinous."

Arianna stepped back. Was it possible he knew about Will? "I don't know what you're talking about."

"Indeed." Barrons reached in his pocket and pulled forth a single piece of paper.

All at once Arianna recognized the long, swift strokes of the writing. It was her mother's hand!

"Where did you get that?"

"From your home, Arianna. I've been having difficulties of late, changes in my health. It was as if an evil spirit was stealing my life away. When I learned of your peculiarities from one of your cousins, I returned to Castin and found this. You've put a spell on me, you devious witch. I mean to have it ended."

He took a step forward, grabbing her arm in a hawk-like clutch.

"I don't know what you're talking about!" Arianna shrank back, but he only tightened his grip.

"Don't play me the fool, you senseless chit! I know the truth. I know what devil you conjured with your heathen magic!"

"I did nothing of the sort," she said, stamping her foot down, just missing his foot. "If you're referring to the ghost of Captain Markham, that was your own doing!"

"My own? I cannot conjure the spirits, miss. It was you, all along. Planning and plotting. But it's to no avail. I know how best to end this."

With that he pulled a sharp blade from the inside of his cloak. "Now where is it?"

"Where is what?"

"Your talisman—the stone, you fool. Where is it? I must see it destroyed as well, thrown to the bottom of the ocean where no hand may ever use it again."

"I don't have it. He has it. Captain Markham."

Barrons shrunk back. "He's here? Now?" Looking around, his eyes fearfully sought out the shadows.

"No. I left him there, on the cliff. He's gone." Her voice broke and she drew in a sharp breath.

"I will see it with my own eyes, if you don't mind." Then, pulling her along behind him, he went back up the path from where Arianna had come. She had no choice but to follow him.

* * *

It was like becoming the wind, Will thought. The drifts of energy flowed around him, his spirit like a leaf caught in the breeze, gentle and indecisive. It was unsettling to the small part of him that remained human and somehow right to the part of him that was spirit.

Knowing full well that it was time to go, Will tried to turn away from his ghostly existence. It should have been easier, he thought. It should have been a simple matter of going wherever his kind went when their work was done. Yet there was still something anchoring him to life.

In front of him was the sea, the shifting waters beyond the cliff churning, impatient for the son that should have been its own. Will once longed for the sailor's death, but that had been denied him and the Fates had chosen otherwise. The waters could not claim him now. If not the sea, he wondered, then what?

As soon as his mind had formed the question, the answer came sweeping across the horizon. The storm approached, black, angry clouds spinning out of control, hissing and clawing through the air as it came. Will's tempest descended from the heavens like a great mythical beast coming at last to devour its prey. The captain knew he should surrender to it, should meet his lifelong enemy once and for all.

But, his unwilling spirit remained rooted to the cliff edge. What gave him the strength to resist such mighty forces?

Glancing down at his pocket, he pulled out the stone once more. Arianna's amulet had drawn him to her like a moth to a flame. It remained dark and mysterious in his hand. No, it wasn't the stone. What was it?

He heard the rustle of the bushes again. Had Arianna returned? His hope soared. Could her need of him be the simple strand that pulled him back to life? Surely if that had been the case, he'd never have left her in the first place, so strong had been his feelings for her.

No. It wasn't just love, he realized when her slim figure came into view. It was something different. That was when he saw that Barrons had latched onto her arm. Anger and fear rose in Will once again, both fighting for dominance.

"I told you, he's gone and he's taken the amulet with him," Arianna said, struggling against her husband. "Now, stop this foolishness and let me go!"

Barrons turned around several times, pulling Arianna with him. His eyes searched every tree, every bush, making certain she'd told him the truth.

"Very well, Arianna," he said, turning back to her. "It looks as though you're telling the truth."

"I am." Again she jerked against him, trying to free herself.

Barrons was of a different mind, tightening his grasp, drawing her closer to him.

Will's anger grew by the moment. At the same time, he knew he couldn't interfere. He was no longer of the living, and had no choice but to leave her to it.

"Perhaps." Barrons watched her a moment longer, his eyes penetrating, as if he could see inside of her skin and discern the truth. "I suppose it no longer matters, though. Lying or telling the truth, your fate will be the same, my lady wife."

"What are you talking about?" Arianna asked, a tremor in her voice.

"Only that I've decided that your usefulness to me is at an end."

"You're going to kill me." Her tone was a statement instead of a question.

Will's anger rose a notch. The storm was near now, its long, icy fingers reaching out to grab at him. But his growing rage was more than a match for it. He would not leave the woman he loved to face the devil alone.

"It will be a most unfortunate accident, sweet Arianna. You see, I have to make sure that you don't have the chance to conjure another spirit to haunt me, duplicitous woman that you are."

As he said that, Barrons raised his hands, first to her arms and then gliding them up her shoulders and finally finding his hold around her throat.

Arianna had tried to back away from him, but his hands now encircled her throat, firmly holding but not yet squeezing her flesh.

"Let me go!" Arianna demanded through clenched teeth.

Will could see the fury mounting in her eyes. Behind him the wind rose and pushed him closer to her, adding his strength to hers. In his pocket, Will felt a stirring of energy begin to grow.

"I will release you, my sweet. Only after I've squeezed the last bit of life from you. I know you'll be concerned about your brother and Markham's brat, but you needn't worry. The three of you will be reunited with him on the other side of the veil, while I return home to mourn the death of my dear wife. Of course, I'll have put down the two scalawags who murdered you all. It will be a tidy end to a troublesome adventure, don't you see?"

"No!" Arianna grasped his wrists and tore at his arms. "Don't hurt them. Do what you will to me, but let Ethan and the child go. They can never do anything to harm you!"

"I know that, but I'm a fastidious man. I don't like leaving a mess behind me, and that's what your little family has become. No, I fear all of you shall be tucked into the grave when I leave."

"Then I curse you, Richard Barrons, for the evil man that you are. May you never find peace or rest! May a thousand demons rise from hell and grind you under their heels!"

Arianna twisted sideways, her face growing crimson at the action.

Barrons's laughter was the final spark that set off the storm. Suddenly a bolt of lightning split the ground beside him. Will once again had form, and from that form burst forth his fury.

"Take your hands off her, you bastard!" Will's voice boomed over the glade.

Barrons instantly turned, still holding Arianna, pulling her sideways like a marionette. Squinting in Will's direction, he took one hand from Arianna, and after reaching inside of his coat pulled out a pistol and brandished it about wildly.

"What? What was that?"

Will stepped into the light. His fury was tempered only by his fear for Arianna's safety.

"It's me, Barrons. Will Markham. I came to exact my vengeance on you."

"Come any closer and I'll kill her, I swear it!" Barrons then pulled Arianna to stand in front of him, the gun held to her temple.

"What do you think will happen then?" Will moved closer.

Barrons took a step back, pulling Arianna with him. "Show yourself, you devil."

Will took in a deep breath, inhaling the charged energy of the air around him. Like a man reborn, he could feel the return of the solidness of muscle and bone, skin wrapped around him like a blanket, barely holding in the force of his emotions.

"I'm here." Will stood, hands outstretched, tilted forward on the balls of his feet. "Let the woman go."

"It's not possible." Barrons slowly pulled the pistol from Arianna's head and pointed it shakily at Will.

"It is indeed. Do you think Arianna did this? It was I who sought her out. I told you I would not rest until I saw you destroyed."

"So you have. Was it you then who taunted me?"

"It was."

Barrons studied him for a moment, lines of concentration deepening on his face. The single scar that rose up Will's neck to his temple glowed a furious red in the afternoon light.

"You think to destroy me?"

"It was my intention. To see your flesh stripped from your back, the way it was for me when you had your man whip me. To cut open your arm and watch while you bled. To put the hangman's noose about your throat and watch the life pulled from your body the same way you watched my final moments. That is what I craved, sure enough."

"And now?" Barrons asked, his gun hand trembling slightly.

"Now I would give it all up if you let Arianna and

the others go. Let my daughter live out her life untouched by your evil. Let Arianna's brother heal if he can. For that, I forfeit my vengeance on you. I'll let you live in peace."

Will waited while Barrons considered his offer. Could the man not see the merit of Will's proposal? A life of peace versus an eternity of torment?

Of course, Will knew instinctively that only hell waited for Barrons, its great maw open to devour the man's soul when his time on earth came to an end. He wondered if Barrons knew that as well.

"You have no say in my life," Barrons said at last. "You are naught but wind and bluster. You're powerless to do anything to me or you would have destroyed me by now. No, I think your threats are empty."

With that, Barrons drew back his hand, and with the pistol still intact, used it to crash against Arianna's head. She instantly crumpled from the blow.

"You beast!" Will roared.

In the next instant, he was flying through the air, his outstretched fists connecting with Barrons. But the fiend didn't go down. Instead, he parried and swinging wildly, twisting, he grappled with Will's form.

The moment the two men joined, a flash of lightning exploded from them, like gunpowder and fire intermixed. It rumbled around them, shaking the ground and tearing at the air.

"No!" Arianna screamed.

Will couldn't take his attention from Barrons, enveloped as he was the same sphere of light and energy. Together they struggled, good and evil, light and darkness, rolling to and fro like a tornado caught in a whirlwind.

The roar of their struggle was almost deafening, and

yet Will could still hear Arianna's sobs. Her pained cries and pleadings sought him out and though they broke his heart, he knew he couldn't turn away from this fight. He had to put the devil away once and for all, even if his own life went down with the cur.

The wind rose in a crescendo, howling and beating until the rain swept in, covering them and whipping the ground with unrelenting fury. Will could no longer deny the tempest's presence, could no longer fight his lifelong foe. The two men, one of the living and one not, struggled in its midst. Will took small comfort in knowing that at least when the gale came to claim him, it would also take one final victim. Not that Richard Barrons was a victim—he was the devil. Will had no problem consigning him to hell.

Somehow in the ensuing moments, Will felt the world slip sideways. One instant, they were on solid ground, and the next they were perilously close to the edge. A low moan rose from the waters beneath them. Will knew the call. It was the voice of the sea beckoning him to her. Of course, he thought, the only other woman to rule his life. He knew in that instant that that was how it must be.

Arianna could have sworn she'd fallen into a nightmare. From the instant that Barrons had appeared at the bottom of the hill until the moment Will had engaged him on the cliff edge, she'd known the outcome of the struggle. Barrons would be destroyed once and for all, Will would have his justice, and she would pay the dearest price of them all.

She'd sat by and watched the spectacle, unable to intervene, unable to stem the flow of circumstance that had wrapped them both in a bolt of energy and then thrown them into the sea below.

Scrambling from her spot, she'd ran to the edge of the cliff. Peering over, she'd seen the huge splash the two of them had made. The instant Will and Barrons hit the water, a giant plume of steam rose upward. Their struggle was only visible for a few seconds and then they sank into the depths of the sea.

Arianna stood there several minutes, hoping beyond hope and praying beyond prayer that Will would arise from the water, whole and unharmed. But the water soon stilled, with the cresting waves rising and then crashing against the rocky side of the overhang.

Only the startled cries of Katherine drew her from her reverie.

"Oh, Arianna, thank heavens I've found you!" the child sobbed, running up the path and straight into Arianna's arms like a bullet shot from a pistol.

"Katherine," Arianna sniffed. "What is it? What's wrong?"

"It's Lord Ethan. I've killed him! I swear it was an accident. I've killed him!"

Chapter Eighteen

Digby climbed out of the longboat and trudged behind Captain Alms and his men. He'd no intention of landing on this godforsaken rock again. The last time he'd been on it a year before had bloody well been enough. The captain had insisted, most likely to have Digby shot if they didn't locate the chests or the remains of Barrons's wife or Lord Halverson. It would be his sorry luck if they didn't, Digby thought. He'd be making his way back to Newgate if the blasted man didn't have him executed on the spot.

Trudging up the beach to the main path, the manse soon came into view.

"It's a wonder the blasted thing is still standing," he muttered as they neared the front of it.

"Indeed. Though it looks as though someone was attempting repairs."

A few yards from the entrance, the first evidence of Barrons's arrival was evident. The body of a man was laying on the ground, his chest covered in blood, unmoving, eyes open and unseeing. Digby crossed himself and muttered both a curse and a prayer.

A woman appeared at the front door. Her bent figure staggered down the stairs to the walk, her hands waving wildly.

"Help us! Please help us! They're dead, I tell you, all dead. Oh, dear heavens above. The devil has come back and shot them all!"

It seemed to take forever to get back to the house. Arianna stumbled blindly through her tears, her hand clutching Katherine's as though it were a lifeline dragging her in from the sea.

"There he is, Arianna! Right there!"

Arianna quickened her pace when she saw Ethan's still body tangled amongst the marigolds.

"Ethan! Ethan, are you all right?" Running ahead of Katherine, she made it to her brother's side. Kneeling down, she picked up his hand, clutching it in both her own.

Suddenly Ethan coughed, his body spasming in the effort.

"Look! He's alive!" Katherine landed beside her, her hands tangling in Arianna's blouse.

"Yes, I know. Thank heavens!"

At that moment, Ethan opened his eyes. His clear blue gaze met hers and a wide smile crossed his face.

"Arieeee!" he muttered. "That you?" Ethan's voice was thick and wavered as he spoke.

"Dear God! Ethan!"

"Yessss. Kit-ten?" His eyes searched about him, not resting until they landed on the child.

"I'm here, Lieutenant! I'm right here." She shot forth and grasped Ethan about the chest.

"Head hurts." He motioned weakly with one hand, pointing upwards. "Get up now?"

"Oh!" Arianna sat back on her heels. Hot tears flowed down her face. Grief from her loss of Will to joy from Ethan's improvement overwhelmed her and despite her intention to be strong for everyone, Arianna folded over on top of her brother, sobbing.

"All right, Arianna. Y'll see."

Arianna felt Ethan's gentle patting on her head. The comfort he tried to give her made her weep all the more.

Will didn't fight the heavy waves as they crashed over him. Indeed, it was all he could do to hang onto Barrons's frantic form. Too late the devil had realized his folly and meant to break away and make for the surface. The freezing water had other ideas it seemed, pulling them both into a deep chasm of darkness. The farther down they went, the more the ocean's walls pressed against them.

Oddly enough, Will didn't mind ending up here. He'd always loved the sea and counted himself lucky to find rest there once and for all. Barrons had other ideas.

Just when Will thought that they were deep enough to never find the surface, Barrons broke away from him. Lashing out with his feet, Will's mortal enemy pushed him back and propelled himself upward. From the quiet depth he watched as an expression of victory replaced the jagged face of fear the other man had worn since they'd fallen into the sea.

Will roared in frustration. Because he was not completely solid, he had no purchase against the water. He lunged forward, just barely able to move, grappling for Barrons, just missing the man's heel, his fingers brushing against his foot.

Even at this depth Will could perceive his enemy's glee. Barrons smirked above him, his face glowing an unearthly shade, his arms making wide circles, his solid form maneuvering in the water. With forceful strokes, he then fled upwards.

Will followed. He would not surrender the struggle with him alone at the bottom of the sea. Fighting on like a man possessed, he chased Barrons.

An eternity seemed to pass as Will forced his way through the water, but he did not relent in his pursuit of the fading figure.

When Will had finally made the surface, he could see Barrons ahead of him, his lean form cutting through the waves. He would soon make the shoreline, and Will knew he would go back to Arianna, Katherine, and Ethan. He would finish the task that had brought him to the island.

"Barrons! You are a coward!" Will called out, still fighting against the sea. His was the harder struggle because he was not fully alive. Relentless, the waves beat against him, exhausting his every attempt to get closer.

As he watched, Barrons got to the beach, struggling to stand upright, the fatigue of his fight with the sea evident in his every move.

Only once did he turn back to Will, his face alight with a triumphant glow. Instead of fleeing, he waited for the ghost, taking ragged breaths, he wiped one damp sleeve across his face.

"It's time to put you down once and for all," he called to Will.

"I will destroy you!" Will finally felt blessed sand

beneath him. Looking up, he saw Barrons smile, his eyes darkening like midnight. With one hand he reached inside his coat and pulled forth his blade.

"I wonder, does a ghost bleed, pirate?"

"You've already killed me once. Do you think yourself lucky enough to do so again?"

Barrons did not answer, instead lunging forward, meeting Will forcefully, this time wildly swinging his knife, cutting at the air around them.

Will ducked sideways, just missing the blade's advance. His arm came up and in one blow, he knocked the weapon from Barrons's hand, throwing his body against the man. Once again when they came close to touching, lightning crackled and the wind rose up against them. Barrons would not be intimidated. Like fire he burst forth, his fist coming down and making contact with Will's chest.

Sparks crackled and lit the air with electricity when living flesh struck ephemeral spirit, present but not quite solid.

Will twisted sideways with the blow, scrambling to miss his enemy's advance. Suddenly, he realized he could not win this battle on land. Barrons had his madness to feed his fury while Will's strength ebbed like the sea pulling away from the shore.

In a final bid to put the devil in his place, Will turned and grabbed the other man around the waist. Surprised, Barrons tried to pull away, his fists beating at Will's back. Again the wind picked up, carrying the rain and sand in a furious whirl about them.

Not willing to be bested, Will threw all of himself forward, pushing Barrons once again into the water, his legs weakening by the second, his power fading at last.

"Let loose of me, you fool!" Barrons screamed,

scrambling against the rising tide which dragged them out to sea.

"You will be destroyed, once and for all," Will ground out, propelling Barrons in front of him now. Deeper and deeper into the water, he forced him, until the land faded behind them and they fell into a chasm beneath the waves. Before he knew what was happening, the water sucked them both down, pushing them to the depths with its oppressive force.

For a brief moment, Will almost lost his grip on his enemy. Barrons continued to strike Will, his blows glancing off with each hit. Will ignored the mounting discomfort, his shape threatening to break apart at any second. He knew that before long he would once again be completely spirit and would likely never return to solid form again.

His muscles weakening by the moment, Will began to fade once again. Unable to hold Barrons any longer, Will felt him finally slip from his grasp. A cry of frustration and anger boiled within him but with the water holding him prisoner he could not even cry out. It looked as though Barrons would win their final battle after all.

With the last of his energies spent, Will waited as the deluge of water pressed him down, holding him to the depth just below Barrons's escape. As Will watched, the other man made for the surface, the dim light of day hovering just above them.

Will saw the final glance Barrons shot down at him. A triumphant expression of a murderer, ready to make his final kill. Barrons had won.

Just as the devil neared closer to the light above, Will saw the water around them change. The murky shallows moved and slipped around him like black oil, like the unnatural form of a snake, slithering upward.

Was it water or beast? Will had no idea, but he watched as the form moved ever up, gaining speed until it slid beneath Barrons's feet. Then, almost too swiftly to see, the form caught one of the man's ankles and then the other. Shock lit Barrons's features and the dark form rose higher and higher, clinging to his legs with a tenacious embrace.

For a few seconds Barrons froze, surprise and fear mixing on his expression he struggled upward. Will was certain he'd make it, but at the last second, he froze. The blackness engulfed him. Like some huge, hungry beast, it swallowed him whole. A single bubble emerged from the blackness and broke against the surface.

Even at his depth, Will heard the scream. The devil was destroyed at last.

Relief and exhaustion coursed through him. Will knew his time was at an end. Nothing held him back. In seconds he would have no more form than a memory. It was time he left his life behind, his victories and defeats, his love of his daughter and Arianna, all of it would reside on the other side of the veil and he had no choice to be satisfied with that.

A single minute passed as the sea embraced him.

Except he did not fade away as he'd expected. Before Will knew what was happening, the water erupted around him. Sparks of light burst on either side, and he had to duck to miss being impaled by them. The water began to move around him, faster and faster until the motion caused a great dizziness to overcome him. Like a child's top, he spun, and a myriad of colors and lights wove around him until his heart cried out.

One word sprang from his lips as the world exploded around him.

"Arianna!"

She didn't know how long she'd wept when another hand touched her. It was a man's hand, the long, cool fingers gripped her sleeve.

"Miss? Are you all right?"

Arianna looked up into the boyish features of a young soldier. His gray eyes questioned her sanity, she was sure, but she really didn't care at the moment. The world had suddenly turned upside down around her and propriety had never mattered that much to her during the best of times.

"Yes. I'm fine," she sniffed and looked over to where Ethan still lay on his back. Katherine had scooted at least three feet away, wary of the stranger. Both looked to her with questioning expressions.

"I'm glad to hear that, madame," he said, straightening up. Turning he called out to his comrades. "Captain Alms, I've found the lady and two others," he shouted. "They're alive."

Around the corner of the house, two men appeared. One was tall and broad-shouldered and wore the blue uniform of a naval officer. The other shorter man was one she knew well.

"Mr. Digby," Arianna spat, her voice full of the venom she felt. "Arrest that man! He was in league with my husband."

"Now, Lady Barrons. We know the whole story and whether you like it or not, 'twas Mr. Digby who led us here. For all of his sins, he is responsible for our finding you."

"That's the truth, missus. I expect to be well paid for it, too," the little man sneered.

Arianna dismissed him with a wave of her hand. "I want to go home," she said, crossing her arms and stamping her foot.

"So you shall, lady," Captain Alms said, bowing deeply. "I'll take you there myself as soon as we gather the goods hidden here by your husband."

"My late husband, sir. If you care to look, you'll find his body at the bottom of the ocean."

The captain raised his chin at her statement, but it was Digby's response that she noticed first. He let out a slow breath, a deep grin crossing his face.

"Well, that is good news," the little man said, a grin spreading across his rodent-like features.

In the end, Arianna chose to make her trip on the *Persuasion*. It had been sitting about a mile off the island's coast. It would be traveling back to England escorted by the *Elkhurst*, though Mr. Digby, after seeing the disdainful look she aimed at him, thought it best to make his trip back with the naval men. For her part, Arianna was satisfied with that. As Barrons's widow, she was the true owner of all his possessions. Except for his personal journals, she turned everything over to the authorities. She'd no wish to be coupled in the conspiracy with Richard Barrons.

For now, Arianna was content to stand on the ship's deck and watch over the sea as the island faded into the distance. For a short time she'd loved the place, but without Will, she knew there would be no reason for her to want to stay or ever return. Her only regret was that she'd not gone back to try and locate the amulet.

She hadn't wanted to face the fact that he was really gone, she decided.

No, the jade stone was best left wherever it had landed. Besides, she'd made a promise to Will to turn away from the dead and find her life among the living. Though she'd no intention of finding a husband as he'd admonished, she had Ethan and Katherine to care for now, and that was more than enough for any woman.

"Man overboard!" The shrill call of a deckhand broke through Arianna's reverie.

"What? What is it?" A sudden dread filled her. What if they'd found her husband alive amongst the waves? Could he come back from the grave as well?

Frantically, she made her way to the railing, through the gathering crowd of sailors. A long boat was being set into the water. Anxiously, she watched the men haul a large body out of the churning sea. Arianna couldn't make out the identity of the man, though as they pulled him up onto the deck, she became more and more certain it wasn't Barrons.

Just as they set him down, the man's head lolled sideways. A thrill shot through her. She knew that face! She barely controlled a squeal of excitement.

By some pure miracle, the impossible had happened. Will Markham had been returned to her!

"Is he alive?" one man asked.

"Is he even breathing?" another chimed in.

"Where in blazes did he come from?"

The man on the wet deck coughed furiously and then fell back into stillness.

Arianna pushed herself between the sailors. "Here, take him to my cabin. He needs these wet clothes stripped from him and plenty of warm blankets."

"Aye, Lady Barrons. Right away," the second in command, a man named Hawkins, ordered at her side.

"Thank you. I'll take care of him."

"Best be careful, ma'am. We don't know if he's a sailor or a pirate."

"Whatever he is, he's been through an ordeal. Did you see the bruises on his arms and chest?" Arianna paused, remembering Katherine. If the child saw him before Arianna had a chance to warn her, she might divulge Will's true identity.

"Would you please have one of your men see to my brother and my husband's charge? I don't think we should let them near the stranger until we establish what his intentions are."

"Very wise, my lady. I shall have two of our best men help you get him settled."

Somewhere in a field of graves, an unmarked plot shivered in the ground. Six feet below, a transformation took place. Where once lay a rotting corpse, two months gone, a new shape appeared. This one was newly deceased, dressed in what once had been fine clothes and expensive leather boots. A shudder passed through the still form and only briefly did his eyes open. Richard Barrons looked up into the coarse weave of his burial shroud and then promptly died. This time, no ghost would rise up out of the grave. He sank into a deeper, darker, burning place.

Once below decks, Arianna settled herself in beside Will. She watched him closely for several hours as he slept. His slumber was fitful at times, and she feared a fever might yet rise up in him. No telling how much sea water he'd taken in. Worse yet, he looked to have received quite a beating. Still, every time she felt his pulse or felt his cheeks, the fire of life still burned within him. For that she was grateful.

For a time, Arianna busied herself with various tasks. When she thought he was resting quietly, she left Will's side long enough to see to Ethan and Katherine. That done, she settled into a chair beside Will's bed and picked up one of the five volumes of her husband's journals and began to read about the life of Richard Barrons as was told by the devil himself.

The morning sun finally broke through the small window. Will awoke with a strong headache and a burning in his chest that made him think he likely swallowed the entire ocean. That was when he felt a pressure, gentle but firm, upon his belly and chest.

Opening a bleary eye, he peered down at the quiet form that was spread across his middle like a comforter. In fact, it was the tangle of pale blond hair, and the shapely neck of someone he knew quite well. Raising a gentle hand, he placed it on her head and took in the silken feel of her tresses.

A sharp hiss escaped him. Surely he was in heaven.

The form stirred and a beautifully mussed Arianna sat bolt upright, wearing a startled expression.

"Will? Are you awake?"

"Yes, but by God, I don't know how. I was dead one minute, split apart the next, and now, here I am. I don't understand it at all."

"Neither do I, but I'm thanking heaven above it's true. Oh, I can hardly believe it's you!"

In one quick motion she was on him again, her body pressed to his, her arms twining around his neck.

"I know. I expected to be dead. I expected to wait an eternity to ever hold you again."

Arianna suddenly pulled back from him. With a firm hand she ran her fingers along his shirt. Will closed his eyes, reveling in her touch. It wasn't until he felt her pause that he opened his eyes. She had found something. Her hand slid between the opening of his shirt and she pulled free the jade amulet, still attached to the gold chain.

"You still have it."

"Yes. I don't know how it happened at all, Arianna. I swear, it's a mystery."

Thoughtfully she closed her hand around it. "Perhaps not." Her eyes gazed up at his for a moment.

The next thing he knew, she had slid upwards, touching her lips to his, drinking his kiss in hungrily. Despite his achiness and the exhaustion he felt, Will returned her passion in kind.

A few moments later, she pulled back, ending their embrace.

"Wait. You're not strong enough yet and I've something to show you."

"If you say so." Will stretched out, his stiff limbs crying out from their recent abuse. Truth be known, he was glad for the time to recover. When he made love to her, he wanted it to be with all of his strength, all of himself. The best maneuvered advances were those well planned. Even in his sorry state, he could make plans.

"This explains it all."

"What is it?"

"Barrons's journal." She settled beside him and opened the book.

Will put his hand on hers. "We no longer have to concern ourselves with him. He's dead, Arianna. I saw him die."

She shook her head. "I never doubted it. But this explains why he hated you so. When we get back, we can use it to prove your innocence."

"And tell them what? That I've arisen from the grave? No. If it's all the same, I'd just rather remain anonymous, if you don't mind. Too many questions."

"I don't mean to do that. I just thought you should know."

Will watched her, realizing that something else simmered beneath the surface of her statements. Anxiety stirred in her deep blue eyes.

"What else have you found?"

Arianna bit her lip. "I think you should hear it."

Settling herself beside him, Arianna began to read. Will listened as the tale unfolded. Closing his eyes, the words rang out and he felt as if his world suddenly righted itself in the telling.

"It begins with this, I think," Arianna said.

When she began reading, her voice took on a deep quality that would have lulled Will to sleep had it not been for the content of her words.

"11th November," she began. *"As I am writing this, my heart is full of glee. I have once and for all dispensed with the brat. He is now sitting in the workhouse kitchen, unknowing just what life awaits for him. With any fortune, the child will be dead in a month. I would have killed him myself, but the chance of blood*

on my hands may ruin my chances later. This way, with Mother's death and Kelly's drunkenness, no one will be the wiser. William will never threaten my position once it is regained.

"*30th December. My stepfather is dead. I have returned from my uncle's house after he ruthlessly cast me out. A public set-down, no less. One day I shall be in the position to depose the old wretch. The Duke of Melbourne may have money and status now, but, given wealth, even I can challenge him. I'll ruin him and make him pay for every disparaging remark he and my faithless father ever made about me.*"

"He had an ax to grind." Will shrugged. "Richard Barrons was not the first child to be thrown out of society. I still have no pity for him."

"Neither do I, but it is the child that I was concerned about. I wondered if it were at all possible that he'd always been so with children."

"So it would seem." Will clamped down on the memory of Katherine's treatment at Barrons's hands.

"No. Only two, specifically, the child in this text and your daughter."

"Why should he be so particular?" Will glanced curiously at Arianna.

Clearing her throat, she returned to the reading after thumbing through several of the volumes.

"Here's where I found it. The passage that reveals everything. It will help you to understand," she said in a soft tone. She read again.

"*2nd June. Damn all the fates that walk the earth! The serpent from my past has risen up once again. The child has grown to be a man. My younger brother has taken on the last name of the very workhouse I'd sent him to years ago. He owns a merchant ship now, and*

*damn it all, if the blighter hasn't dared to oppose me in
business. I must put him down once and for all."*

Will sat upright in the bed. "What the devil?"

"It's you, Will. Here, he reveals your name." She
pushed the text in front of him. Will took a moment to
focus on the bleary print, but it was indeed his own
name that was scrawled across the page.

"Damn and blast," he muttered, though the power of
his curses faltered in the early morning.

"I'm sorry, Will. In this journal, he details his plans
for both your betrayal and hanging. He'd arranged it
all. He even had plans to raise Katherine, to use her
against the duke and force the old man to reinstate him
into the family. Your cousin, Viscount of Mallorton,
had been stricken ill at this time. With his death, the
Duke had no one to pass his title to. Barrons wanted to
make sure you would never inherit so much as a farthing. Killing you was the only way to make that happen. He knew if the title descended to him, you also
had a claim to it."

"My mother and father's name was written in the
workhouse records," Will said quietly. "I was listed as
an orphan. We both must have been so."

"Have you no memory of your childhood?"

Will shook his head. "Only of living in that squalid
place. Of wanting every day to run away and become a
sailor." He shook his head, weary in the knowledge of
how much of his life had been hidden from him. He'd
had a mother that had cared for him, even if his father
had not. It would have been enough to lift the heavi-
ness from his heart these many years.

* * *

An hour later, Will's eyes remained closed. The thoughts of what circumstances and fates had brought him this far spun in his head.

"Will?" Arianna said beside him. "Are you all right?"

"I'm just trying to understand."

"What? That the reason Barrons hated you so much was his fear of your learning your identity? Or your mother's reasons for throwing away her position and family?"

"No. I've long since given up on those particular puzzles. My life was what it was, and now, it is what it is. I'm just trying to understand what fate brought me here, from death to life again. You'll have to admit, it's not the usual way of things."

Arianna smiled and settled herself beside him once again. Her fingers glided across his chest and found the amulet once more.

"It's magic, Will. I don't even try to understand it, I know my mother never really did. She just depended on it, I suppose."

Will shook his head. "It's not the stone's powers that brought me back, Arianna. There is only one magic that can cause such miracles to happen. That is love. Our love."

"I will have to consider that, my captain. And what of the jade? Didn't you see its glow when we were together?"

"I did." He took the stone from her hand and held it up to the light. A small, warm fire shone within its depths. "I think it is more like a compass, helping us to navigate, each toward the other. The true power that has brought us together is our love. Strong, like the wind blowing over the horizon . . . it filled our sails and pushed us along the same course."

"And now we travel together?" Arianna asked, her clear green eyes searching his.

Will took a deep breath. Glancing toward the porthole he caught a glimpse of the sky kissing a calm sea. No storm waited for him upon the horizon . . . the tempest had been put down with his enemy's death. Peace had come to him at last. A sense of wonder and joy filled him as he pulled Arianna close and held her in a warm embrace.

"Indeed we do. Now and forever more." Will sealed his promise with a kiss.

Chapter Nineteen

Two months later . . .

Will paced anxiously in the corridor. His anger rose with every step. He glanced at Arianna, knowing instinctively that her usual calm manner covered a hint of anxiety.

"Damn and blast," he muttered his sailor's oath. "I don't like this one bit."

Arianna gave him a sympathetic smile. "I know it's inconvenient, but a summons by a duke is nothing to scoff at, as much as you may want to. Don't forget, not just your future is at stake here but Katherine's as well." She is his great-grandniece." She thought a moment more. "Yes, that's right."

Will huffed. "I don't know what makes you think he'll believe our story, let alone agree to what you propose."

"He'll have to agree with it. Or at least part of it. Whether he chooses to recognize you or not, you are the rightful heir to the title. If he wants to cast you aside, so be it. But first, he must know of Katherine's existence. He must know that when your grandfather cast off your mother, he also lost more than just her two children."

"Yes, yes, he threw away a legacy. I understand all that."

"Do you also realize how hard it would be for the man to carry out his brother's decree when the loveliest child ever born would be his to adore? I had heard that the old man goes quite potty over children. Donates a great sum to orphanages the year round. It's said that he's still searching for the family he'd lost."

"A bit late for that, don't you think?"

"Be fair, Will. As a younger brother, he couldn't possibly have begun the search when your grandfather was still alive. He had to make certain that enough time had passed before even trying. By then, you were a grown man and Barrons's machinations were already set in place. We can only hope that he'll accept our explanation for what happened without asking too many questions."

"I won't subject her to the old scoundrel's scrutiny. Her mistreatment at Barrons's hands was enough." Will growled.

"Nor do I expect you to. But we owe it to Katherine to make sure."

Will knew she was correct. When it came to matters of the aristocracy, Arianna was the expert. No matter that she hadn't involved herself with much of the *ton*, she knew its intricacies quite well.

"After all this is finished, you'll still agree to be my wife?" Will asked, his heart rate bounding at the thought.

Arianna smiled. "I will become your wife even if

you decide to become a fishmonger. However, I do think it wise to establish your identity first. I've already been wed to one commoner. If it's revealed that you are his brother, it might make it somewhat uncomfortable for us both."

Will nodded. "At least it will give Katherine a mother once more and your brother some comfort, I think. Though I am loath to take my grandfather's title. If it must be done, then so be it. I can do anything for Katherine's sake. I just hope your brother's support will be enough to erase the damage Barrons did to us all."

Will's thoughts went back to that morning when they'd left his daughter and Ethan at the breakfast table. Katherine was excited beyond words, to be reunited with her father. Now recovered, she chattered away most of the morning, regaling him with the details of how she'd planned to outfit her new quarters.

It was Ethan who most concerned Will, however. Though his condition was improving, as he was now able to speak more words than previously, he still had a long recovery ahead of him. His body had weakened considerably over time and the pain of his reawakening flesh was written all over his expression. He seemed happy enough, though, that Arianna had found her love and not the least bit surprised at Will's appearance. He confided that, he had seen the ghost on a few occasions so he was not altogether disapproving of their affection for one another.

Still, Will could see a hauntedness of another kind behind the earl's eyes and it saddened him greatly. He supposed that in his own elevated circumstance, he wanted everyone around him to be as happy.

Will's thoughts were interrupted when the great hall's doors finally opened. A immaculately liveried butler appeared at the doorway and motioned them forward.

"His grace will see you now."

Will glanced at Arianna. She was already moving, her bearing that of a noblewoman. Damn, but he loved her. Like a hapless puppy he followed in her wake.

"Incredible story, Lady Barrons."

Arianna nodded, a picture of relief easing the lines of worry around her eyes. "It is, your grace."

"I don't believe a word of it."

The three of them were seated in the dining room, at the duke's breakfast table. Though mostly cleared of the morning's fare, there sat before each of them a steaming cup of the duke's favorite treat, hot chocolate.

At the duke's declaration, Arianna was barely able to remain upright. She felt Will tense beside her and quickly put her hand on his arm. He needed to remain calm if they were to have any success at all. Under her touch, he instantly relaxed. She spared him a glance. This was her battlefield, her eyes informed him.

Will only blinked once, then turned his attention back to the Melbourne.

"Why is that?" she asked the old man. "I told you, we rescued William from the sea. He'd been abandoned on the island—as had his daughter for a longer time— along with Ethan, and myself. I thought he'd been killed when he and my late husband struggled on the cliff edge. Certainly you can see the family resemblance. I assure you, William Markham is your grandnephew."

The old man gave them a disparaging look. "I can bloody well see who he is. I still have eyes, you know. What I don't believe is that you are only my niece's son. There was a man who accompanied the ship that rescued you. A partner of Barrons, and dare I say, just as much a criminal. I made a deal with the devil the day I shook his hand, I can tell you. Name was Digby."

It was Arianna's turn to startle. Her hand went to her mouth in surprise. Was it possible that Will's true identity might be made public? The sudden vision of his being hung a second time swam before her eyes. She felt herself begin to swoon.

"Here now, Lady Arianna, calm yourself!" Melbourne's brusque command cut through her faint.

"I'm calm," she said after several deep breaths and pushing away Will's offer of water.

"Now. Back to the facts. The truth is, when that blackguard saw this gentleman, he went near to mad. Said as how he'd been hanged several months ago, as Captain William Markham, the pirate now four months in the grave."

"Surely you don't believe such a tale?" Will asked, his voice rougher than before.

"In fact, I am inclined to do so, young man. I was frantic to know the truth, you see. I'd been aware of Barrons's dealings for some time. The arrogant scoundrel tried to maneuver me right out of my title, he did. Anyway, I had my man of affairs locate the body and then commission an exhumation. Imagine my surprise at finding who it was that inhabited the pirate's grave."

Both Will and Arianna leaned closer.

"Who was it?" Arianna barely breathed, her grip tightening on Will's arm.

"None other than Richard Barrons. And not four months dead, but newly deceased. Still had an expression of terror on his face, the medical examiner reported. Imagine that."

Arianna swallowed. "How do you explain it?"

The duke eyed her cautiously. "How, indeed? Except to say that somehow, divine providence intervened and that young man at your side is indeed my grandnephew. The one I've spent half my life searching for. Except to say that he was dead and now he lives again."

"Surely, your grace, you can't go spreading such a story."

"And see him lost again? Or even have my own sanity suspect? No, I will not. But I will know the truth. This is William, the son of my niece, is it not?"

Will nodded. "I am."

"Come to claim the same inheritance that your older brother tried to extract from me since he was of an age to desire it?"

"No." Will's denial was like a fist slamming on a table. "I wanted only to tell you of my daughter. She's far more deserving of anything than I. I thought that if you recognized her, she might somehow be taken under your wing, sponsored if you will. I want her to have the life I never had."

Arianna felt the tears gather in her eyes. "Katherine is a beautiful child, your grace, spirited and loving. You have only to look at her to know it. Already my brother has instructed his attorneys to include her in our family. She will be raised well and want for nothing. I even plan to wed her father as soon as the mourning period allows. While it may not include all that you could offer her, there's no question of her having a good life. I just thought to give you the chance to meet her. A chance to repair your family."

The duke gave her a suspicious look. "Why would you care, young lady?"

"Why, indeed. I have had a talent, your grace. Because

of a gift I'd inherited from my mother, I've seen what such heartache can do to the souls of a family. I only wanted you and, if possible, your brother to see the fine man who grew out of the strife his decree has caused. Perhaps to give you all a chance to heal the rift. Nothing eases a wound better than a child. She is a new promise for your souls, sir."

The duke leaned forward. "Have you spoken with my late brother, George? His ghost, I mean."

Arianna shook her head. "I'm afraid not. I wish that I could. Since my involvement with Will, I've not had so much as a summons. But I can tell you from experience that you're throwing away a chance at a whole family if you don't at least attempt a reconciliation."

The old man sat back in his seat, his opaque gaze darting back and forth between them.

"Damn my eyes, if I don't believe you," he said, the beginnings of a smile upon his lips.

"You do?" Will asked, an incredulous expression growing on his face.

"Indeed." He turned to Arianna. "Not only did I once have the chance to meet your mother, I made the acquaintance of your grandmother as well. A charming lady, though I thought her a bit daft at the time. She'd told me that your family was descended from fairies, of all things. I daresay I believe it now."

Arianna couldn't hold back her smile. "Thank you, your grace."

"No, I thank you. Both of you. It takes a great deal of courage to face an old beast in his lair. Now, we've plans to make. A ball must be held announcing the return of my grandnephew to society. I must say, a good tailor will go a long way in disguising your pirate persona . . ."

"You'll be choosing my wardrobe?"

Arianna couldn't hold back her laughter. Will's glee fled and a new state of agitation took hold.

"Darling, it will be necessary, if you are to be announced as the duke's heir."

"This is some foul joke, is it not? I've never heard such a thing."

"Yes. We'll have to find you a suitable valet, a man of affairs, an entire new staff to run your estate . . ." the duke began.

"I don't have an estate," Will said pointedly.

"You do now. My brother's home on Peach Street will be a good start. We'll have to see about finding you an appropriate country house, though. Oh, and a few thousand acres around it. I'll set my man to it immediately."

Will sat back in his chair, a look of pure panic on his face.

"I imagine facing the hangman wasn't nearly as frightful as this," Arianna whispered to him.

"Indeed." Will huffed, his face turning slightly pinkish.

"Welcome to the aristocracy, my love," she said and then leaning forward, lightly kissed his cheek.

"I dare say, it was much easier being a ghost," he muttered.

Epilogue

Hours later Arianna sat with her husband-to-be in front of the fireplace, watching as the last tongues of the blaze died out into smoldering ash. Naked and wrapped in a quilt, they'd remained on the chaise longue, utterly sated from their lovemaking. For the first time in her life, Arianna felt as though she were a part of the world and not just a spectator.

"What are you thinking?" she asked, breathing deeply and inhaling the scent of him. Flattening her palms, she ran her hands up his chest to rest them on his broad shoulders. The muscles under her touch quivered slightly. A deep sensation of arousal coursed through her in response. She delighted in the power his body had over her.

In truth, she had always known he would feel this way. She knew the essence of him as completely as she knew her own. In some ways he was still her Will, the specter who came one night and spirited her heart away. And though he'd been real enough for her before, now he consumed every bit of her—her senses, her heart, her emotions. It made little sense when one tried to form these strange, wonderful feelings into words, but Arianna didn't care. She simply luxuriated in his presence and knew full well that her desire for him would never fully be quenched.

"I'm thinking about you," he said quietly.

"You are? Are they good thoughts?"

His chest rumbled slightly as a small laugh escaped him. "Very good thoughts."

"Really? Could they be that I'm the most beautiful, desirable woman you've ever known?"

"Ah, fishing for compliments, are we?"

It was Arianna's turn to smile. "In case you haven't noticed, you're not very forthcoming with your praises, captain."

He laughed again. "That's because words don't begin to describe how beautiful or desirable I think you are."

"That's a very nice try, Will. Still, you've not told me what's on your mind."

"I know." He sobered. "Many things. The swell of the ocean, the warmth of a tropical breeze, the incredible way your skin feels against mine when we make love."

"Mmmm. That's all?"

He sighed. "That, and how incredible life is. I've been given the gift of it a second time when I'm sure I didn't deserve it. Yet here I am, in the arms of, yes, the most beautiful and desirable woman I've ever known, about to make passionate love to her for the second time tonight."

Arianna pulled away from his embrace and gazed into his eyes. They were wide and dark and he was watching her with such intensity that she nearly melted from his scrutiny. She trembled.

"Do you want to know what I'm thinking?"

"Always."

"I'm thinking that you think too much. Make love to me again, Will."

He smiled then, his hands gently kneading her shoulders, his breath warm and heavy on her skin. "With pleasure."